A NEW NA
SEPTOLOGY Vɪ-VII
Jon Fosse

Translated from the Norwegian by
Damion Searls

**TRANSIT
BOOKS**

Published by Transit Books
2301 Telegraph Avenue, Oakland, California 94612
www.transitbooks.org

© Jon Fosse, 2019
Translation copyright © Damion Searls, 2021
All rights reserved by and controlled through Gina Winje Agency
Originally published in English translation by Fitzcarraldo Editions in the UK in 2021

ISBN: 978-1-945492-57-0 (paperback)

LIBRARY OF CONGRESS CONTROL NUMBER
2021947714

DESIGN & TYPESETTING
Justin Carder

DISTRIBUTED BY
Consortium Book Sales & Distribution
(800) 283-3572 | cbsd.com

Printed in the United States of America

9 8 7 6 5 4 3 2 1

 The translation has been published with the financial support of NORLA.

 This project is supported in part by a grant from the National Endowment for the Arts.

A NEW NAME: SEPTOLOGY VI–VII

'Just a fool! Just a poet!'
—Friedrich Nietzsche

VI

AND I SEE MYSELF STANDING there looking at the two lines that cross in the middle, one brown and one purple, and I see that I've painted the lines slowly, with a lot of thick oil paint, and the paint has run, and where the brown and purple lines cross the colours have blended beautifully and I think that I can't look at this picture anymore, it's been sitting on the easel for a long time now, a couple of weeks maybe, so now I have to either paint over it in white or else put it up in the attic, in the crates where I keep the pictures I don't want to sell, but I've already thought that thought day after day, I think and then I take hold of the stretcher and let go of it again and I realize that I, who have spent my whole life painting, oil paint on canvas, yes, ever since I was a boy, I don't want to paint anymore, ever, all the pleasure I used to take in painting is gone, I think and for a couple of weeks now I haven't painted anything, and I haven't once taken my sketchpad out of the brown leather shoulderbag hanging above the stack of paintings I've set aside, over there between the hall door and the bedroom door, and I think that I want to get rid of this painting and get rid of the easel, the tubes of oil paint, yes, everything, yes, I want to get rid of everything on the table in the main room, everything that has to do with painting in this room that's been both a living room and a painting studio, and that's how it's been since Ales and I moved in here so long ago, so long ago, because it's all just disturbing me now and I need to get rid of it, get it out of here, and I don't understand what's happened to me but something has, something's happened, and what it is doesn't really matter, I think and I hear Åsleik say *St Andreas Cross*, emphasizing the words, saying it with that revolting stress on the words, he's proving he knows something too so he says it like that, with pride, yes, he's simple, Åsleik is, that's the right word for it, simple, I think and I think that I told him I'd go to Øygna with him to celebrate Christmas with Sister, as he calls her, this woman whose name is Guro, at her house, and that's really the best thing for me since if I stay home alone all I'll do is lie in bed, I won't even get up, yes well maybe get up to get myself some water if I'm thirsty and food if I'm hungry, other than that I'll just lie in bed in the bedroom without even turning the light on and I'll keep it as dark as I can, and then I'll try to get some sleep, and I'll try not to think about anything, because I want to let everything be empty, yes, empty and silent, yes silent, yes, silent and dark, because the only thing I long for is silence, yes, I want everything to stay perfectly silent, I want a silence to come down over me like snow and cover me, yes, I want a silence to come falling down over everything that exists, and also me, yes, over me, yes, let a silence snow down and cover me, make me invisible, make everything invisible, make everything go away, I think and all these thoughts will go away, all the pictures I have, all the pictures gathered up in my memory tormenting me will go away and I will be empty, just empty, I will become a silent nothing, a silent darkness, and maybe what I'm thinking about now is God's peace, or maybe it isn't? maybe it has nothing to do with what people call God? I think, if it's even possible to talk about God, if that even means anything, because isn't God just something that is, not something you can say anything about? I think and I think that still, praying is good for me, yes, praying with a rosary the way I do, and going to mass is too, but it's a long drive to Bjørgvin, anyway driving there and back the same day is a lot of driving, I don't like doing that, I think, and I've spent the night at The Country Inn so many times too, I think, but every year I've gone to mass on Christmas Day, and I would have done that this year too if I wasn't going to go celebrate Christmas Eve at Sister's house with Åsleik, so there's not going to be any Christmas Mass for me this year, I think and I stand there in front of the easel and then I go and sit down by the window and I look out the window and even though it's dark I see the driveway that I had built running down to the country road and I see snow, just snow and the islets and reefs, the holms and skerries, yes, the Sygne Sea, and I can see all the way out to the mouth of the fjord and the open sea, even when it's dark I can see it all well and I think that I need to get rid of that picture, I need to put it away, I don't want to look at it anymore, I don't want it in the main room anymore, I need to get rid of it, I think and then I go over to the easel and I take the stretcher and I lift the picture off the easel and I put it in the stack of unfinished pictures under the peg where my brown leather shoulderbag is hanging, between the bedroom door and the hall door and above the stack of paintings I'm still not satisfied with, and I look at the wall next to the kitchen door and there aren't any pictures there since I drove them down to Bjørgvin a couple of weeks ago, down to The Beyer Gallery, I think and I see Bragi standing there by the kitchen door looking at me, and it's like he's feeling sorry for me, I think, yes, it's like Bragi wants to comfort me but he doesn't know how to do it, and I see his dog eyes, and it's like they understand everything, yes, like nothing is hidden from them, I think, and Bragi is always near me, when I'm lying on the bench he comes and lies down next to me and as soon as I lie down in bed in the bedroom at night he follows me and jumps up into bed, no, life was never so good without a dog, without Bragi, I think, but Asle will get better soon and I'll have to give Bragi back, I think and then I'll get myself a dog of my own, that's for sure, I think, because I've never had a dog before, even though I've thought so many times that I wanted one, I kept thinking I should get a dog, and a boat too, a Barmen boat, but up until now all I did was think about it

Yes, good boy Bragi, I say

and right away he starts wagging his tail and I think he needs to go outside

You can go outside for a bit now, Bragi, yes, I say

and I go and open the front door and Bragi runs out into the snow, but it's not snowing now, and it's colder, yes, it's really a cold clear night and I see the stars shining clearly up in space, and I see the moon, it's big and round and yellow, I think and I think that it's God shining from the moon, and from the stars, yes, in a way, even if he isn't anything, and doesn't have any how, and doesn't have any why, yes, because God doesn't have a why any more than, yes, than the moon does, or the stars, the moon is just there, the stars are just there, yes, a flower is just there, and a deer, because both the moon and the stars and flowers and deer just are what they are, but they have their how in opposition to God, I think and I'm cold, and it's Friday today and it's nighttime and tomorrow is Little Christmas Eve, the day before Christmas Eve, and this year on Christmas Eve day I'm going to go with Åsleik to Øygna to celebrate Christmas with his sister Guro, and every year, since The Fiddler left Sister, Åsleik has asked me if I'd come with him, because when Sister and The Fiddler lived together Åsleik didn't spend Christmas at Sister's, and for at least ten years I've said that I'd rather spend Christmas alone but this year I don't want to be alone, I don't want anything, to tell the truth, and in any case I really don't want to paint anymore, and that's very strange, I think and I call for Bragi and he comes padding over and we go inside and he shakes himself off, shakes the snow off, and I shut the front door and I go into what's now the living room and the studio and what'll soon be just the living room and then I realize I'm tired, I should have lain down, I think and then I go and sit down in my chair next to the round table and I look out into the darkness, look at my landmark, my spot out there in the Sygne Sea and I look at the waves and I see Asle leave the apartment at 7 University Street where there's the room he's renting from Herdis Åsen and walk to The Art School and he thinks that he draws from a model every day, for three hours, sketching it's called, and then there's art history class two hours a week, and that may be what he gets the most out of, yes, the professor who gives the lectures, Professor Christie, is an Art History professor at the University of Bjørgvin, and what sticks with him is less what Professor Christie says than the slides of artworks he shows, Asle thinks, and Professor Christie says that it's obvious that the greatest artists do something different, they bring something new into the world with their own unique quality, their entirely unique art, yes, they create a new way of seeing that no one had ever known before, and after an artist like that has finished his work the world looks different, Professor Christie said, but it was the pictures he showed that made the biggest impression on Asle, and the books he referred to, which you could borrow from The Art School, because there was a big library there, but there was a long waiting list, for example he'd put himself on the list for a book of paintings by Lars Hertervig and it had taken three months before he could borrow the book, and then he could keep it for just a month, Asle thinks, but then he ran across a smaller book of paintings by Lars Hertervig in a bookshop in Bjørgvin and he bought the book and it was small enough to fit in the inside pocket of his black velvet jacket and then he started going around with it in his pocket all the time, he took it with him everywhere and looked at the pictures whenever he could, when he was sitting on a bench in a park, or when he was sitting alone in The Coffeehouse or The Alehouse, and then there was The Bjørgvin Museum of Art, yes, that may have been what Asle got the most of all out of, because the truth is he had never seen any real paintings before he moved to Bjørgvin, and students always learned that in their first few days at The Art School, yes, it was Eiliv Pedersen who said that, that they had to go to The Bjørgvin Museum of Art as much as they could, and they should really stay there for an hour, yes, or several hours, looking at one single picture, but if they'd never been there before they might as well get a general impression of the whole collection sooner rather than later, he said, and then they should pick one picture and really get to know it, and it was good to sketch it, or for that matter make a sketch in dialogue with the picture, Eiliv Pedersen had said, Asle thinks and if they were good enough painters maybe The Bjørgvin Museum of Art would end up buying one of their own paintings someday, or more than one, and that was a great honour, he'd said, yes, the greatest honour aside from being The Festival Artist in Bjørgvin and aside from The National Museum of Art in Oslo buying one or more of your paintings, he'd said, Asle thinks and he thinks that anyway he'll be satisfied if he can just paint pictures and if he can make enough money to live on just by painting, he thinks and I sit there at the round table and I look out into the darkness and even though it's dark I can see the water, see the waves out there at my spot in the middle of the Sygne Sea, yes, I can see the water, see the waves, as clearly as if it were daylight, and tonight the water is pretty calm, I think sitting there and taking my bearings from that same spot in the water, yes, there's a spot near the middle of the Sygne Sea that's my place, I think and I think that tonight Åsleik's going to come over and have lutefisk at my house, and I'm not in much of a mood to have a visitor, because it's like I can't manage to do anything, no, not even sit here in my chair, I think, but I have to be somewhere, and I have to be doing something, and tomorrow it'll be Little Christmas Eve and then it'll be Christmas Eve itself, and I told Åsleik I'll go with him to celebrate Christmas at Sister's house, and on Christmas Eve morning or maybe early afternoon we're going to go in his Boat to Øygna, that's what we've arranged, I think and I look at my landmark, I look at the waves there, and then I see Ales and Asle walking there, hand in hand

I can't believe we met, Ales says

Yes, Asle says

It's incredible, she says

Yes, he says

and they keep walking, hand in hand

And that we became a couple the moment we saw each other, Ales says

Yes, right in The Bus Café, she says

Yes, Asle says

It just happened, she says

and Ales laughs and Asle feels how good it is to be holding Ales's hand in his hand and he doesn't entirely understand what's happening and what happened, he thinks, because he was just sitting there in The Bus Café and then suddenly Ales was there, yes, she showed up as if out of nowhere and then sat down and then their eyes met, he thinks and Ales says that it's very strange, she never goes to that café usually, The Bus Café, because it doesn't have the best reputation, she says, so she was there for the very first time today, to tell the truth, she says, and why would she have gone to The Bus Café today of all days, and why was Asle sitting there today of all days, no, she can't understand it, or rather she can understand it, because it was God's will, she says and Asle hears what she's saying but he is entirely in the good warmth from her hand and they walk out onto a wide street and Ales says this is High Street, and there, at 1 High Street, and she points, in the big white building there, that's The Beyer Gallery, yes, there's no question it's the biggest and most important gallery in Bjørgvin, and she's gone to all the exhibitions there since she was a little girl, because her mother Judit likes to go to exhibitions, she's from Austria, she comes from a small town outside of Vienna, a town with the big name Hainburg an der Donau, while Ales's father was Norwegian, from West Norway, he was like people from there are, he came from a place called Dylgja where almost no one lives, but his sister, old Alise, still lives there in a nice old white house, she says and Asle says that he's heard the name Dylgja but he doesn't know quite where it is and Ales says that it's nice there, it's in a good location on the Sygne Sea, yes, the sea that Sygnefjord opens out into, before it goes out to the ocean, she says and then she says that her father was a good man, and he, a country boy as he always liked to call himself, especially after he'd had a little something to drink, yes, he, the country boy, became a doctor, and it was while he was in Austria studying to become a doctor that he and her mother Judit met, and when he was done with medical school they moved to Norway and to Bjørgvin and then they both started working at The Hospital in Bjørgvin, and her mother Judit still works there, yes, she's a nurse, Ales says, and, as her father liked to say, that wasn't the worst thing in the world for a boy from Dylgja to be, a doctor, but, Ales says, last year he died suddenly, and he wasn't that old, and it was definitely because he drank so much, he drank so much that he died of it, Ales says, but she doesn't want to talk about that or think about that now, not today when she and Asle have just met, she says and Asle looks at his watch and he asks if they can go to 1 University Street right away, he's worried about getting there too late, he says, the woman who wants to rent him the room and he have agreed to meet there at three o'clock, he says and Ales says of course they can, but they have plenty of time, she says and they walk down the street called High Street and then Ales practically drags him down into a little alleyway called The Lane and Asle sees The Lane written on a street sign and wow is it narrow

This is one of the narrowest alleyways in Bjørgvin, she says

and Asle doesn't say anything and they walk hand in hand down The Lane and then Ales suddenly stops and then she puts her arms around Asle and presses her mouth to his and then they stand there and they have their tongues in each other's mouths and then they suddenly let go of each other and they hold hands again and then they walk down The Lane and Ales says that if they take a right and go down that street they'll be able to see The Country Inn, the hotel where people visiting Bjørgvin from the nearby countryside often stay, and on the ground floor there's The Coffeehouse, one of the cosiest cafés in Bjørgvin, she often goes there herself, she sits there and sketches, she says, and what she actually likes to do there is sit at a table and secretly look up at this or that person and then she tries to do a drawing of him or her, Ales says, and then she says that Asle is really lucky to have a place at The Art School already, and then she says that today they won't turn right and go to The Coffeehouse, they can do that another day, they'll go left and when they get to the end of the street they'll see The Fishmarket, and once they've reached the end of that street they can just take a right and go straight and then they'll be at University Street, Ales says and she says that his name is Asle and her name is Ales but that's all they know about each other, or almost all anyway, he says, so maybe they can sit down somewhere and just sort of be together, Ales says and they've reached The Fishmarket and she points to a bench near the water's edge, with a view of The Bay, and they go sit down on the bench and Asle puts his shoulderbag in his lap and he opens it and he takes out his sketchpad and then he writes down his address in Aga, and then he writes 7 University Street, and he says that they need to go to 7 University Street soon and Ales says that if she remembers correctly he'd said 1 not 7 and Asle says that he has the letter from the woman who wants to rent him the room in his jacket pocket so he can always check, he says and then he takes out the letter and it says 7 University Street, he says and he says that the woman he'll be renting a room from is named Herdis Åsen and Ales says that she feels a little jealous just hearing him say her name and Asle says that she's an old woman and Ales asks how he knows that and Asle says that he knows because he's talked to her on the phone and he could hear from her voice that she was an old woman from Bjørgvin and he says that this Herdis Åsen had said she'd rented a room to a student from Hardanger for years but now he was done with his studies, she'd said, and so she'd be glad to have someone else from Hardanger as her next renter, Asle says and then he tears the page he's written the addresses on out of his sketchpad and hands the page to Ales and then he hands her the sketchpad and the pencil and she writes down her name and her address and a telephone number and she says that this is where she lives with her mother Judit, the two of them live alone in an apartment not far from The Coffeehouse, that's why she goes there a lot to sit in peace and quiet and do her sketching, like she'd been planning to do today for instance, but then she decided to take a walk first and she walked by The Bus Station and she saw the sign saying The Bus Café and then she thought she'd never been there, it might be nice to go see how it is in there, she'd thought, because she'd heard different things about that café, she says and luckily she went in so that the two of them could meet and now they'll have to write letters to each other, yes, until Asle moves to Bjørgvin, and he says that that won't be long, as soon as he rents the room from that woman Herdis Åsen he'll quit The Academic High School right away and give notice at his room in Aga and he'll put everything he owns in the luggage area in the back of the bus, and then he'll just take a taxi from The Bus Station over to his room on University Street, he says, and Ales says she can certainly help him move in, when the time comes, she says, and Asle takes back the sketchpad and pencil that Ales is holding out to him

Yes, that's my mother's phone number, but of course you can call me there, she says

and Asle says that he doesn't have his own phone number, but the woman he's probably renting the room from had said that she has a phone and Asle could use it, as long as he didn't make too many calls, or receive too many calls, that's what she'd said, and he thought he'd never use the phone at all but now that Ales has given him her phone number she can have his, he'll give it to her, Asle says and Ales says that's great, it's good that they'll be able to reach each other by phone, she says and then she hands the torn-out page to Asle and he copies the phone number from the letter Herdis Åsen sent him onto it and gives it to Ales and she says that now they probably should get going soon if he wants to keep his appointment with this Herdis Åsen, up on 7 University Street, she says and Asle puts the sketchpad and pencil back in the shoulderbag and then Ales and Asle walk hand in hand across The Fishmarket and then up a street Asle doesn't recognize

It's really unbelievable that we met each other today, Ales says

I feel so happy, so lucky, she says

It was an act of God, she says

and Asle doesn't say anything but he feels how good it is to feel the warmth from Ales's hand, and how well their hands fit together, in a way, everything feels right somehow, and everything is so simple, and nothing is embarrassing or wrong or difficult, everything is clear and obvious, Asle thinks walking along with Ales and not saying anything and then Ales points and says there it is, in that courtyard, that's where this Herdis Åsen woman lives, and Asle says it's on the sixth floor and Ales says she can go up with him and then Asle puts his hand on the handle of the front door and it's unlocked and Ales says that Herdis Åsen must have left the door open because he was coming, she says and I sit in the chair by the window and I look at my spot out in the Sygne Sea, the spot I always look at, my landmark, I look at the waves there and I think that it's like time has just stopped, something I've never experienced before, and I look at the empty chair where Ales used to sit, the one that was her chair, and it's empty, and yet Ales is sitting there, I think, because now I can clearly feel that Ales is sitting there, the way I can so often see her, I think and I look out at the water again, at the Sygne Sea, at my spot there and I can feel so clearly that Ales is sitting there in the chair next to me and I think that it's already been many years since Ales died, she died and I lost her much too soon, we didn't get to spend that many years together, and children, no, we didn't have children, so now I'm alone, and it's already been many years since my parents died, first Mother, and not long after that Father died, and my sister Alida died all the way back when I was just a boy, I think, and she died so suddenly, she was just lying there dead in her bed, I think and I don't want to think about that, and I think that I should have called The Hospital and asked how Asle is doing, but now it's too late, now it's night and I've called so many times, and I always get the same answer, that he needs his rest and can't have visitors, I think, so I'll just call tomorrow, on Little Christmas Eve, I think, because almost every single day in the past couple of weeks I've called and asked if I can come see Asle and the woman I talk to at reception at The Hospital always says that the best thing for him would be not to get visitors, she says and when I ask how he's doing she always

says that there's no news, she says everything's about the same, I
think, but Asle has children, I think, there's The Boy who's grown
up and lives in Oslo, yes, the son he had with Liv is all grown up,
and then there's The Son and The Daughter, the children from his
second marriage, with Siv, but their mother took them with her
when she moved to be with a man in Trøndelag, and those children aren't grown up yet, I think and I think that Åsleik's coming
over tonight to have lutefisk at my house, since this year it's my
turn to host the lutefisk dinner, because we have lutefisk together
once every Advent and lamb ribs together too, one year I serve
lutefisk and Åsleik serves lamb ribs and the next year it's the other
way around, and every year we have lamb ribs together again on
New Year's Eve, one year at Åsleik's house and the next year at
mine, and this year it's me who's going to be hosting the lamb ribs
dinner on New Year's Eve, I think, and I usually look forward to
these meals, but this year the lamb ribs I ate at Åsleik's didn't taste
so special, and now it feels like a bit of a chore to have to prepare
the meal, it's like I don't know how to peel potatoes and carrots
anymore, how to dice bacon, but I just need to do it, I think and I
look at my watch and when I do I think about Ales, because I got
the watch as a Christmas present from her once, I think, yes, for
years before that I used to wear a watch I got from Grandmother
as a confirmation present, and then I got this watch from Ales and
that's the one I've had ever since, I think and I see that Åsleik will
be here any minute so I need to set the table and put the potatoes
on to boil, I think, and I get up and I go away from the window
and I look at the empty easel and I'm sort of filled with happiness
and then I go out to the kitchen and I get out plates and knives
and forks and I set the kitchen table like I always do, and next to
Åsleik's plate I put a beer glass and a shot glass and next to my plate
I put just an ordinary water glass and I think that I can probably
put the potatoes on right away, I think and I peel the potatoes and
carrots and I put the potatoes in a pot of water with salt and then I
turn on the stove, and it's a good quick stove so it won't take long

for the water to boil and then I turn the stove down to the lowest heat, and even then the water is boiling more than it really needs to, but that's how it is now, yes, it probably doesn't matter, I think, and I put the carrots in the pot and now I can fry up some bacon at once, I think and I dice the bacon and I put it in the frying pan and I turn on that burner and it doesn't take long for it to start to crackle and sizzle in the pan, it's a good old cast-iron pan that was there when Ales and I moved into the house, yes, it was here like so many other things, and like so many other things that were in the house it also stayed, I think and I've been feeling kind of rough today, I think, but the good smell of frying bacon kind of brings me back to life, and I suddenly realize I'm hungry, because I haven't eaten anything all day, have I, I think, and despite everything lutefisk is one of the best foods I know of, maybe the very best, I think and I see the big pieces of fish lying there and I put a big pot on the stove, with lots of salt in the water, and I turn up the stove full strength, but I'll put the pieces of fish in the boiling water only when Åsleik gets here, because you have to be really precise when you're cooking lutefisk, you have to pay close attention the whole time so that the fish gets cooked just right, not too much, so that it falls apart, and not too little, so that it's hard and inedible, I think, and obviously you have to make sure at all costs that the bacon doesn't get burnt, so it's important to keep an eye on that, I think and I turn off the burner that the frying pan is on and then I stir the bacon and I stand there and look at it and I stir it several times and then I move the frying pan onto a cold burner and then I hear the screeching and grinding of Åsleik's tractor and I go out into the hall and I stand in the front doorway and Bragi comes and stands next to me and I see Åsleik's tractor come around the corner and stop and then I see Åsleik get out of the driver's cab and he comes walking towards me

Dinner'll be ready soon, I say

It'll be good to eat something, Åsleik says

I'm really hungry, he says

and we go inside into the hall and Åsleik takes off his boots and his snowsuit and his fur hat with earflaps and then he goes into the main room and I follow him and then he says that it sure is a bit cold in the room and he goes over to the stove and he says that the embers are still glowing and he puts a log on and I go out to the kitchen and I look at the water boiling and I put the lutefisk in the boiling water piece by piece and Åsleik comes into the kitchen and he says he forgot the beer and spirits in the tractor so he'll just go get the bottles

Because there's nothing like that in your house, he says

I've had my allotted portion, I say

Yes yes, Åsleik says

and he goes out and I've put all the pieces of lutefisk into the boiling water and I stand there looking at them and Åsleik comes into the kitchen and he says Sister sure was happy when she heard that I'm going to come celebrate Christmas with them this year, really strangely happy, he says and I say that he should just pour his own glass

Yes I've already set the table as you can see, I say

And the food's almost ready, I say

and Åsleik asks for an opener and I find one for him and then he opens his bottle of beer and he goes and sits down on the bench along the side of the kitchen table, by the wall, and he pours himself some beer and spirits and he takes a little sip of the spirits and then he says again that yes, Sister sure was happy I was going to come for Christmas this year, no, he can't believe how happy she was, he says and then I go get the food and I put it on the table and then I sit down at the head of the table and we serve ourselves and eat and neither of us says anything

You're a bit out of it today, Åsleik says

Yes I feel a bit tired, maybe, I say

But that's how it should be on Little Little Christmas Eve, as we used to say when we were kids, he says

Maybe you said that too, he says

and I say that we did

That was part of the rush to get everything ready for Christmas, he says

and then we sit there and eat without saying anything and Åsleik drinks beer and sips his spirits and I think maybe Åsleik can help me carry my paintings and painting supplies up to the attic, because now I can't paint anymore, not that either, and as for why I should have suddenly just felt that I didn't want to paint anymore, that's something else I can't say anything about, and I think that I can ask Åsleik if he'll help me carry the pile of paintings leaning there between the bedroom door and the door to the main room up to the attic, to the storage space where I keep the paintings I didn't want to sell

Yes, that was good food, Åsleik says

and I don't say anything and we eat and the food doesn't taste especially good to me and I see Åsleik drink down the rest of his beer

That sure tasted good, he says

and then he finishes his spirits in one gulp and I don't say anything

Thanks for dinner, Åsleik says

It really tasted great, he says

and then we sit there and we don't say anything

Not too chatty today are you, Åsleik says

and I don't say anything and then we sit there in silence and then Åsleik says well he'll probably just head home so I can lie down if I'm tired and then he says thanks for the meal and we'll see each other on Christmas Eve, in the morning or early afternoon, it would be best if we set out as soon as it's light, so if I could come over to his house at around nine that would be good, Åsleik says, but actually the best thing would be if he called me when he thought it was almost time to head out, he says and then he again says thanks for dinner, it really tasted great and then he takes his bottle of spirits with him and he leaves the empty beer bottle behind and I say we'll talk soon and I see Åsleik go out into the hall and I get up and I start to clear the table and I think that Åsleik left almost as soon as he came, I think and then I hear the sound of his tractor motor and I go and sit down in my chair by the round table and I look at the sea, at the Sygne Sea, at my spot there and I think why do I sit here all the time looking and looking at my fixed spot, at the waves there, even though it's dark now, and it's night, and I should have gone and lain down, I think and I think that I don't understand this, no more than I understand how when I wake up in the middle of the night it's always like Ales is lying in bed next to me, always, I wake up and then it takes some time before I understand that she's not there, but that's not true, because she is there actually, we're lying next to each other like we did when she was alive, I think and then I think that I don't know anything, but nothing means anything, yes, the only thing that gives meaning is what doesn't mean anything in the normal sense, that Jesus Christ was nailed to the cross, died, and was resurrected, and when that happened death, that came into the world when the world became the world as we know it with its endless cycle of life and death, was banished from human reality, of course a person dies in this visible world, in the world as it's been ever since the incomprehensible thing that we now call The Fall, and the body disappears, either it crumbles away in the earth or gets burnt up in an oven, it disappears one way or another, the visible disappears, but the soul is raised up by the spirit, it is reborn in and with God because Jesus Christ invalidated the old world, Jesus Christ, God's son, and people think that literally, as if God were a kind of human father and Jesus Christ a kind of human son of a human father and it's no wonder that people then think that that's foolish nonsense, because obviously it's just an image to say that God is a father and Jesus Christ is a son and The Holy Spirit is the creative power that mediates between the two, that's just a way of trying to put something into words, and it doesn't really matter whether or not it really happened like that, as long as it happens in the heart, in the soul, because the spirit, The Spirit, is real, and so is The Fall, whatever that might be, that's also just a way of saying that there was a break between God and humankind when death came into the world, and what the cause of that was, no, we can't know, certum est quia impossibile est, but, yes well I think and think and I don't understand what I'm thinking, and I don't know what I believe or don't believe, but for me God is near, and at the same time far, completely near and completely far, and somehow you get closer to God in Jesus Christ than you do by thinking about God entirely without human characteristics, yes, in thinking about God as a person who at one point in time you could talk to and be with like any other person, yes, the way I can be with Åsleik now, I think, because after I met Ales and she took me to St Paul's Church, yes, yes, then, I think and I think that I don't want to think more about Ales and I think that it's obvious that you can't come to faith through reason, belief is grace, a gift of grace as it's called, and if someone has faith then they also know what grace is but if they don't have faith then they don't know either what grace is or what a gift of grace is, they don't know that everything is a gift, I think, but anyway those are just words, and words always lie, I never believe in words, and I also don't believe in what I think in words, I think and I think that it's only in my pictures, when I've painted well, that something can be said, yes, a little something, about what I've experienced and what I know, and then it's said not by the picture itself, not by the colours, the shapes, yes, well, everything that's in the picture, and also not by what the picture represents somehow or another, but only by the picture's own distinct unity of form and content in one, like the spirit, and this unity, this spirit is as invisible as the picture, the painting, is visible, and what the picture is in reality is this spirit, that's what a picture really is, neither matter nor soul but both parts at the same time and together they make up what I think of as spirit, and maybe that's why my good paintings, yes, all good paintings, have something to do with what I, what Christians, call The Holy Spirit, because all good art has this spirit, good pictures, good poems, good music, and what makes it good is not the material, not matter, and it's not the content, the idea, the thought, no, what makes it good is just this unity of matter and form and soul that becomes spirit, I think, no I'm not thinking clearly now, I think and I've thought thoughts like this so many times, I think, that because pictures have a spirit painting can be compared to praying, that a picture is a prayer, I think, that the pictures I paint are prayer and confession and penance all at once, the way good poems are too, yes, you could say all good art is like that in the end because all good art finds its way to the same place, I think and I think that these thoughts are probably just as stupid as all the other thoughts I think, I think, sitting there looking out the window, out into the darkness, at my landmark there in the Sygne Sea, at the waves and I see Asle sitting in The Alehouse and he raises his pint and says cheers and Siv raises her glass and they toast and then Asle says that there are a bunch of cafés and restaurants and bars in Bjørgvin but he likes it better at The Alehouse than for example at The Artist Café, because there are real people at The Alehouse while there's nothing but climbers at The Artist Café, it's like everyone's always chasing after something, all the regulars there seem to want something, without it being a real longing, it's just something artificial, something rigid, just willed, something worldly with nothing of heaven in it, Asle says and also it's like everyone's supposed to be friends and like each other, and they act like they do, but actually they're all competing with each other, in a way that sort of doesn't look like competing, and everyone is supposed to somehow be their own person, be original or whatever, and that's why everyone is actually like everyone else and none of them is their own person, they're all imitators, because everybody trying to be original just makes everybody an imitator, and that's what culture is, probably, he says, it's probably just one person being like another person that creates a culture, for example wearing a suit and tie, while what art is, yes, art is everyone just being like themselves, and totally themselves, Asle says and there's not a single person in The Alehouse who's like any other person here, except for the fact that they're drinking beer and smoking and the fact that most of them are or have been sailors, but it's like life itself has forced them to be what they've become, life made them become themselves, Asle says and Siv says now don't exaggerate and then she holds his hand and then they sit there holding hands

And you're married and everything, she says

A father even, she says

and Asle doesn't know what to answer and Siv says she won't keep this up much longer now, either he has to leave Liv or else it needs to be over between them, she says and something in Asle rips and breaks and he doesn't know what to say or what to do and then he says that he'll try to rent a room for himself and Siv says that they can live together, the two of them, she's rented an apartment and they can live there together and his son could come visit them, it's probably too expensive for her to pay for the whole apartment alone but if there were two of them to pay the rent it would probably work, because artist stipends aren't that much to live on, she says and Asle feels such love for Siv it almost drives him crazy and he just can't go home to Liv and their son and try to act normal and then Siv says that she doesn't like it very much at The Alehouse and Asle says that it's probably just a place for old sea dogs and not for young women and Siv says that they can go home to the apartment she's rented and she says she can make dinner for them and she has wine at home and beer too, Siv says and Asle says that he'll just finish his pint and then they can go, and Siv says he can finish her pint too, and then she asks what Liv is up to and Asle says that she's working shifts at a hospice now but that she's talked about getting the high-school certificate she needs to enrol in The Nursing School

She could do that, she's smart, Siv says

Yes, Asle says

and he finishes his pint and Siv takes a little sip of hers and then puts it down in front of Asle and they each roll a cigarette and then they sit there smoking and Siv says that she's starting to wonder if she should drop out of The Art School, now that she's seen what the other students can do, yes, it's like what she can do is so little, and Asle asks what she'll do then and she says that she's interested in literature, and she's always been good at languages, so maybe she'd be better off going to The University, she says, and she can study literature there, or languages, she says, but then she'll probably become a teacher, and if there's anything she has no desire to be it's a teacher, so she doesn't know, Siv says and she stubs out her cigarette and then she says that it's time for them to go, now they'll go home to the apartment she's rented, she says, and she was lucky to find it, she says, but it was too expensive for her even though her parents were nice and gave her some money every month, she says and Asle finishes Siv's pint and then they get up and leave and they're walking next to each other

Don't you want to hold my hand? Siv says

Yeah, Asle says

and I sit here in my chair and I look at my spot out there in the Sygne Sea, and even though it's dark I see the water so clearly, I see the waves, and at night they're not so high, I think and then I get up and I see the empty easel and then I go over to it and I stand there and look at the easel and now there's no picture there, and I can't remember the last time there wasn't a canvas on a stretcher there and I look at the empty easel and I see Asle walk down the street away from The Alehouse, in his black velvet jacket, with his brown shoulderbag, and he's holding Siv's hand and he thinks that he and Liv are officially married now, they got married at The Courthouse, Liv was there with him and their best man and maid of honour, and Liv had picked her sister to be maid of honour and so Asle thought he could ask a childhood friend of his, his best friend from childhood, Tor, if he'd be his best man, and he'd agree to even though he and Asle hadn't spoken since middle school, yes, since Asle dropped out early in tenth grade and moved to Stranda, but Asle didn't really have anyone else he could ask and so he called

Tor and it was an easy conversation, everything was like it was before, and Tor told him that after middle school he'd gone to The Agricultural School in Utvik for a year and now he'd taken over the family farm since his father wasn't in such good health anymore, he didn't exactly know what was wrong with him but it was one thing and another and so now he was a farmer with three cows and over a hundred sheep, so really he was a sheepfarmer, and he liked being a farmer, Tor had said, yes, it was much better being a farmer than going to school, and he'd probably never be rich but he made enough to live on, maybe a little more, he said and then Asle said that it was going to be a very simple wedding, a so-called civil ceremony, because while other people were getting confirmed he had left The National Church, so it wasn't going to be any kind of church wedding, Asle said and Tor said Asle had probably been the first person ever in their village not to be confirmed, and there was no one in the village who had longer hair than he'd had, Tor said and Asle said that that was something he was proud of, yes, that he'd done it, yes, refused to get confirmed and left The National Church, and he wasn't sorry that he'd dropped out of school in tenth grade either, at first it had been hard, he just got yelled at at home, not by Father, but Mother scolded him nonstop, and then he rented himself a basement room in Stranda, and then everything came together, and to make some money for a little food and his painting supplies he'd started painting pictures called *Boat in a Storm* and he'd propped them up by the stairs of The Stranda Hotel to sell them, and they were mostly pictures of sailboats in storms and damn if he didn't sell them, and that's how he made enough money to get by and then he met a girl named Liv who worked as a chambermaid in The Stranda Hotel and then she got pregnant and they had a son and now they were going to get married, it was Mother who'd nagged them to get married and eventually they thought it might be nice since Mother had said that she and Father would pay for the wedding, and, yes well, now he'd started at The Art School in Bjørgvin, because he got in, just from his pictures, and then he and Liv had rented an apartment at The Student Home, yes, it was because they had a child that they were able to get a place there, yes, well, so now they were going to get married at The Courthouse and he needed a best man and he was happy and grateful that Tor was thinking he might be willing to do it, he was worried about calling up out of the blue and asking him and Tor said of course he would be his best man but that he hadn't been to Bjørgvin since he was a kid so he'd never be able to find his way around there, he said and Asle said he should just take the bus to The Bus Station and then he'd fetch him there and when it was time to go back home Asle would bring him to The Bus Station so he didn't need to worry about that, he said, and Asle said they'd found a neighbour in The Student Home who would look after their son while they got married at The Courthouse, he said and afterwards they'd have the reception at The Grand Café, in a separate room, just the four of them, they'd have a big meal there with everything and then they'd head home to the apartment in The Student Home and Tor could spend the night there, and Liv had asked one of her sisters if she'd be the maid of honour, and she'd said yes, so that's four, Asle said on the phone and he told Tor what day the wedding would be and Tor came to Bjørgvin in his best suit and Asle had bought himself a suit at The Second-Hand Shop in Sailor's Cove, that was where he'd bought all his clothes since he'd moved to Bjørgvin, and Liv had borrowed a wedding dress from her sister that fit her almost perfectly, and then Asle had bought a bridal bouquet for her and the wedding party took a taxi to a photographer first, because they wanted a real wedding photo, and he didn't really know why but that's how it was, Asle thinks, and then they took another taxi to The Courthouse and they were married and then they took a taxi to The Grand Café and got their private room, and they ordered a full menu and drank a lot of wine and then Liv started saying that Asle had only married her because he kind of had to, since his parents wanted him to, and because they had a child together and he said well they were married now anyway and she kept going and kept going and then they drank cognac with their coffee and Asle's father had given him money to pay with, and he paid for the private room and the good food and the good drinks, and then the wedding party took a taxi to The Student Home, it was him and Liv and Tor and Liv's sister, and when they got out of the taxi Liv screamed loud in the darkness and then she threw the bridal bouquet right into Asle's face and he managed to catch it before it hit the ground and they hurried through the rain to the apartment in The Student Home and Asle was carrying the bridal bouquet and Liv was almost howling as she walked and her sister was trying to comfort her and Tor and Asle walked next to each other after Liv and her sister and they stayed outside until Liv and her sister had taken the lift and then they went inside and took the lift upstairs and when they entered the apartment Liv was lying on the sofa and her sister looked at them and she shook her head and Asle put the bouquet down on the kitchen table and he said so now they were married, he and Liv, and Liv's sister told her now she was married and Liv said goddammit if this was what it was like to be married then she wasn't interested, because Asle didn't care about her at all, she'd never realized it, not as clearly as she did today, on her own wedding day of all days, she said and her sister said she didn't know what she was talking about, everything had gone so well, and the wedding picture will definitely be beautiful and then Liv got up and she picked the bouquet up from the kitchen table and threw it on the floor and her sister went and picked it up and she said now she needed to rest, probably the best thing to do would be to go and lie down, she said, and she'd help her take off her wedding dress and they went into the bedroom and Asle heard Liv crying and her sister comforting her and then he said that he'd bought a bottle of whisky and then he poured a big glass for Tor and a big glass for himself and then he said that they needed a little water so that it would be the right strength but Tor had to decide for himself how strong he wanted his to be, Asle said and he turned the tap on and put a little water in his glass, had a taste, and then put a little more water in the glass and Tor did the same thing and then they went into the living room and sat down and Tor said that this was a nice apartment and Asle said they'd really been lucky to get an apartment in The Student Home, and it wasn't too expensive, it was expensive enough, but he was getting something called an artist stipend and Liv was working a few shifts at a hospice so they were managing fine, and his parents had paid for the wedding, because Mother had nagged and nagged them to get married, so finally he'd said yes, they'd just do it and then Tor asked if he'd proposed to her and Asle said he never proposed and he said it just happened, they would get married because everything would be the same as it was before, he said and Tor said that he wasn't exactly looking forward to getting married himself after having been to this wedding and then they both started laughing and they laughed and laughed until finally Asle managed to stop laughing and he said that probably not all weddings were necessarily like this and Tor said he certainly hoped not, but obviously they couldn't be, he said and then they sat in silence for a bit and then Asle asked if Tor wanted to go to sleep, there was a blanket and pillow under the sofa they were sitting on, it was what they call a sofa-bed, he said and Tor said he was actually extremely tired, and he could feel that he'd certainly drunk enough, he said and then they got up and Alse opened up the sofa and Tor said yes that sure is a sofa-bed and while Tor stood there holding his glass and taking a cautious little sip of his drink every now and then Asle made up the bed and now there was only the sound of sobbing from the bedroom and then Liv's sister came out and said that her husband was still outside waiting for her and she said that it was too bad Liv had gotten so drunk, and so out of control, she said, but she'd come back tomorrow, she said, or in any case the day after tomorrow, she said and laughed and Asle thanked her very much for having agreed to be Liv's maid of honour and Liv's sister said there was no reason to thank her and she congratulated him on becoming a married man and then she said that she'd kept her husband waiting long enough, and besides it was a long drive back to Sartor, she said, so they said goodbye and then Asle walked Liv's sister out to the entryway and they said goodbye and he went back into the apartment and when he walked into the living room Tor was there in just his underpants and he'd put his clothes on the armchair and Tor said he was tired and he emptied his glass and went and put it on the kitchen counter and Asle said that he'd take him to The Bus Station tomorrow morning or early afternoon of course and Tor said thanks and then Asle said that he was the one who should be thanking him for helping, for agreeing to be his best man, and Tor said there was no reason to thank him, but it had been quite a wedding, Tor said and then Asle drank the rest of the drink in his glass and then they said good night to each other and then Asle went quietly into the bedroom and he saw Liv lying outstretched on the bed, on top of the covers, in her wedding dress, and he left the door open and got undressed in the light from the hall and put his clothes on a chair and then gingerly closed the door and then he lay down on the bed as quietly and carefully as he could and he lay on his side and he thought that it was really stupid getting married, he and Liv, but anyway it'd been nice to see Tor again and get to talk with him a little, Asle thought and he thought how was this all going to end? no, he didn't know, he thought, Asle thinks walking down the street in his black velvet jacket, with his brown shoulderbag, holding Siv's hand, and he thinks that he lay there on his wedding night and saw pictures before his eyes and he saw six different pictures that he had to paint away, pictures that had lodged in his mind and that he now saw before his eyes one after the other, there was one picture of Tor's hands and then one of just one of Tor's hands, both from when he'd picked Tor up at The Bus Station, and then one of Liv bending forward to straighten her wedding dress, and then one of the photographer's face when he told them he was about to take a picture and one of the waiter's face as he looked at the table right before he served the first course and then one of Liv's sister holding

Liv in her arms after she'd thrown the bridal bouquet at him, these
pictures were painted inside his skull as it were, it was like his skull
was a canvas, Asle thinks and he's tried to paint them all away, but
he hasn't been able to, he thinks walking down the street there in
his black velvet jacket, and with his brown shoulderbag, and holding Siv's hand and neither of them says anything and I sit in my
chair and I look out into the darkness at my landmark there in the
Sygne Sea, and I see the water so clearly, I see the waves, and I
don't understand how I can see the water, the waves, yes, even
though it's totally dark, I think and tomorrow is Little Christmas
Eve and then it'll be Christmas Eve and I'll go with Åsleik to celebrate Christmas with him and Sister in Øygna, I think and I really have no desire to do that but I did say yes, yes well I said yes, I
think and I think that it's like all my strength has been taken away
from me and I need to go lie down, I feel so exhausted, it's like I
don't even have the strength to get up and go lie down, I think
sitting there in the chair looking at my spot out there in the middle
of the Sygne Sea and I look at the waves and I see Asle and Siv
walking hand in hand down a street in Bjørgvin and then they go
up some stairs and Siv unlocks the door to the apartment she's
renting and Asle goes inside and he shuts the door after him and
then Siv throws her arms around him and she holds him close and
they kiss each other, a long kiss, and then Siv says that it's nothing
special but it's somewhere to live, she says and then they go into a
room that's both a studio and a living room, and the floor is almost
covered with drawings and paintings
    I like painting on the floor, Siv says
    Looks that way, Asle says
    I should try that too, he says
    You've never tried it? Siv says
    No, never, Asle says
    and Siv says he really needs to try it, it's almost like a totally
different surface, plus you can use thick paint without the colours
running together, and the surface of the picture can be much more

built up too, she says and Asle says yes of course and then Asle lies down on the sofa and then Siv comes over and lies next to him

Now it's you and me, Siv says

Yes, Asle says

and then they lie there and hold each other and Siv says that it's a little cold and she still hasn't shown him the bedroom and then they get up and they go into the bedroom and there's a mattress on the floor and Asle lies down on it and Siv says that it's a little cold in there and she gets a blanket and spreads it over Asle and he lies there and he thinks that he needs to leave Liv, and leave The Boy, and move out, and it hurts so much to think that he's going to leave him, but they'll have to still see each other, at least once a week they'll have to still be able to see each other, Asle thinks and then he says that he has to go home and Siv says she can't bear to think about him going home to her and that his home is here now and he can, yes, he has to move in with her whenever he wants, because there's more than enough room for them both, she says, and she'll straighten up, since she's spread her stuff out everywhere, but he can paint in the main room and she can paint in the bedroom and then they'll have the kitchen as a kind of common room, she says, and she says that sounds so stupid, she can hear how dumb she sounds, she says and Asle gets up and goes and gets dressed and he says that he needs to go now and Siv says well then talk to you tomorrow and she says that she'll miss him and that she thinks about him all the time, she doesn't do anything else, just thinks about him, she can't get herself to think about anything else, she says and the thought that he's going home to another woman drives her completely crazy, Siv says and Asle says that he'll come here, he'll move in with her and Siv says that he and Liv are married and he says he'll have to get a divorce and she says that'll take a long time, first he'll have to separate and then it takes a year or so and only then will he be able to get divorced, Siv says and Asle says he'll tell Liv everything tonight, that he's found another woman, and that sounds so stupid, found another woman, yes that does sound stupid, Siv says and they really don't need to talk about it too much, because it'll go badly no matter what they say, everything just has to happen, she says and then she asks when they'll see each other again and Asle says probably tomorrow at The Art School and she says no, she wants to see him tonight, can't he come over tonight so that everything's over and done with, Siv says and Asle says he needs to go and Siv asks can't she make him a little dinner and Asle gets embarrassed and then Siv says that she bought enough food for dinner for them both

That sounds great, he says

Well it's not all that, Siv says

It's just normal food, she says

That's what I like best, normal food, Asle says

and Siv says she knows, that's why she bought pork chops, since she knows he likes that, because lots of times when they've eaten together at the café he's ordered pork chops, she says and Asle says that that was nice of her and then she says she'll start cooking then and Asle can just sketch or whatever he wants to do and then Asle goes and takes his sketchpad out of the brown leather shoulderbag in the hall and he goes and lies back down on the sofa and then he just lies there and looks at the pencil and at the blank white page in the sketchpad and then he draws the face of a screaming baby, and then he draws it seen from various angles, and he wants it just to be a rough sketch, just practice, but it sort of doesn't turn out that way, it turns into real drawings that are really saying something, and he doesn't like it, and now he wants to draw something else and he starts to draw a boat and he gives it nice lines and three strakes and an old-fashioned pointed bow, it's a traditional Barmen boat he's drawn, just the boat, and with a couple of oars lying on the seats, and it's a nice boat, and now there's the good smell of cooking meat from the kitchen and then Siv is standing in the doorway and she asks him if he wants a bottle of beer

See, I planned everything, she says

Yes, thanks, Asle says

and Siv goes back out to the kitchen and then she comes back in with a half bottle of beer and a glass and Asle puts the sketchpad down

You don't want me to see what you've been drawing? Siv says

and Asle doesn't answer and he picks up the bottle and the glass and he pours the beer into the glass and he tastes it and then he puts it down on the coffee table and Siv says that the table is ugly as hell but she got it for next to nothing at The Second-Hand Shop, the sofa too, she says

And now I've got it all dirty with paint on it too, she says

and tubes of oil paint and brushes are sitting on the table and Asle takes a sip of beer and Siv says she has to check on the food so the chops don't burn and then she goes back out to the kitchen and Asle thinks that he's never been there, in the kitchen, and he drinks more beer and then he sketches a big empty open boat in a rough sea and he thinks that it's almost a bit like the paintings he painted and sold to make money when he was living in Stranda and then Siv is standing in the doorway and she says dinner's ready and they pretty much have to eat in the living room, she says, because the kitchen's so small that there's no room to eat in there, she says and Asle gets up and then he's standing in the kitchen doorway and he sees a short kitchen counter with two cupboard doors under it and a stove and a cupboard hanging over the stove and then there's a window and Siv takes a plate out of the cupboard and then she puts a pork chop on the plate and then a kind of red mashed vegetables he's never seen before and he asks what it is and Siv says does he really not know what it is? it's red-carrot mash, yes, it was totally normal at her house when she was growing up, she says and then she puts a couple of potatoes on the plate and then she asks if he wants melted butter on his potatoes and he says yes and then Siv takes a spoon and scoops some up and pours it over the potatoes and then she gives him a knife and fork and Asle goes out to the living room and he clears a space in front of him on the coffee table for his and Siv's plates and then Siv comes in with her plate and

she says enjoy and Asle takes a bite of the food and it tastes great,
and the carrot mash is sweet and goes perfectly with the fried pork
chops, and they eat in silence

That was really good, Asle says

Just normal food, nothing special, Siv says

and they eat and don't say anything and Asle thinks damn he
was hungry, but now, now he has to go home to Liv, she's maybe
waiting for him

I hope it was good, Siv says

It was definitely good, Asle says

and then he says thank you for dinner and that he has to go
now and Siv asks him if he's coming back tonight and he says
maybe, and she says just maybe and then Asle leaves and I sit in my
chair here and look at the sea, at my landmark, I'm looking straight
ahead the whole time, just at the water, at the waves there at one
spot in the middle of the Sygne Sea and I think I should have called
to find out how Asle is doing, but I probably wouldn't have found
out anything, every time I call they just say that he's pretty much
the same and that he needs his rest and that it's better for him if
he doesn't have any visitors now, the woman who answers the
phone always says that, because it's always a woman who answers
the phone, but the voices are always different, I think, and one of
them said that his three children had come to see him but he'd had
hardly any contact with his children after his two divorces, a little
with The Boy, as he called him, the one who lives in Oslo, his son
from his first marriage, but he'd had almost no contact with The
Daughter and The Son, at first after the divorce The Daughter and
The Son had stayed with him every other weekend, but then Siv,
their mother, found another man and moved to Trøndelag or some
other city with The Daughter and The Son, and then the two
women he'd once been married to had come to see him, she said
and she said that he was doing much worse after one of the women
he'd once been married to had visited, and she probably shouldn't
have said that, she said, but since she knew that he and I were close

38

friends she sort of decided she could tell me, she said, but I mustn't tell anyone that she'd said that, she said and I think that still I should call The Hospital and I get up and go out into the hall and I pick up the phone and I dial The Hospital's number and I say, like I always do, every time, that I'm a good friend of Asle's and I'd like to come see him, because maybe there's something he needs? I say, and yes, I've already gone and picked up his dog, someone from The Hospital came with me and unlocked the door to his apartment, so maybe I can bring him something? I say and I say that it was me who got Asle admitted, and who has his dog now, I say and I look down and I see Bragi sitting on his haunches right in front of me and looking at me with his dog's eyes and she says that she'll ask and I just stand there with the telephone in my hand and then after a while the voice comes back and she says that Asle isn't well enough to have visitors yet, so, unfortunately, she says and I ask if I can call again tomorrow and she says of course I can and I say thank you and she says it was nothing and I hang up the phone and I go into the main room and I look at the empty easel and then I go over to the round table and I put on my black velvet jacket, because it's so cold in the room, I think, but I can't bring myself to light the stove, and I haven't even turned on the electric heater, I think and I go back out into the hall and I put on my long black coat, and I put on a scarf, and then I go get the grey blanket that's on the bench and I drape it over my shoulders, the blanket Grandma had around her when she lay on the bench back in The Old House and couldn't talk or walk, the one she handed to me when they put her on a stretcher to carry her out to the ambulance, I think, that blanket has stayed with me, wherever I lived I had that blanket with me, I think and I sit down again in my chair by the round table and I tuck the blanket tight around me and I take my bearings and then I sit there and look at the waves and I see Asle standing there and he's holding The Boy in his arms and he's rocking him back and forth and Liv is sitting there on the sofa and she's crying and crying and then Asle goes into the bedroom carrying The Boy and he puts him down on the bed and then he gets the sketchpad and pencil from the leather shoulderbag in the hall and then he sits down on the edge of the bed and he starts drawing a girl about twenty years old lying outstretched on the floor and it's hard to tell if she's alive or dead and he draws a girl who's sitting on a sofa and crying and crying and the whole time he hears Liv crying and crying and Asle shuts his eyes and he looks straight ahead into the nothingness and then he sees three new pictures lodge themselves forever in his mind, there's one of a young woman lying on the floor who looks more dead than alive, and then there's one of a young woman who's sitting on a sofa crying and crying and then there's a picture of a boy not even one year old lying with his hands and feet spread out on a double bed and crying and crying and Asle thinks that he needs to paint these pictures away, but maybe he can't, because there are some pictures that just stay there, he thinks and then he sees Grandfather's black boots in the rain, always that picture comes to him, he'll never be rid of it, no matter how many times he's tried to paint a boot in the rain he has never been able to get rid of that picture, Asle thinks and he'll probably never really be able to get rid of a picture, that's just something he wants to do, or imagines he can do, because once a picture has lodged inside him it's stuck there, but when one of the painful pictures turns up it's less painful if he's tried to paint it away, it becomes fainter then somehow, he thinks and he thinks that he's tired, because he doesn't think he's slept at all tonight, or maybe a little, he thinks and he thinks that it was good he got home in time, if he'd come home any later Liv might be dead now, because he got her to The Hospital and there they pumped her stomach, got all the pills she'd taken out of her, he thinks, but The Boy had slept well and heavily all night, he thinks and he hears Liv crying and crying and he picks up The Boy and goes into the living room and then he stands there and rocks The Boy back and forth and he looks at Liv who's sitting there on the sofa and crying and crying and Asle asks if she wants anything, because someone has to say something, he thinks and Liv

just shakes her head and Asle sits down next to her and he puts his
arm around her shoulders and she lets it just stay there and then
she twists away a little so that his arm falls down off her shoulders
and Asle takes his arm back and he asks where Liv got the pills
from and she doesn't answer, she just cries and cries and Asle gets
up and he stands there and rocks The Boy back and forth and he
thinks that he didn't take off his black velvet jacket when he got
home last night or since, he sleeps in it sometimes, he thinks and
Liv just cries and cries and Asle rocks The Boy back and forth and
he asks if Liv feels like holding The Boy and she doesn't answer,
she just keeps crying and Asle asks where Liv got the pills from and
she doesn't answer and Asle rocks The Boy back and forth and Liv
cries and cries and now she really needs to stop this crying soon, he
thinks, she hasn't said a word since she got back from The Hospital
she's just sat there on the sofa crying and crying and Asle asks again
where she got the pills from

My mother, Liv says

From your mother? Asle says

You took them from your mother? he says

and Liv doesn't answer

I took the pills from Mother, she says

and Liv cries and cries and Asle can tell that she's trying to stop
but the tears just keep flowing and flowing

Gradually, over a long time, she says

and Asle rocks The Boy back and forth and he thinks that Liv
stole medicine from her mother over a long time, every time she
went to visit her on Sartor, maybe all the way back to the first time
they went there she did that and he'd never noticed anything, he'd
noticed nothing, nothing, he thinks, because he's just been caught
up with drawing and painting, and with these pictures he has in his
head, Asle thinks and he thinks that when The Boy was born he
had just started at The Art School and they were living with Liv's
parents out on Sartor before they were told they could move into
the apartment at The Student Home, he thinks and he looks at

the easel there in the living room, and his painting supplies are on
the coffee table, and hanging on the walls in the living room and
in the hall and in the bedroom are the paintings he's finished or is
still working on and Liv is sitting on the sofa crying and crying and
Asle rocks The Boy back and forth and he thinks that Liv can't just
keep crying and crying, he has to do something, he thinks and I
sit and look at my landmark out there in the Sygne Sea, I look at
the waves there and I think that Åsleik came over and had lutefisk
at my house today, and I usually always look forward to that meal,
but today I was so exhausted, or whatever it was, but Åsleik took
it well and I think he liked the food even if not that much was said
during the meal, I think and look at the water, at my landmark, at
the waves there, and I think that today it felt like nothing had any
meaning for me anymore, and painting, no, I can't paint anymore,
so I'll just have to live with these pictures in my head as best I can,
I think and I look at my landmark, at the waves and I see Asle
standing and holding The Boy in his arms and he's rocking him
back and forth and I look at my landmark out there in the middle
of the Sygne Sea and I close my eyes and I feel that Ales is near me
now, and then I feel her take my hand and then we sit there holding hands, and it's so good to feel Ales's hand, I think and I think
that sometimes it's hard to know if what's there is God's nearness
or Ales, and maybe there's no difference? I think and I think that
I read in a poem once that God is my dead friend, that's what it
said, and there's something true in that, I think and I look at my
landmark, at the waves and I see Asle standing in front of the open
front door at 7 University Street and Ales is standing next to him
and suddenly it's like something comes over her, Asle sees, and Ales
says that she has to go soon, so if it takes a long time, yes, at Herdis
Åsen's house, then, yes, she might not be able to wait for him, but
they'll absolutely see each other again soon, because starting today
they are a pair, they're Asle and Ales, she says, and she'll write a
letter to him every night, she promises, Ales says and Asle just looks
at her and then Ales jumps into his arms and she hugs him tight

and Asle hugs her tight and then they pull away from each other
and then Ales says anyway, she has to go now, she says, and so Asle
can settle into the apartment in peace and quiet and then they'll
see each other again soon, she says, yes, now he just needs to go
rent that room from that Herdis Åsen or whatever her name is, she
says and Ales says she sincerely hopes she's an ugly old hag, she says
and Asle says well she's definitely old, judging from her voice on
the phone, and judging from her handwriting in the letter he got
she's no spring chicken, no, he says and then Ales throws her arms
around him and gives him a quick kiss on the mouth and then she
says she's just kidding

I can't believe we found each other today, she says

And it'll be for our whole lives, she says

And maybe it was decided by providence, she says

Or maybe it just happened by chance, she says

and she says that it seems like some things are decided by providence while others aren't, yes, they just happen by chance, but
even if it was just by chance then it happened anyway and now it's
up to them, to her, to him, to make what's happened, that they
met, as beautiful as possible, Ales says and Asle says that he can't
show up late to his appointment with Herdis Åsen and Ales says
that he better go and look at the apartment then and get that out of
the way, she says, and it's probably best if he goes alone, she says, or
else he probably won't get the room since this Herdis Åsen woman
will probably think he's going to have women over all the time and
she probably won't like that, that's probably what this Herdis Åsen
is like, Ales says

Women over, right, Asle says

Now I need to go, Ales says

and she says she has something she needs to do, she says, so
she needs to go, and she says that she wonders if he's going to live
in that room there at all, at Herdis Åsen's, anyway it won't be for
long, Ales says and Asle doesn't understand what she means and
then he sees Ales stand there and Asle opens the front door and

he goes inside and he goes up all those stairs changing direction at every landing, and at every landing there are two doors, one on the left, one on the right, and all in all there are twelve apartments in the building, and Herdis Åsen lives in one of the apartments on the top floor, Herdis Åsen who will rent him a room if she thinks he deserves it and if she wants him living in her apartment, Asle thinks and he rings the doorbell under the nameplate that says Herdis Åsen and after a moment he hears light footsteps coming and then the door opens and a little old woman, probably around seventy, opens the door and looks at him, and she's wearing glasses, and her hair is pretty short, and she has lots of wrinkles in her face, and a heavy smell of cigarette smoke comes out of the apartment

No I don't believe my eyes, Herdis Åsen says

and she says Asle should come in and he walks into the entry-way and she holds out her hand to him, and her fingers are long and thin, and she's wearing lots of rings, and her nails are painted a dark red colour and Asle holds out his hand and they shake hands and he feels that her hand is cold and she stays standing there holding his hand for a long time, and then she lets go of his hand and Asle thinks that it's no doubt already decided that he'll rent a room at Herdis Åsen's because she goes over to a door next to the front door and she opens it and invites him into the room and there's a bed and a desk and a bookshelf and a wardrobe and then a dresser, and on the dresser is a hot plate with one burner, a breadbox, a cutting board, and then a kind of basin to wash the dishes in, and there's a dishtowel hanging on the wall and all the furniture is nice old furniture, well-made city furniture, Asle thinks, and he sees that the bed is made, everything's tucked in tight and Herdis Åsen says that this is what she has to offer, she says, and then she goes out into the hall and Asle follows her and she shows him a room with a toilet and another with a shower, and she says that since she showers in the morning it would be nice if he could shower at night, and in the room with the shower there's also a washing machine and she'll explain how to use it later, she usually washes her clothes every Friday and then hangs them up to dry on the lines there, she says and she points at a few cords hung from one wall to the other under the ceiling, more or less over their heads, so it would be nice if for example he could wash his clothes on Mondays, she says, yes yes, she says and then she opens a door and Herdis Åsen says he should come right in and then she walks into a living room, and there is good well-made old city furniture in that room too, a sofa and coffee table, a big table with chairs, a secretaire, and there are paintings on the walls, hung right next to each other, and Asle sees at once that they're good paintings, but he can't tell who painted them, and she says that she's interested in art so she's had enough money to buy a few pictures over the years, or really she didn't have enough money but she bought them anyway, and to be honest she's bought a lot of pictures over the years, she has a lot more than are hanging on the walls, there are stacks of them in the wardrobe in her bedroom, Herdis Åsen says and Asle sees that there's a big heavy bookshelf in the living room, and Herdis Åsen says that she used to be a high-school teacher, her subjects were Norwegian and German, but now she's retired, of course every now and then she still teaches, if someone needs a substitute, she says, and her father was a professor of Nynorsk at The University in Bjørgvin, and even though she grew up in Bjørgvin she's always had a good feel for Nynorsk, and for the dialects related to Nynorsk, yes, that's why she's always taken in renters from Hardanger, and the most recent one lived there for the whole time he was a student, and now, like the otherpeople who'd rented a room from her, he'd become a teacher at a rural high school, Herdis Åsen says and she says that all her previous renters have been male students at The University, humanities students one and all, and now they're scattered around the country at various high schools, and one of them has meanwhile become a professor of Nordic Literature at The University in Oslo, Herdis Åsen says and she goes into the kitchen and she says that she'd rather keep this room for herself, but there are cafés at The Art School and he can probably buy his food there? and he can keep bread and cold cuts and milk and things like that in his room, she doesn't know if he noticed, she says, but there was a breadbox on the dresser and a cutting board and a basin for washing dishes, and in the bottom drawer there are a couple of pots and a frying pan and some dishes and cups and mugs, everything a person might need to make a little food, but all her earlier renters bought food at the cafeteria at The University and he probably can too, maybe? if not then there's a cafeteria at The Art School? because even if he's going to The Art School he'll be allowed to go to The Cafeteria at The University, she says, or else there are more than enough reasonable cafés in Bjørgvin, and the people who've stayed in her rented room before usually went to The Coffeehouse, in any case you used to be able to get a reasonably priced dinner there, but they've probably raised the prices in recent years, she says, and she herself never goes there, when she eats out she always goes to The Grand Café, the prices there are affordable enough for her and the food is good, and besides she can get nice wine there that isn't too expensive, she says, and she has to have wine with her food, every day she has wine with her food, yes, and even if she skips the food sometimes she doesn't skip the wine, she takes a glass every day, at least one, Herdis Åsen says and she goes back into the living room and she says that she has a little collection of books and she points at the bookshelf, she'd inherited thousands of books from her father, she says, but she sold most of them to The Holberg Antiquariat down by The Fishmarket, and if he was interested in books at all he had to stop by there someday, she says, but, as he can see, yes, she kept some books, yes, it was mostly the Nynorsk and German literature she was interested in, even when she was young, she says, so both the Nynorsk classics and some of the contemporary Nynorsk writers are there on her shelf, and then the German classics, she's less familiar with contemporary German literature, but she has some of the most well-known contemporary German writers on her shelves too, and she's probably read most of the books there, she says, because she reads constantly, but now it's one book in one book out, and either she gives the book that needs to go out to someone as a gift or else she sets it aside and when she has enough books set aside she takes them to The Holberg Antiquariat down by The Fishmarket and she gets paid next to nothing for them, but that doesn't matter, she has her pension so she gets by, and then she makes a little money from these hours she's substitute teaching, she says, and then she'll also get a little rental money from the room, she says and she looks at Asle, but, yes, he should know it's not for the money that she rents out a room, not at all, she says and then Herdis Åsen opens another door and she invites Asle to step inside and Asle sees in front of him a rosemaling canopy bed, it's high and quite wide and there's a high-backed chair by the side of the bed, and it has carved dragons on the ends of the arms

I inherited the bed and the chair from my parents, Herdis Åsen says

and she's lit a cigarette and she holds out a pack of cigarettes to Asle and she asks if he smokes and he says he does, and Asle takes a cigarette and says thank you and then Herdis Åsen takes her lighter and holds out a light for Asle and he takes a good drag on his cigarette and she says he probably hand-rolls his cigarettes, doesn't he, and Asle says he does and then Herdis Åsen picks up an ashtray from the nightstand next to the other side of the bed, there's a high-backed chair next to one side of the bed and a nightstand next to the other, and the nightstand too is rosemaling, and first she taps the ash off her cigarette then she holds out the ashtray to Asle who taps his ash off, and then she asks when he can move in and Asle says that he's not entirely sure but as soon as possible, actually, he says and Herdis Åsen asks if he's starting at The Art School right away and Asle says yes and she asks isn't he going to high school, and Asle says that he went to The Academic High School, in Aga, yes, but that he didn't like it there and that's why he tried to get into The Art School before he was done with The Academic High School and he got a spot thanks to the paintings he showed them

Then you must have real talent, Herdis Åsen says

Well I don't know, Asle says

Yes you do, she says

Yes I guess I do, he says

and she says wouldn't it have been better for him if he'd finished high school with an examen artium, something he'd have for
later in life? because being able to live as an artist, to live off his art,
live off selling paintings, well, that's not so easy, she says, even if
there are galleries in all the big cities in Norway now, and even if
The Beyer Gallery in Bjørgvin has no problem selling pictures, she
says, but Beyer is very particular about which artists he takes on at
his gallery, yes, it's much harder to get an exhibition at The Beyer
Gallery than to get into The Art School, she says and they go into
the living room and Herdis Åsen says that all the pictures, except
the old ones, in the thick frames, yes he can see which ones are old
and which are new, she bought all the new pictures from Beyer,
and anyway they were family, he used to be married to her sister,
so he was technically her brother-in-law, but, yes well, it's been
many years since her sister died, so Beyer was a widower now,
Herdis Åsen says and because she was single she'd often, when her
dear departed sister was alive, gone on holiday with them, yes, to
the big cities of Europe, so she'd been inside a lot of art museums,
but most of the time they'd travelled to Italy, to Rome, because
Rome was the place Beyer liked best, but if Asle had talent and
painted good pictures she'd be happy to introduce him to Beyer
one evening, she could invite him over for dinner and then he
could have a look at Asle's paintings and if he showed at The Beyer Gallery then that would really be something, to tell the truth,
because lots of graduating classes from The Art School can go by
before Beyer finally thinks anyone's paintings are good enough for
their own exhibition, Herdis Åsen says and she stubs out her cigarette and Asle stubs out his and he says that if she wants to have him
in her apartment he'd be happy to rent the room from her, as long
as it's all right for him to paint pictures in the room, he says and

Herdis Åsen says that that's fine, but he should call her before he comes with his things and moves in, she says and Asle says of course he'll do that and I sit there in my chair and I look at the sea, at the waves, instead of standing by the easel looking at the picture I now just sit and look at the sea, I think and I feel no need to paint anymore, none at all, and again I think that I need to call The Hospital to find out how Asle is doing, and if I can come visit him soon, because now he's been in The Hospital for weeks and he surely has to get better soon, better enough for me to visit him anyway, but I just called, so I can't call again right away, I think, something must be wrong with me for me to even think of it, I think and even if I did call I'd only hear that it was best for Asle if I don't come and see him, so I should drive to Bjørgvin instead on Christmas Day, but no, I can't, because this year I'm going with Åsleik to celebrate Christmas at Sister's house, I forgot about that, I think, and that'll make it a long time since I've been to mass, I think and I feel a strong need to take part in the mass again, and be forgiven, and take communion, and usually I always drive to Bjørgvin on Christmas Day to go to mass, even though I like the simple mass on normal weekdays better, I go to high mass on Christmas Day but there's a completely different spirit in the simple everyday masses, almost no one goes to those masses as opposed to high masses on Sunday mornings, then it's almost full in St Paul's Church, and there's singing, yes, a choir, and full organ music, yes, all things considered it was very nice but for me it was the quiet moments with just the words from the priest and the answers from the people that were the best masses, and when the people there, five or six or seven of us, stood up to take communion there was a wonderful sense of atonement, yes, of peace that came over everything, I think, and maybe I'll want to paint pictures again if I just go to mass and sit peacefully and pray a silent prayer as the host, Christ's transfigured body, dissolves in my mouth and I become part of Christ's mystical body, become part of the communion of saints, and when as a part of it I turn towards God, in silence, and then I

always pray for people I've known who are dead now, and especially for Ales, and then I pray for the living people who I feel
might need someone to pray for them, and it would be so good, as
the host dissolves in my mouth, to pray for Asle, pray that he'll get
better, or pray that God takes him back if that's what would be best
and lets Asle find peace in God, in God's peace and God's light,
because Asle never really fit in in this world, and something bigger
than life spoke from his pictures with such a clear and silent voice,
but that's how it is with all good pictures, I think and I look at my
landmark, at the waves and I see Asle lying in a bed and he's shaking, his body is trembling, and The Doctor says that he doesn't
understand why it's not stopping, and it's strange too, that the
spasms haven't stopped, they've been going on for a long time now,
yes, days, weeks, The Doctor says and they've given him as much
medicine as they can, and that's helped, and most of the time he's
asleep, The Doctor says and I see that Asle is getting fed intrave-
nously, as they say, and he's peeing through a catheter, as they call
it, I see and Asle's just lying there and when he wakes up he just
thinks confusedly that he might as well die and finally be done
with it, so that he's done, Asle thinks and then he disappears into a
doze again and the shaking takes hold of his body and he thinks
that she's standing there saying she can't do it anymore and The
Doctor says and she says she wants a divorce and a little room of
painting supplies and he thinks that really he didn't need any more
room yes even after their son was born yes the apartment in The
Student Home yes before he was born Liv's father and it was good
to move in and she lies there and she's just barely breathing and Siv
and to be at The Student Home and paint and The Boy and Liv lay
on the floor a glass of alcohol diluted with water drink the whole
glass and Siv comes into the living room and she can't stand looking at him standing there painting anymore become a teacher have
children paint and then drink and she is so exhausted she might
collapse at any time painting and she just can't imagine and
Bjørgviner Bjørgvin Bjørgviner and she lets go of his arm and

never been in love before no never and the paintbrush the kitchen vodka and she went to get The Son from nursery school bought toilet paper dinner that meat a glass of vodka no she can't stand it anymore and bread milk The Son and The Daughter sleep in that morning a two-room apartment forcing her he just taking and doesn't know and never come back and never been in love quiet in love that was gone and never should have moved in together and she walks down the street and her long black hair flows her long black raincoat flutters on her back vodka and her long black hair flows down her back her long black raincoat flutters out to either side teacher and that big apartment and The Son and The Daughter and a door slams shut boiled carrots and then good mashed potatoes there's nothing like she makes good mashed potatoes and he never does anything around the house and Mama wants a little food and one day Papa and plates and knives and forks and I want a divorce and looking down at the floor and lying there thinking it over for a long time probably have to him too and then he has to learn to pick up a child from nursery school he and people he and a half bottle of vodka go to a shop an advance on mother's inheritance gives her economic and moral support and love he's always known and never cared he just stands there and then a black raincoat and the door opens and going over to the window just like that flowing hair the black raincoat open and fluttering to each side the sofa her body moving the fluttering black raincoat vodka and he's not worth much of anything not worth living be alone die and he can decide to go out to sea the waves and The Son and The Daughter vodka and there's a little left in the bottle take a walk divide up the things lie down and now it's finally decided not saying anything and going to The Alehouse and going to bed her flowing black raincoat hair and The Doctor says won't this shaking ever stop and The Nurse says yes it's so strange, yes, he's just lying there shaking and shaking and The Doctor says won't these spasms stop and I get up and I think I need to call The Hospital and hear how Asle is doing and I go out into the hall and pick up the phone and I hold it to my ear and I see the phone number for The Hospital written on a slip of paper that's on the telephone stand and I think now I've called there every day for a long time, and I called just now, what's wrong with me? I think and I always get the same answer, and I can't call The Hospital again already, I think and I'd rather drive to Bjørgvin on Christmas Day and go to Christmas mass in the morning, the way I usually do, but no, I can't this year, because I'll be in Øygna with Åsleik celebrating Christmas at Sister's, I think, but maybe I can drive down to Bjørgvin after Åsleik and I get home on The Boat? because the plan is to go to Øygna in The Boat as soon as it's light in the morning on Christmas Eve day, probably around noon, and come back home from Øygna to Dylgja the next day, yes, as early as we can, and then after we get home I can drive to The Hospital and check on Asle, and when I say how long a drive it was to come see him they'll probably have to let me in, I think, and maybe there's an evening mass too that I can go to on Christmas Day? I think and I go and sit back down in my chair by the round table and I look out the window at my spot there in the Sygne Sea and I think that it's my own darkness I'm sitting and looking into and that's why I can see the water, the waves, in spite of the darkness and I look at my landmark, at the waves and I see Asle running down the stairs in 7 University Street and he's happy and carefree, because now he not only has a place at The Art School, he's rented a room too, right in the middle of Bjørgvin, just a short walk from The Art School, yes, Herdis Åsen said so when he was leaving and she thanked him for wanting to rent a room from her and then Herdis Åsen said she was looking forward to him moving in, the only thing, yes, the only thing she asked was that he take the trash out for her, well, for her and for himself, it had to be done every Wednesday night, she said and Asle had said of course he could do that, and then they said so long until next time and Asle ran off down the stairs and he thinks that he'll be living at Herdis Åsen's for a long time, she sort of won't want to let him go, he thinks, and Ales had said that she had to

52

leave, she had to do something, but she never said what, he thinks, and he never got to ask her either, and he runs down the stairs because now he'll maybe see Ales again, he thinks, but maybe she left when he went up to look at the room, she said she had something to do, that's all she said, and that she'd write to him, Asle thinks and he thinks that since he spent so long at Herdis Åsen's she definitely must have left, he thinks and he runs down the stairs and he opens the front door of 7 University Street and he goes out and he can't see Ales anywhere, and she did say she had something to do, and said something about how she couldn't wait for him if he was going to be too long, or did she say that? and what did she have to do? why is she gone? why did she leave? Asle thinks, because there's no Ales to be seen, nowhere, and why didn't he hurry up? why did he spend such a long time up at Herdis Åsen's? but he couldn't just leave, could he? she wanted to just show him the apartment and the room and as soon as she did that he left, Asle thinks, and is it really true in reality that he and Ales met today? that they met at The Bus Café? and that they became boyfriend and girlfriend? or is that just something he imagined? because it can't be possible, things like that aren't possible, Asle thinks and he thinks that Ales gave him her address and he reaches into the pocket of his black velvet jacket and he takes out a slip of paper where Ales wrote her name and address and phone number, and she lives with her mother, so that's where he can reach her, but had they said goodbye to each other? and didn't Ales say that she'd wait for him? and now there's no Ales here, Asle thinks, and he looks at his watch and it's two hours before the bus to Aga leaves from The Bus Station, and, no, he doesn't understand why there's no Ales here, did she regret what she'd said and just leave him? what's happened? he thinks and I look at my landmark there in the Sygne Sea, I look at the waves and I see Asle walk into The Newsstand at The Bus Station and he thinks that now he'll buy a *Northern Herald* and then he'll go to The Bus Café and buy a pint and then he'll sit there, because it's a long time, yes, almost two hours that he has to wait for the bus to leave for Aga, but he'll drink a pint, slowly, and he can read the newspaper, and if he feels like it he can draw a sketch or two, because there are lots of pictures that lodged in him today, yes, so many that he feels almost overwhelmed and desperate when he thinks about all the pictures that got into his head today and it's like every one of them weighs so much, Asle thinks and now he's at The Newsstand and he buys a copy of *The Northern Herald* and then he goes into The Bus Café and he sees that there's almost no one there, but sitting at a window in the back of the café with her back to the wall is a woman with medium-length blonde hair, and she looks like she's a few years older than Asle and she sits there looking out the window, and there's a glass of wine in front of her, and then, at the other end of the café, there's the man with long dark hair who looks just like Asle, who's always wearing a black velvet jacket and carrying a brown leather shoulderbag, and who hangs around and paints, just like Asle, the guy Asle met at The Stranda Hotel when he and Sigve went there, and ran into at The Paint Shop, and he too is sitting by a window, and he's sitting with his back to the woman with the medium-length blonde hair and there's a pint of beer in front of him and Asle thinks that it's really strange that he's sitting there, because he's the one who made Asle think about applying for a spot at The Art School just with the pictures he'd painted, without an examen artium, Asle thinks and it's sort of like he doesn't like seeing him sitting there, and he doesn't know why he doesn't like it, and Asle thinks that he hopes this Namesake, because his name is Asle too, hasn't noticed him, but of course he will, Asle thinks and then he goes to the counter and says he'd like to buy a pint please and the man standing behind the counter who can't be much older than Asle looks suspiciously at him and then he pours a pint from the tap and Asle pays and he notices that the woman with the medium-length blonde hair is looking at him and he doesn't look at her, he looks straight ahead and then he looks at The Namesake and he sees that he's sitting with a sketchpad in front of him and he's lost in the drawing he's working on and Asle goes and sits down by a window a few tables away from the woman with the medium-length blonde hair with his back to her and so that The Namesake has his back to him, and then he takes a sip of beer and he looks out the window and he sees people arriving at and leaving The Bus Station, some are carrying suitcases and shopping bags, some are empty-handed, some are walking with a spring in their step, some are limping, now and then there's someone walking with a cane, and then he sees a man with long grey hair tied back in a hairtie, and he's dressed in a black velvet jacket, just like Asle, and he's wearing a brown leather shoulderbag, and he's walking with a cane, and Asle doesn't know why a picture of this man gets lodged inside him but now he has a picture of him lodged in his mind, yes, it's like he has a camera in his head, Asle thinks, no, he mustn't think things like that, but still that's kind of how it is, in a way, yes, and every so often this camera takes a picture entirely by itself and the picture gets stored in his head, or it's like it gets glued into a photo album in there, and then it pops up every now and then, and then he sees it perfectly clearly before his eyes, and when a picture like that pops up it's like everything that's happening around him, in the real world, goes away and it's like he sees nothing but that picture, and why do pictures get stuck in his head like that? no, he doesn't know, and he doesn't know why they suddenly pop up in his head either, he doesn't understand, why would he be like that? and it's to get rid of these pictures that he paints, actually that's the only reason why, because it's always one of these pictures that he, no, not paints, but he tries to get rid of one of these pictures by painting a picture that's like it, Asle thinks, and the reason a picture gets stuck inside him must be that it says something to him, and it's what the picture says that he tries to paint, yes, to make it go away, and in a way the picture kind of turns into part of himself, something he in a way understands and that anyway doesn't bother him anymore, or bothers him less anyway, Asle thinks and he raises his glass and he takes a good sip of beer and he thinks that at least two maybe three pictures have lodged in his head since he got to The Bus Café and he looks at The Namesake's back and he sees the door of The Bus Café open and a woman with long black hair walks in and she goes straight to The Namesake and he gets up and then they give each other a hug and then they kiss each other and Asle hears The Namesake say it's nice to see you Siv and she says it's nice to see you too Asle, because, no, this can't go on, she says, I miss you all the time, she says and she sits down across from The Namesake and he says he's missed her too and it's so good to see you again Siv, he says

It can't go on like this anymore, Siv says

and The Namesake says that soon now, yes, he'll tell Liv about them soon, but she must know about it already, and it probably wasn't because of the two of them that she wanted to kill herself, because she'd been stealing pills from her mother for a long time, she'd said, and storing them up, he says and trying to kill yourself while there's a baby not even a year old lying there crying all alone is just wrong, he says

No it's unbelievable, he says

And of course I think it's my fault, he says

and the woman named Siv says it's not his fault, he's tried to take care of Liv as best he could, that's all, they just met and then she lived with him in his room there in Stranda and then she got pregnant, she says, but he must have liked her? have been in love with her? been attracted to her anyway?, and fuck, fuck, fuck, Siv says and it almost looks like she's about to leave and The Namesake says she needs to calm down, because it's just her now, but he does have to think about The Boy too, he says, yes, Liv's better now, and now she can take care of the baby, so soon, very soon, he'll tell her about the two of them, The Namesake says and Asle thinks why are The Namesake and the woman named Siv sitting in The Bus Café talking loud enough for other people to hear them about things that are none of anybody else's business? things that are only for the two of them? things that it only disturbs other people to have to listen to? Asle thinks and he looks up and he turns around and his eyes meet the eyes of the woman with the medium-length blonde hair, she is sitting and looking at him, and Asle turns back around right away and he looks down at the table and he starts to flip through the newspaper and he pages through the whole newspaper and there's nothing in there he especially pays attention to, and he flips back to the death notices and he reads through them, and it's strange how many people have died, both young and old, people from all the cities in West Norway, Asle thinks and he doesn't understand it, people are born, people die, just a few years of struggle and toil to get through their life one way or another and then they die, they come from nothing, they're just born, and they go back to nothing, they're just gone, and then there're these years they call life, a life, a human life, Asle thinks and he sees The Namesake get up and the woman who'd sat down across from him gets up too, and then The Namesake puts the sketchpad and pencil into the brown leather shoulderbag and puts it on and Asle looks down at the newspaper, at the page with the death notices and then he hears a voice say no it's you and Asle looks up and he sees The Namesake standing there looking at him

It's been a while, Asle says

Yeah, remember those days at The Stranda Hotel? The Namesake says

Yeah, Asle says

And the last time we talked was probably at The Paint Shop back in Stranda, The Namesake says

and there's silence and Asle sees that the woman named Siv has walked to the door of The Bus Café and stopped

And all sorts of things have happened to me since then, The Namesake says

Yes, Asle says

and to him it's unbearable how much the two of them look alike but The Namesake doesn't seem to notice or care, for him it's just like they're two people the same age and that they wear similar clothes and look a little like each other, Asle thinks and The

Namesake tells him that maybe he remembers him telling him that he was going to be a father and Asle nods and he says he's become a father, yes, the father of a baby boy not even one year old, he says and he's started at The Art School and he and Liv, yes, that's the name of the woman he lives with, he probably told him about her back at The Stranda Hotel? The Namesake says, yes, first they moved to Sartor, yes, to her parents' place, and then they moved to Bjørgvin, when they got an apartment at The Student Home, and now they live there, he says and the woman named Siv comes walking back to The Namesake

Let's go, she says

and she takes The Namesake's arm and Asle looks at her and he sees that she looks like she's totally mixed up, she's sad and she's angry and everything you can imagine, he thinks

Take care, The Namesake says

And give my regards to The Stranda Hotel, he says

and The Namesake laughs and he says Asle should say hi to his friend too, the guy with the tattoos, his name was Sigve right, The Namesake says and he looks at Siv and points with his left hand to the spot between the thumb and index finger of his right hand and he says that the guy he's talking about had a heart, an anchor, and a cross tattooed between the thumb and index finger of one hand and on the other, he says, and he points with his other hand to the same spot on the other hand, he had a tattoo of three dots in a triangle

A beggar's mark, he says

Bet you didn't know that, he says

and Siv shakes her head and she tugs at The Namesake's arm

We need to go now, she says

Yes well take care, The Namesake says

Take care, Asle says

and he sees Siv almost drag The Namesake to the door with her and Asle hears her say something about how he doesn't need to tell people about things like that and then she says something about it scaring people and Asle turns around and looks behind him and he sees the woman with the medium-length blonde hair still sitting and looking at him and then he turns to face forwards again and looks down at the page with the death notices and he thinks why is she sitting there looking at him, he thinks and he takes out his tobacco pouch and he rolls himself a cigarette, lights it, and takes a good drag of it and he feels a kind of well-being spread through his body, he thinks and he puts down the paper and he drinks his beer and he looks at his watch and he sees that there's only about an hour now until the bus is supposed to leave, and he thinks he'll just go to the gate the buses to Aga leave from and there was nothing worth reading in *The Northern Herald*, so he'll just leave the newspaper here, Asle thinks and then he gets up and he puts on his brown leather shoulderbag and he thinks he won't look at the woman with the medium-length blonde hair and he walks out the door and I sit there in my chair by the round table and now I've closed my eyes, and I just sit there, and I think that nothing has any point, any meaning, but what kind of empty weightless words are these? point? meaning? nothing like that exists because credibile est quia ineptum est, that's how it is, or certum est quia impossibile est, so it was said and that's how it is, and it's so cold that I can't even get undressed to go lie down, I just sit there in my chair, next to the round table, in my black coat and with the grey blanket wrapped around me, I sit there and Bragi is lying in my lap and I think that God is so far away that no one can say anything about him and that's why all ideas about God are wrong, and at the same time he is so close that we almost can't notice him, because he is the foundation in a person, or the abyss, you can call it whatever you want, I think and I often think about the picture that's kind of innermost inside me, and it's good and bad equally, it doesn't matter what you call it, or I think about God's shining darkness inside me, a darkness that's also a light, and that's also a nothing, that is not a thing, I think and we come from God and we go back to God, I think and I think that now I need to stop with these thoughts of mine, they don't go anywhere, I think and I think that I want to lie down on the bench and I get up and Bragi falls to the floor, yes, every time, I think and I think that I'm so tired so tired and I lie down on the bench and I spread the grey blanket over me and Bragi jumps up and lies down next to my feet and I feel how good it is to have him lying here next to me and I take out the rosary I always have hanging around my neck, that I got from Ales a long time ago, it's brown, with wooden beads and a wooden cross, and now I'll pray with my rosary the way I often do, not for any reason except that it gives me calm, gives me peace, I think and I always pray with my eyes closed, and with silence inside me, first I make the sign of the cross and then I pray the Apostles' Creed while holding the cross, and then an Our Father while holding the first bead, then an Ave Maria three times while holding the next three beads one by one, then the shorter Gloria, as it's called, in the space before the next bead where I pray the Our Father again and then I pray the doxology, as it's called, in the Our Father at the first bead above the cross and then finally I recite Salve Regina while I hold the cross, and I switch back and forth between using Nynorsk and using Latin but I always recite Salve Regina in Latin, because it's impossible to translate it, all you can do is make a version of it, I think and then I usually make a sign of the cross at the end and I make a sign of the cross and I start to say The Apostles' Creed silently inside me and I say I believe in God the Father almighty and I think that actually I don't believe in what I'm saying, or else I believe in it in a certain sense, so I can't exactly say that I don't believe in it, but it's good to think about the fact that the apostles said these words too, yes, the first Christians, the ones who were called the humble, I think, and if God isn't almighty, but is more likely powerless, still he's there in everything that is and everything that happens, because that's how it has to be if God put limits on himself by giving human beings free will, since God is love and love is inconceivable without free will, so he can't be all-powerful, and the same thing is true of nature, if God created the laws that

nature follows then the laws are what's in control, I think and if
God hadn't given himself limits, for whatever reason, then he
wouldn't be all-powerful either, not in any thinkable way, I think,
because that can't be thought, but there's one thing I'm sure of and
that's that the greater the despair and suffering is, the closer God is,
I think and I say Who created the heavens and the earth and the
words are simple, they're words everyone can understand, and
that's why the meaning too of these words is something for everyone, but if you get hung up on the literal meaning, to the extent
you can, then the words become meaningless, and I used to do that
myself, because it's almost like the people who spoke these words
when I was growing up believed it, believed in the literal meaning
of what they said, in God a father who lived up in the sky somewhere, who was all-powerful and who used that power to even
exterminate millions of Jews, I think, but those who think of God
like that are truly sinning, misusing God's name, or maybe they're
not, they don't know any better, and I shouldn't judge them, because judge not lest ye be judged, as is written, but I can't help it,
I think it's blasphemous to think like that, and the people who
believe in the God they told us about when I was growing up in
Barmen believe in a false idol, they're misusing God's name, pure
and simple, and may God forgive them, and he does, for God's
grace is so all-encompassing that it's wrong to distinguish the grace
as something particular, as grace, I think, and now how can I know
that? I think, and it's equally wrong to say that God is almighty, yes,
all-powerful, because then how does it make sense that God became human and shared our powerless condition? for such is the
foolishness we preach, as Paul wrote, I think and I say to myself
inside myself And in Jesus Christ His only son Our Lord He was
conceived by the power of The Holy Spirit and born of the Virgin
Mary He suffered under Pontius Pilate, Was crucified, died, and
was buried He descended to the dead On the third day he rose
again He ascended to heaven Is seated at the right hand of God the
Father He will come again to judge the living and the dead and I

think that when Jesus Christ in the utmost powerlessness died on the cross it was God himself who died, because The Father and I are one, it says in scripture, yes, then it was the old God, the vengeful God as described in The Old Testament who died, the God of vengeance died with Jesus Christ dead on the cross, and rose up again with Jesus Christ, the resurrection of God, and with his disappearing from the created world a new connection between God and humanity was formed, but not in this world, or rather it was like an annihilation of this world, it was like in opposition to this world that the good Lord now existed in humanity, yes, like a shining darkness deep inside people, yes, maybe you can think of it as like The Holy Spirit, I think and I say to myself I believe in the Holy Spirit The Holy Catholic Church The communion of saints The forgiveness of sins The resurrection of the body And the life everlasting and I think that the humble Christians have thought about and pondered all this, all these things, for more than two thousand years, how God can be all-powerful, be all-knowing, and be love at the same time, and I think that it's wrong to think like this, because in a certain sense God isn't anything, he is a dark shining nothingness, a nothing, a not, and at the same time he is also in everything that is, he is being, a distance that is also closeness, because God is both in and gone from the created world, which is outside the creator, outside of God, I think, all of space with our little planet where human beings exist is in a certain sense there so that God can exist, because without human beings God would not have become God but something else instead, I think, and when what we know as our earth, and the space we're in, is gone, then nothing will be there, the nothingness will be there, the nothingness that God is, because God is eternal, and eternity can't be any thing, anything finite, anything in space, so God is the whole past, the whole present, the whole future outside time and space, and that is why God reaches from eternity to eternity, and he knows everything, he is all-knowing, and that's why everything that happens is in a way predetermined because it already exists in God's eternity, in God's mind, even the freely willed actions are all in God's everything and nothing, because even after all of creation is gone there will be nothing there, nothingness, that's how it is with everything that is, with each individual person, after the individual, the person is gone from creation they will be in God's eternity, as nothing, there in God's shining darkness, in his nothingness, because everything comes from nothing and to nothing it will return, it comes from God, who is therefore so close, so close, since he is inside every single person, yes, he is the foundation, the abyss, yes, the innermost picture in everyone, like a full void, like a shining darkness, I think, and this was why everything came into existence, so that God could exist, because he is in every human being, because God becomes God in the soul and the soul becomes the soul in God, as Meister Eckhart wrote, and no one else has made belief more understandable, more comprehensibly incomprehensible, no one else has opened up the kingdom of God to me like Meister Eckhart, and if it wasn't for him I would never have found words for the closeness of God, for the closeness that God in his silence gives me, yes, gives to all people, whether they realize it or not, and of course Meister Eckhart is right about how many of the people who don't believe in God are people who really do, while the ones who are doing all kinds of things to show that they believe in God actually believe in something other than God, they believe in an idol, because they believe in good works, in repentance and fasting, in sacraments, in the liturgy, in this or that conduct bringing them closer to God, yes, most of those who are inside are outside, and most who are outside are inside, the first shall be last, as is written, but even so both prayer and mass, and most of all the eucharist, can lead us closer to God, closer to eternity and nothingness, closer to the shining darkness inside us, because I experience that every time I go to mass or see the halo around the host, or the glimmer coming from it, the light, in the transfiguration happening, in the consecration, I think and I think and think and there's probably nothing especially smart about what I'm thinking, I think and I

think why does the fjord exist? and the ocean? and the sky? and
why do I exist? why is there anything rather than nothing? I think
and everything exists at some point and stops existing at some
point, not just me, because obviously both my paintings and I myself will cease to be, how ridiculous is it to think that anything in
creation won't disappear and turn into nothing, even the most
beautiful painting, the most worthwhile painting in the world will
be gone someday, the same way whoever painted it will be long
gone, and the greatest poem will disappear, because everything
disappears, and eventually there'll be nothing left, and then the
kingdom of God will have come, yes, Let thy kingdom come, I
think, but right now, yes, right now the kingdom of God is in
everyone, and God's being, his uncreated darkness and light, his
nothingness, speaks and is silent from what exists, from the water,
from the sky, from the good paintings, yes, from the round table
right here next to me God silently speaks, and from the two chairs
next to the table, yes, God is looking at me from the table, from the
chairs, I think, because, yes, Nah ist und schwer zu fassen der Gott
Wo aber Gefahr ist wächst das Rettende auch, I think and I think
that to think like I'm doing now doesn't go anywhere, because my
thinking is so muddled, I'm so tired that the thoughts just keep
going and going and turn what is utterly simple and clear into
something incomprehensible and unclear, I think, but no, I always
think like this, whether I'm tired or not, and I think as clearly as I
can, but I'm not up to it, so it just turns into meaningless irrational
words, maybe, I think, and really I'm just trying to say in words
what I know, know for sure and for certain, I think and I think that
Jesus Christ will come again to pass judgment on the living and the
dead, and then I think that those are just words, words, because
Jesus Christ is always coming back, in every single moment, in
every single instant and he is judging, both in life and in death, and
turning everything evil into nothingness while everything good,
all love, everything from God and with God, continues to exist, I
think and then I say to myself I believe in the communion of saints,

and I think that yes I do believe in a communion of all people who have been freed from their evil, who have become their own nothingness, who have become the part of God that is inside them, everyone who has ever lived and who is now dead make up a community, a communion of the saints, because the evil has been taken from them and turned into nothing, yes, I like to think that that's what burns up in hell, evil is what disappears there, not people! because a person is so much more than evil, a person is created in God's image! I think, and insofar as evil becomes nothing, becomes not, it, yes, in a way it falls out of time and space, the evil and the good together, and they become one in the kingdom of God, I think and here again are these clumsy words, these words that separate a person from God, and at the same time in some incomprehensible way connect a person to God and then I say to myself The resurrection of the body and the life everlasting and I think that what I'm saying is that a person is not just body and soul, there is spirit that connects the body and the soul, the same connection, the same undifferentiating connection, between what we like to call form and what we like to call content that makes a painting good, or makes a good poem good, and that makes good music good, yes, that exists when one thing can't be separated from the other, when form can't be separated from content, it's precisely when they meet that the spirit in a work of art becomes something particular, that at the same time is totally universal, I think and it is this unity that's resurrected when the flesh is resurrected, as a transfigured body, as a spiritualized body, as Paul wrote, and this happens as soon as a person dies and leaves time and space, not at some point somewhere or other in the future, because time, with its before and now and after, is a part of this evil, fallen world, the same way space is too, with its proximities and distances, but when a person dies and leaves time, leaves space, goes to God, as something completely particular and completely universal at the same time, not mixed, not divided up, that's what I think and I think how can I know that? I can't know whether or not things are like what I say they're like, maybe they're totally different, but that's how I'm able to think about it, or keep trying to at least, it's probably impossible for anyone else to understand what I think and the truth exists in the unspoken, since it disappears and goes away when someone tries to say it, because thou shalt not make any image of God, as stands written, and that's probably exactly what I'm doing now, and precisely what I'm not doing when I'm painting and manage to paint well, then I make an image of something totally different and in that way maybe an image of God, but I can't think such things, I think and then I close my eyes and am so tired so tired and I pray God forgive me my sins, because God is near whether a person prays or not, and in a way praying brings a person farther from God, as Meister Eckhart wrote, and that's because a human being is a prayer in himself or herself, in his or her yearning, I think and I think that's enough now and then I call Bragi and he jumps up from where he's lying next to my feet and he looks at me and his eyes sparkle in the darkness

I don't understand anything, I don't, I say

and Bragi looks at me with those sparkling eyes, his dog's eyes, and then I close my eyes

Good boy, Bragi, I say

and I think that I think thoughts but they were all thought better by Meister Eckhart, He From Whom God Hid Nothing, that's what they called him, and if it wasn't for his writings, and for Ales, I would never have converted and become Catholic, that's for sure, I think, but maybe in that case I would have been closer to God than I am now? maybe I was closer to God before I converted and became Catholic? I think

You're a nice dog, Bragi, yes, I say

and I think that I'm tired but I still can't get to sleep and I think that I'm in bad shape, I feel so tired and weak that I'm not sure how much more I'll be able to do, and I don't want to paint more paintings in any case, what's done is good, I think, but what am I supposed to do if I don't paint? I think, because aside from Åsleik, well, who is there to talk to? yes well I talk to Beyer a couple times a year, but other than that I have no contact with anyone, and there aren't so many people in Dylgja, and I can't even imagine moving away and leaving Dylgja, it's in Dylgja that I've lived my life, and my life is the life I lived with Ales, the time before that and the time after that don't count somehow, they're somehow not my life, I think and I make another sign of the cross, how many times a day do I do that? no, I don't know, but every time I feel a kind of pain, yes, I make the sign of the cross and I think that without really understanding why I've now lost all my desire to paint, it's like I've finished the painting I'm supposed to do, ever since Asle was admitted to The Hospital and they didn't let me see him I've had no more desire to paint, and the bad picture, the one with the two lines that cross, luckily it's not on the easel anymore, I've put it away, put it at the front of the stack of the unfinished paintings, with the stretcher facing out, I think and I think that it's probably going to be morning soon, I think and I close my eyes and I see Asle sitting on the bus to Bjørgvin and he's thinking that everything he owns is packed in two boxes he got at The Co-op Store, and he put his sheets and blankets in the burlap sack Mother put them in when he moved to Aga, and he has his painting supplies in the old suitcase that used to be in the attic of The Old House and then there's the easel and everything fit in the luggage compartment in the back of the bus going to Bjørgvin and Asle thinks that when he was there to rent his room he met Ales, they met entirely by chance at The Bus Café there, and as soon as they met they were boyfriend and girlfriend, and since then they'd written letters to each other every day, as soon as he got a letter from Ales he wrote one to her, and as soon as she got a letter from him she wrote one to him, Asle thinks and now when he gets to The Bus Station in Bjørgvin Ales will be there waiting for him at the gate, that's what she wrote, and then they'll take a taxi to 7 University Street, because even though it's expensive there's no way they can carry all the things, and anyway it wasn't that far from The Bus Station to 7 University Street, was what Ales wrote, and now Asle is sitting on the bus and everything he owns is in the luggage area and he thinks how lucky he's been, not only did he get a spot at The Art School without his examen artium, without having to finish all three years of The Academic High School, but he found and rented a room in Bjørgvin not too far from The Art School, and so he could quit The Academic High School, and the day he did that was a great day for him, Asle thinks, yes, there've been several great days in his life recently, but the greatest was the day he met Ales, and next was the day he got into The Art School, and in third place was the day a few days ago when he went to The Principal of The Academic High School and told him he was leaving, Asle thinks and I lie there on the bench with my black coat on, with the blanket tucked tight around me, and it's so cold in the room, but I don't have the strength to get up and light the stove, and I'm so tired but I can't get to sleep, I think and Åsleik came over and had lutefisk here last night, and now it's probably already midnight, maybe, I think, it's probably Little Christmas Eve already, maybe, I think, and the lutefisk was as it should be but somehow it didn't taste good to me, I think and I lie there with my eyes closed and I see Asle walking from The Shoemaker's Workshop and he stops at the door to The Landlady's house and he rings the doorbell and she comes and opens the door and she says no, is it you, and Asle says he has to tell her that he's going to move to Bjørgvin to start at The Art School there, and that he's already found a room in Bjørgvin, so he's come to give up his room, he says and The Landlady says that it's too bad Asle's leaving, she'd liked having him living there at The Shoemaker's Workshop, it felt safer, to be honest, she says, but if he's moving to Bjørgvin then that's the way it is of course, yes, she says and then she asks him if she can offer him a little coffee or a roll and Asle has no choice but to say yes, he thinks and The Landlady says he should come in and Asle takes off his shoes in the hall and goes into the living room and The Landlady says he should sit down on the sofa and then she walks on her slightly stiff feet out to the kitchen and she comes back in with a flower-pattern tablecloth and carefully puts it down on the coffee table and spreads it, and then she goes out to the kitchen again and then comes back with some rolls on a flower-pattern dish, and the tablecloth and dish have the same kind of flowers on them, and then she goes out to the kitchen and gets a coffeepot and she pours coffee, first Asle's then her own, and then she says enjoy and Asle takes a roll, since really he has no choice, even though he doesn't like rolls, and he takes a bite and he chews and chews and then he raises his coffee cup to his mouth and takes a sip

Milk and sugar? The Landlady says

I forgot to ask you, didn't I, she says

Maybe a little milk, Asle says

Since I don't take any myself I forgot to offer any, she says

I like it black, she says

and then The Landlady goes out to the kitchen and she comes back with a little pitcher of milk that she puts down in front of Asle and he pours a little milk into his cup and then there's silence for a bit and then The Landlady says it's strange isn't it, how some people like milk in their coffee, and some people like sugar, and some both, and some neither, she says

Yes, Asle says

People are different, he says

and after that there's silence again and then The Landlady says that she doesn't entirely understand why she never rented out the room upstairs in The Shoemaker's Workshop before, it just never happened, she sort of never realized she could, because The Shoemaker's Workshop sort of belonged totally and completely to her husband, her good husband, now long since passed, so she sort of had nothing to do with the house, that's how it was when her dear husband was alive and then that's how it stayed afterwards too, when he was gone, but now, yes, now that she's had a renter for the first time she'll keep doing it in future too, that's for sure, because in a strange way it was like having a little company in her life having a young man living up there in The Shoemaker's Workshop, it made her feel safe, and it's hard to believe but in a strange way it gave her a feeling like her husband was still alive, even though he's been dead all these years, she says, and she tends to his grave as best she can, for as long as she lives he'll have a well-tended grave, The Landlady says and when her own time comes she will lie in the same grave as him, and, yes, that'll feel safe too, yes, death loses a bit of its sting when she thinks that she'll be sleeping in the same grave as her husband for all eternity, she says, because everything else, well, the stuff about the resurrection of the flesh and all that, no, she can't quite picture that or bring herself to believe in it, but lying in the same grave as her husband, that feels right and safe, The Landlady says and Asle has managed to eat almost the whole roll and he drinks his coffee

Are you taking the bus to Bjørgvin tomorrow already? The Landlady says then

and Asle nods and says that yes he's going to Bjørgvin tomorrow

Then you probably have a lot to do, The Landlady says

Packing and tidying up and cleaning, because you do need to make sure you clean up after yourself, you know, she says

and then The Landlady says that she used to be able to do things like that herself but she's now so stiff and sore that it's more than she can manage to keep her own house clean, isn't it, she says, and having things spick and span in her house had always been especially important for her, not being slovenly in any way, because she was never slovenly, no indeed, she says and it's like there's a kind of anger flaring up in her voice

I'm no slob, no, she says

and Asle doesn't know what to say, because he sort of can't say you're right you're not slovenly because then it's kind of like she is in a way, he thinks, and so he doesn't say anything and he chews at the rest of his roll and then The Landlady holds up the dish to him and says he should take another roll and Asle says no thank you, thank you so much

This is plenty, he says

You'll have a little more coffee, though, won't you? she says

and Asle shakes his head and says that now he has to get busy packing and getting everything ready so he can take the bus to Bjørgvin tomorrow, he says

I suppose you do, The Landlady says

and Asle hears that there's something hurt in her voice and then she says that he can take a few rolls, for the road, yes, The Landlady says and isn't it strange that today when she went shopping at The Co-op Store she bought herself a bag of rolls, now why would she have done that? yes, it's as if she knew someone would be paying her a visit today, but she didn't know, now did she, she says and then she gets up and she takes the flower-patterned dish of rolls and goes out to the kitchen and then she comes back in with a paper bag and she hands it to Asle and he says thanks thanks and The Landlady says that it's too bad he couldn't live here longer, but since he got a spot at The Art School over in Bjørgvin well what has to be must be, she says and Asle holds out his hand to her and he and The Landlady shake hands and then he says thank you so much for everything, and for the coffee and rolls, he says and The Landlady says it was nothing and then Asle leaves and he turns around in the doorway and he sees that The Landlady has raised her hand and is waving to him and he raises his hand and waves back and then he's out of the house and he thinks it was good to get that over with, but what in the world is he going to do with these rolls? he doesn't like rolls, and it would be too bad just to throw them away, he thinks and he's almost done with his packing already, he's already packed everything he owns in two boxes he got from The Co-op Store, and then he packed his painting supplies in the old suitcase that used to belong to his grandparents that he'd brought with him from the attic in The Old House when he moved into his room, and he'd layered the grey blanket he got from Grandma between the paintings as best he could, he thinks and now he needs to go over to Sigve's and give him back the two books he'd borrowed from him such a long time ago, he mustn't forget that, and truth be told he's barely opened them, and he doesn't even remember who wrote them, but he did read a couple of pages of each of them, and the rolls, yes, maybe Sigve likes rolls and so he can give them to him? Asle thinks and he puts the two books and the bag with the rolls in his shoulderbag and he goes out and he thinks that he has to go see Grandma today, he thinks, he has to do that today even if she doesn't even notice when he comes in the room anymore, so that's why he's been going to see her less and less often, Asle thinks and he goes over to Sigve's place and he knocks on the door, he is knocking on Sigve's door for maybe the last time, Asle thinks and Sigve opens the door and Asle asks if Sigve likes rolls and Sigve answers what kind of question is that, but, sure yeah and Asle says he doesn't like rolls so if Sigve wants these rolls he can have them, he says and Asle takes the bag of rolls out of his shoulderbag, he got these rolls from The Landlady, he says and he hands Sigve the bag and Sigve says thanks, thank you, he says

But come in, Sigve says

and Asle goes inside and shuts the door behind him

And tomorrow you're off, Sigve says

Yes, Asle says

and then no one says anything and Sigve puts the bag of rolls down on the kitchen counter and then he says that he's going to still be living in this little old house the rest of his days, but he didn't pay Asle enough for the painting, he says and he takes out a few banknotes and hands them to Asle and he says thank you for painting a picture of my house and there's a kind of embarrassing silence, and it's as if Sigve is sorry he took the picture, because it's nowhere to be seen since Sigve never hung it up, but what did he do with it? Asle thinks, maybe it's under the sofa? he thinks, because he can't just have thrown it away can he? he thinks, but Sigve thought it was too dark and too sad, that painting, because it was a sad painting, to tell the truth, but it was a good painting, maybe one of the best he's painted, and then in black and white, yes, in just black and white and grey and with the tiniest bit of blue in one or two places, Asle thinks and he doesn't really think Sigve threw out the painting

Thanks a lot, Asle says

Don't mention it, Sigve says

and he says that since Asle is moving to Bjørgvin tomorrow they probably don't have time to head over to The Hotel and have a farewell glass together, but he does have a couple of bottles of beer here, he says and then Sigve goes and gets two glasses and one bottle of beer and he opens the bottle and hands it to Asle who pours some for both Sigve and himself and then he puts the bottle down on the table and they drink and Asle looks at the chessboard, there at the end of the table, with the pieces in various positions on it and Asle thinks he doesn't understand how Sigve can spend so much of his time thinking about how he's going to move one of his pieces on his next turn, but he probably needs something like that to think about so as not to think about something else, Asle thinks, and he himself doesn't even know how to play chess, he thinks

I'll miss you, Sigve says

And it's not an easy career you've chosen, if you want to make a living painting pictures, he says

and Asle says all he wants to do is paint, everything else will happen however it happens, he says

It's probably more of a calling than a normal job that puts food on the table, Sigve says

and there's a silence and then Sigve says that maybe they can meet up in Bjørgvin sometime, because when he has time off he sometimes takes a trip there, and when he gets out of the bus at The Bus Station there the first thing he always does is go to a place called The Bus Café to get a pint or two or three and then he walks over to The Fishmarket and on the way there he buys himself a bottle of something stronger and then he sits down at The Fishmarket and secretly takes a sip every so often, and he looks at the people, at the boats, and then he glances up at The Prison and feels how good it is to not be locked up in there anymore, and sometimes he drops by The Alehouse, because they have good beer and good food there at a reasonable price, so Asle should go there, Sigve says and Asle says that he has to look in on Grandma and Sigve says he understands, that he has to say goodbye to her, and that'll probably be another loss for her, not to have Asle come see her, because he goes to see her so often, he says, but after he's seen his Grandmother they could probably meet up afterwards and have a farewell glass of something at The Hotel, he says, because he's going over to The Hotel right now, he says and then Asle says he can't forget, he has the two books he borrowed with him, he says and he says that he read a little of them, and he liked what he read, but he didn't read enough to get that much out of them, Asle says and he takes the books out of the shoulderbag and hands them to Sigve and says thanks for loaning them to him and Sigve says it was nice to hear that Asle read a little of them anyway and then Sigve says it sure will be lonely for his Grandmother now once Asle stops going by to say hello to her and Asle says that he can't talk with Grandma anymore, she just lies there, she doesn't even notice that he's there, that he's come, but even so he still likes to say a few words and then hold her hand, he says and Sigve says well all right then and then Asle says bye and that he'll see him at The Hotel after he's gone and seen Grandma and Sigve says good and then Asle goes to The Hospice and to the room where Grandma is lying and he knocks on the door and as usual no one answers and he opens the door and he sees that the bed is empty, and he thinks now that's strange, he thinks and he stays standing there for a moment looking at the empty bed and then someone who works at The Hospice comes and she says she's so sorry but his grandmother died today, earlier today, around eight o'clock, she says and Asle just nods and then he quietly leaves and he thinks now Grandma is gone, now the best friend he ever had in his life is gone forever, he thinks and he thinks that he has no desire to go to The Hotel to drink beer with Sigve, but he probably has to go anyway, because a promise

is a promise, he thinks and then he walks into The Hotel and he
sees Sigve sitting there with his glass of beer and Asle says Grandma
died and he'd rather just go back to his room now and Sigve says
it's really sad to hear that, his Grandmother was old and sick but
she was his Grandmother, and it's always terrible when someone is
gone forever, Sigve says and Asle says that he doesn't know what to
say but he wants to go back home to his room, he says and Sigve
says he understands, Asle would rather be alone since his Grandmother just died, he says and then Sigve says that he'll miss Asle, it
was a lot nicer for him since Asle moved to Aga, he says, because
before Asle came he had no one to talk to or have a beer with, he
says, and now things'll go back to how they were before, he says,
yes, he'll drink his beers and smoke his cigarettes alone, Sigve says
and Asle says again that he's going back to his room and Sigve says
well then he'll just stay here alone at his table with his glass of beer
and have a good long think about what his next move should be in
the chess game, because he needs to send the card tonight, he says
and then Sigve says they'll see each other again, wherever it might
be, but maybe in Bjørgvin sometime, he says

I'm going home now, Asle says

It's sad about your Grandmother, Sigve says

and he stands up and then Sigve and Asle shake hands and he
says bye and then Asle goes home to his room and he notices that
he's tired and sad and he thinks again and again that his Grandma
is dead now, she is gone forever, he thinks and he thinks that he
wants to go lie down right now, and he lies down, but he doesn't
fall asleep, because he's thinking the whole time about Grandma
who's lying there cold and dead in The Hospice and he thinks
that in a week he'll have to go to Barmen and go to her funeral,
because she'll be laid to rest in the grave next to Grandpa's, Asle
thinks, and he thinks that he needs to get up early tomorrow, he
thinks, because the bus leaves at eight o'clock, he thinks and he'll
have to make two trips to bring everything to the bus stop, he
thinks, so he needs to set the alarm clock for seven, he thinks, and

he still has his clothes on, Asle thinks and then he stands up and gets undressed and he sets the alarm clock for seven and then he thinks that he should get the grey blanket Grandma gave him when she was being sent to The Hospice and wrap it tight around him and then he realizes that he can't, he's already packed it in the suitcase, wrapped it around the paintings in the suitcase, Asle thinks and I lie there on the bench, and Bragi is lying up next to me, and now it'll be morning soon, and I should have stood up and gone and lit a fire in the stove, I think, but I'm so tired I just can't, I think and I shut my eyes and I see Asle sit up in bed and the alarm clock is ringing and he turns the alarm off and he gets up right away and he puts his clothes on, and he thinks that he has everything packed and ready, he's carried it bit by bit down to the ground floor, now there's nothing left but the sheets, and obviously he has to just roll them up and put them in the burlap sack, he thinks, and the sack is already lying there folded up on the table, and if The Landlady doesn't answer when he rings the bell to drop off the keys he'll just leave them in her mailbox, Asle thinks, but he doesn't have all that much time, he thinks and he rolls up the duvet and the sheet and he pushes the roll down into the sack and then he puts the alarm clock in the sack and he looks at the hot-plate he got from Father and he thinks that he'll just leave that behind, he can't drag it along with him and he can't really use it in the room he's renting from Herdis Åsen anyway, Asle thinks and then he turns off the light and he locks the door and he thinks that Grandma died yesterday, that suddenly comes to him, and he feels a surge of loss inside him and he goes down the stairs and he goes and puts the bag outside The Shoemaker's Workshop's door and then he gets his other things and puts them there too, and then he locks the door and he thinks he just has to do everything as he'd planned even if Grandma is dead and he goes and rings The Landlady's doorbell and he stands there waiting and then he hears footsteps and then the door opens

Yes I just wanted to, Asle says

and he holds out the keys

I wanted to drop these off, he says

Yes thank you, The Landlady says

and then there's silence

Good luck in Bjørgvin, she says

I've been to Bjørgvin too, you know, but that was many years ago, she says

Back when I was young, yes, just a girl, she says

and Asle just stands there

Yes, thank you, he says

It was a pleasure to have you living there in The Shoemaker's Workshop, The Landlady says

and Asle holds out his hand and they shake hands and then Asle walks away and he hears The Landlady turn the key in the door and now he takes the boxes first, both of them, and they're pretty heavy, and it's quite a chore to carry them to the bus stop, and then he goes back and gets his easel and burlap sack and it's much easier to carry those and finally he gets the suitcase and then he stands there at the bus stop with everything he owns and he's also a bit worried about whether there'll be room for everything in the luggage area of the bus and he's thinking the whole time that Grandma is dead, she died yesterday and now she's lying there in The Hospice cold and dead, he thinks and the bus comes and Asle holds out his hand and the bus stops and The Bus Driver gets out and he says well now that's quite a load he has with him there, this is a bus, you know, not a truck, a moving truck, he says, but we can always try, he says, and then hope that there aren't too many other people today with so many things, he says and then they put the boxes and the burlap sack and the suitcase and the easel up into the empty baggage area in the back of the bus and The Bus Driver gets into the bus and Asle goes in after him and he says he's going to Bjørgvin and The Bus Driver says so he's moving to Bjørgvin too, almost every single young person from the country is moving to Bjørgvin nowadays, and he doesn't see what's so much better about living there than in some place or another in the country, The Bus

Driver says and Asle doesn't say anything and he goes and sits down at the back of the bus like he usually does, in the back seat, and there's just one other passenger, an old woman, and she's sitting all the way in the front, and she looks a little like his Grandma, he thinks, and now Grandma is dead, she's gone forever, he thinks and the bus starts and he looks at The Shoemaker's Workshop and Asle thinks that he forgot to wash up in the room the way The Land-lady asked him to, and that's terrible, he thinks, because now it's too late, he thinks and then he looks at The Fjord, and at Gallows Holm out there in The Fjord and he looks across The Fjord, at the mountains on the other side, one mountain behind another in a line reaching back, and all the way at the top of the highest moun-tain he sees the big white snowdrifts, and above that the sky and it's deep blue today and there are almost no clouds, he thinks, and it's like the sky is his Grandmother, he thinks, but no it's Ales who's the sky, he thinks, because Ales is the sky too above his dead Grandmother, Asle thinks and he feels deep inside that this is his country, his landscape, and it always will be, because he has so so many pictures of this landscape fixed in his mind, some are of the landscape itself but most are of a face, or of people where some-thing or another can somehow be seen in a face, in a movement, in a look, whatever it is, those black boots of Grandfather's in the rain, a dark rowboat on a beach at low tide, a heavy slate slab on a boathouse roof, he thinks and all the pictures are so clear, and he can get rid of them one by one, and all the pictures say something more than themselves, it's impossible to understand, Asle thinks, and they're disturbing, these pictures, he thinks, but it helps to paint, because he always paints one of the pictures he has in his mind, but he never paints it the way it is in his mind, he starts off from it, he makes the silent voice in the picture he has in his head become clearer, he gets what he's seen to say what it wants to say, just clearer, because a painting is a silent voice that speaks, and the voice says that there is a silence that at the same time brings some-thing close, no, now he's thinking beyond his abilities, Asle thinks and he closes his eyes and he hears the engine rumbling and The Bus Driver shifts gears up and down and he notices how the bus moves down the winding roads in short bursts, and every so often the bus stops, or has to move to the side to let another vehicle pass, either a car behind him or a car coming towards him, Asle thinks and he thinks again and again that Grandma's dead now, she's lying there alone now, cold and dead in The Hospice, he thinks and then he thinks about Ales, because now it's she who is the sky over everything in the world, he thinks, yes, Ales is even the sky over his dead Grandmother now, Asle thinks and he doesn't really know what's going to happen, how life will be, but he knows that he wants to paint pictures, and he knows that he wants to get the silence, yes, the silent mute language into the pictures, to make them talk in their silent way, he thinks, and he has to, because that's the only way he can live with all the pictures he has lodged in his mind, he thinks and just today there are at least five, maybe ten, that have lodged there, he can't count them, but his things sitting next to the ground-floor wall of The Shoemaker's Workshop, the arms coming into view when The Landlady opened the door, her face with something moving over it, something came, was there, was gone, all at once, and then the other pictures, how The Bus Driver's body moved when he put the suitcase up into the bus, no he can't tell how many of these pictures have joined the collection he has in his head today, Asle thinks and he closes his eyes and he sees Grandma lying there in bed at The Hospice and her face is grey and light blue, her lips are a different blue, and he's holding her hand and he feels how sleepy he is and yesterday Grandma died, he thinks and he feels grief, you'd have to call it, but maybe he felt more grief when Grandma was driven away from the house, from The Old House, where she'd lived her whole life, to The Hospice, when she handed him the grey blanket, Asle thinks, and he thinks that he doesn't want to tell Ales that his Grandma died yesterday, or he wants to tell her but not today, he thinks and he stretches out on the back seat and half lies down there, and then he must have fallen asleep, because he jolts and sits up and he sees that the bus is pulling into a gate at The Bus Station in Bjørgvin and Asle looks out the window and he sees Ales is there, but she doesn't see him, she's standing on the opposite side of the bus from where he's sitting and Asle gets out of the bus and he goes over to Ales and then she sees him and they go up to each other and they give each other a hug and it feels like they've never been apart, that's how it feels in a way, and it feels safer somehow that they'll be in the same city from now on, Asle thinks and then their mouths find each other, right there at the gate, and then they stand there and kiss and it feels entirely right, and it's like they never want to stop, they let the kiss just go on and on and it's like time doesn't exist, Asle thinks and then he thinks that they can't really just stand here like this kissing in broad daylight and at The Bus Station too, he thinks and I lie there and now the sun must be coming up soon, I think, and it's Little Christmas Eve today and I really have to get up soon, but it's so dark, and it's so cold in the room, I think and I close my eyes and I see Ales and Asle standing in front of 7 University Street and Ales goes and opens the front door and she stands there with the suit-case in one hand and holds the door open with the other and she says she knew the door wouldn't be locked and Asle carries the easel and the two boxes and the burlap sack inside and puts them on the floor under the mailboxes and Ales says it was good they took a taxi, it would have been too much to carry, even though it's not exactly a huge amount to move, and even though it's not that far a walk from The Bus Station, and even though the taxi ride wasn't exactly cheap, she says and she says that it's probably better to carry it upstairs in two trips and then Asle starts walking up the stairs with the two boxes and Ales walks behind him with the suit-case and they don't say anything and then an older man in a hat and coat and with a cane comes walking stiffly down the stairs and he says good day and both Ales and Asle say good day and then they keep going and Ales says that that was a fine example of an older Bjørgviner, a real Bjørgvin man, you don't see many like him around anymore, but when she was a girl there were lots of them, older men always went out in either a hat or a sailor's cap with a visor, she says and they carry the things up from one landing to the next and then they put the things down outside the door with the nameplate saying Herdis Åsen and then they take each other's hands and they go downstairs and Asle lets go of Ales and picks up the easel in one empty hand and the burlap sack in the other and Ales says that she can carry the easel or the sack and Asle says no, he'll carry them himself, he says and then they go back up all the stairs to the sixth floor and Asle puts the easel and sack down and then Ales says that maybe she should leave and wait for him outside and Asle gets almost scared

No you can't leave, Asle says

I can wait outside, Ales says

No, Asle says

and he thinks about the last time, yes, when Ales was gone when he got outside, and doesn't want that to happen again today, he thinks and he thinks that he doesn't want to ask Ales why she left so suddenly last time and wasn't there, it feels wrong to ask, he thinks and he thinks about Grandma, about how she's gone forever now, and he'll tell Ales about that, but not today, he thinks and Asle rings the doorbell and they hear footsteps and the door opens and Asle and Herdis Åsen look straight at each other and she says welcome and she holds out her hand and she and Asle shake hands and he thinks that it's strange that Herdis Åsen sort of doesn't notice Ales, or at least she's acting like she doesn't, and it's like Ales shrinks in on herself and tries to be as small and invisible as she can, she really turns almost invisible, Asle thinks and he feels that Ales doesn't want him to point her out to Herdis Åsen, she wants to be as invisible as she can manage to be and then he sees Herdis Åsen look at Ales and a dislike comes over her face, as though what she was seeing was somehow disgusting, but Herdis Åsen doesn't say a single word, she just looks away from Ales towards Asle and says he should bring his things inside, this wasn't a huge amount for someone moving, she says and she opens the door wider and Asle picks up the two boxes and then he goes inside and Herdis Åsen opens the door next to the front door and she says that this is his room, here it is, his room, his home, so to speak, now the two of them will be sharing house and home, in a way, Herdis Åsen says and she laughs and Asle goes out and gets the easel and burlap sack and Ales says that she'll go downstairs and wait outside, she doesn't feel exactly welcome here, she says and Asle feels anxiety, yes, fear grip him and he says she can't leave and Ales says no, really, she'll wait outside, she absolutely will, she says and then Herdis Åsen is standing in the doorway and she says that she doesn't like rules, not too many rules, but there's one rule that has applied to all the renters she's ever had, and she's had quite a few over the years, and that is that they can't bring girls to the room, she says and then Herdis Åsen looks straight at Ales standing there and Ales looks down and then Asle says this is Ales, his girlfriend and Herdis Åsen doesn't say anything and already she is heading back inside and Ales says she's going to go wait outside now and Asle says that he'll come as soon as he can and Ales nods and then she starts to walk down the stairs and Asle watches her go and he's filled with an unbelievable love like nothing he's ever felt and he hears Herdis Åsen say that he should come inside now and then Asle goes into the entryway and Herdis Åsen says that she already took him through the apartment when he was here before and she'd said what he could and couldn't do, and she doesn't want to go through it again, but anyway he needs to remember to take out the garbage every Wednesday afternoon or evening, that was the most important thing, aside from not having girls in the room, and, well, maybe she forgot to tell him that when he was here, but she takes for granted that people know the rules of proper behaviour, she would have thought they'd go without saying, actually, because otherwise what would her apartment turn into? Herdis Åsen says, there'd be some, she says and she stops short and Asle doesn't say anything and so, yes, so he mustn't lose the keys of course, Herdis

Åsen says and she holds up a keyring and she holds up one key on the ring and she says this is for the apartment door, and she holds up another key and she says this is for the street door, and then she holds up a third key and she says this is to his room, but none of her previous renters have ever used it, they left the door to the room unlocked, and in any case there was one thing that was absolutely certain, she would never rummage around in there, in his room, she says and Asle nods and then he walks into the room, into his own rented room, and he says he has his sheets in the burlap sack and Herdis Åsen laughs and says yes yes, yes, you have to carry them in something, why not a burlap sack? she says and then she says that he should just get settled in and then she says that she's baked a cake and would love to offer him cake and coffee and then a glass of wine afterwards would be nice to celebrate his moving in, she says, yes, once he's relaxed a bit, made himself at home a bit, they'd have a little celebration, Herdis Åsen says and Asle says thank you, thanks so much, but his girlfriend is standing outside waiting for him, he says

So, you have a girlfriend? Herdis Åsen says

Yes, Asle says

and Herdis Åsen shakes her head and she says that she's stayed away from that sort of thing her whole life, she'd managed to get through life unmarried and if there was one thing she was proud of it was probably that, she says, but the cake will keep, so later, tonight, if he doesn't spend too long mooning around with that girlfriend of his, he's welcome to have a little welcome party, she says, and in the worst case, if he can't get rid of that female of his, yes, she hopes he forgives her for talking like this, they can just have their welcome party tomorrow, because the cake will keep until tomorrow, Herdis Åsen says and she turns around and Asle sees her cross the hall and go into the living room and then he leaves the apartment and he finds his key and he locks the door behind him and then he runs as fast as he can down the stairs, he jumps down the stairs and he thinks as long as Ales is there now, and she's not gone like last time, he'd thought so many times about why she didn't wait for him that time, but he didn't, and doesn't, want to ask Ales why she didn't wait for him, Asle thinks and he thinks that the thing about not being allowed to have girls in the room was definitely just something Herdis Åsen came up with on the spot when she saw Ales, because it didn't exactly seem like the two of them liked each other very much, no, Herdis Åsen didn't like Ales and Ales didn't like Herdis Åsen, and it must have been because she didn't like Ales for whatever reason that Herdis Åsen brought up this rule, this rule of proper behaviour as she put it, that he wasn't allowed to have girls in the room, Asle thinks, and Herdis Åsen wasn't exactly insulted when he said that Ales was waiting for him outside but she was a little sorry, somehow, he'd noticed that, Asle thinks, and of course it was stupid that she'd baked a cake and everything, and bought wine, and then he just left without letting them have the moving-in party she'd planned, Asle thinks, but he's going to eat cake and drink coffee and wine with Herdis Åsen tomorrow instead, because now he wants to see Ales again, Asle thinks as he jumps down the stairs and goes out the front door and then he sees Ales standing there on the pavement and a lightness comes over him like pure happiness and Ales looks straight at him and Ales says that he can't stay living there at Herdis Åsen's for long if she can't come see him and Asle says that Herdis Åsen hadn't said anything about that before when he came and looked at the room, when it was being decided if he'd rent the room or not, he says and I lie there on the bench, and it's dark in the room, but I'm sure that it's morning now, and today is Saturday and it's Little Christmas Eve, I think and now I need to get up, and I can't remember ever having put on my long black coat and gone and lain down on the bench without getting undressed, just spreading the grey blanket over me, I think and I think that I'm so tired so tired, it's like I can only just stand up, because I didn't get to sleep at all, I think, and it's so cold in the room and I can't bear to light the stove, but I have my coat on and it's good against the cold and Bragi's lying here next to me, curled tight against me and I've spread the grey blanket over us both and I think that I'm so tired so tired and I close my eyes and I see Asle walking down the hall in The Student Home and he's thinking he told Siv they'd talk tomorrow and he said goodbye and Siv didn't answer and then he went to the bus stop as fast as he could without running and then he took the bus to The Student Home, Asle thinks and he walks down the hall to the apartment he and Liv are renting at The Student Home and he hears a baby crying and crying and he walks down the hall and the crying gets louder and he unlocks the door to the apartment he and Liv are renting at The Student Home and it's The Boy who's crying and he goes into the bedroom and he sees The Boy lying there alone in the middle of the double bed with his arms and legs stretched out to the sides and Asle picks him up and holds him close and he rubs The Boy's back and the crying gets softer and then he starts to walk with The Boy around the bedroom and he goes into the living room and he can't see Liv anywhere, maybe she just went out and left The Boy lying all alone? Asle thinks, but she can't have done that, can she? he thinks and he doesn't understand why Liv isn't home and The Boy cries and cries and Asle goes into the bathroom and Liv is lying there on the floor and Asle bends down and he shakes her and she doesn't wake up and Asle puts his hand up to her mouth and he checks if she's breathing and she's breathing but just barely and The Boy is screaming like never before and Asle is like a pole of fear and what should he do? and he shakes Liv's shoulder again, and she doesn't wake up, and he tries to open her eyelids and they fall back closed and he takes a glass of cold water and he throws water in her face and she just lies there like nothing happened and then he sees there's an empty pillbox on the washstand and he thinks Liv took all the pills that were in the box and he thinks he has to call for an ambulance, now, right away, and The Boy cries and cries and Asle strokes his back and he says shh, calm down, Papa's home now, quiet down now like a good boy just quiet down now, Asle says and he says to himself that he has to take everything calmly and I lie there on the bench and I think that it's morning now, yes, definitely, and it's Little Christmas Eve today, I think, so I'll just get up now, but before I get up I want to pray and I cross myself and then I take out the rosary I have hanging around my neck, under my sweater, the rosary I got from Ales once and I hold the brown wooden cross between my thumb and index finger and I say inside myself Pater noster Qui es in cælis Sanctificetur nomen tuum Adveniat regnum tuum Fiat voluntas tua sicut in cælo et in terra Panem nostrum cotidianum da nobis hodie et dimitte nobis debita nostra sicut et nos dimittimus debitoribus nostris Et ne nos inducas in tentationem sed libera nos a malo and I move my thumb and index finger up to the first bead and I say Our Father Who art in heaven Hallowed be thy name Thy kingdom come Thy will be done on earth as it is in heaven Give us this day our daily bread and forgive us our trespasses as we forgive those who trespass against us And lead us not into temptation but deliver us from evil and I move my thumb and index finger back down and I hold onto the brown wooden cross and then I say, again and again inside myself, while I breathe in deeply Lord and while I breathe out slowly Jesus and while I breathe in deeply Christ and while I breathe out slowly Have mercy and while I breathe in deeply On me

VII

AND I SEE MYSELF STANDING there looking at the painting in the pile with the stretcher facing out, it's morning and I got up and turned on the light in the room, but I still have my black coat on, and Bragi is next to me, and I think that today is Saturday and it's Little Christmas Eve and I look at the stretcher of the outermost painting in the stack and St Andrew's Cross is painted on the stretcher in thick black oil paint, impasto, they call it, and I think again that I don't want to keep these paintings that I don't think are totally finished here in the main room anymore, because strictly speaking they are finished, or as finished as they'll ever be, they're as finished as I can make them, I think and I think that I don't have any desire to paint anymore, yes, I have a real aversion to even the thought of painting anymore and I don't understand what changed so suddenly inside me, because it used to be that I had to paint, not just to support myself but to get rid of all these pictures lodged in my head, I think and I realize that there are still pictures in my head but I also realize that they are about to fade away on their own, they are about to come together into one slow picture that doesn't need to be painted and won't be and can't be, yes, the pictures are about to come together into a stillness, a calm silence, I think and I feel filled with something like peace, it's strange how suddenly something can change, I think and I think that I want to carry the stack of paintings that I thought I wasn't done with but that actually I am done with up to the attic and put them with the paintings I've set aside in the storage space in one of the attic rooms, and that

I go up to the attic to look at now and then when I get stuck and can't paint, and then I've always had one of those pictures out, leaning against the back of a chair between the two little windows, in the middle, under the peak of the gable, I think and I see that there are five paintings I thought I wasn't finished with, and all of them are big, or among the bigger ones, because usually I have two stacks there, one with bigger paintings and one with smaller paintings, with my leather shoulderbag hanging between the two stacks, on its peg, but now there's just one stack in the middle, under the shoulderbag, and then I take the pictures under my arms and go up to the attic and I look at the portrait of Ales that's leaning against the back of the chair there between the two little windows in the gable, and then I go into the storage space and I put the pictures down, leaning them against the other pictures that are stacked there, and now there are nine pictures there in all, all with their stretchers facing out, so there were only four pictures along with the portrait of Ales that I kept and didn't want to sell, I think and two of them are some of the first pictures I painted, I think, so now I have nine paintings I can sell, that's enough for one more exhibition, but only one, I think, and the portrait of Ales is the only picture I want to keep, I think and I think that I committed to one exhibition in six months at The Kleinheinrich Gallery in Oslo, but Beyer has all the pictures they need for that, paintings that weren't sold in Bjørgvin, and strangely enough several of them are some of the best pictures I've painted, in my opinion, and in Beyer's opinion too, and then there's an exhibition planned in Nidaros, at The Huysmann Gallery, and they've been talking about that forever, yes, almost as long as I've known Beyer, I think, and Beyer's been keeping for that show the paintings that didn't sell in Bjørgvin or in Oslo, and truth be told they are all some of the best I've ever painted, so the pictures I have up in the storage space will be for my next and last exhibition at The Beyer Gallery, I think, and then it's over, my exhibition next year will be the last one I have at The Beyer Gallery, and the pictures I've painted that Beyer will have to sell off after the exhibition will be the ones that weren't sold in Oslo or in Nidaros or that won't have sold in next year's exhibition at The Beyer Gallery, I think, and, I think, yes, I can just take all the pictures I have stored now and bring them to Beyer's right away, he called me a few days ago and told me that we were selling well this year, and that there were just three pictures that hadn't sold, he said, and he thought they'd get sold before he closed the gallery for Christmas Eve day, or in any case on one of the days between Christmas and New Year's, so I'd made a nice sum of money, he said, and then I'll probably make some more money from the three exhibitions I still have planned, I think and I've always lived modestly and set aside part of my money, so I won't starve even if I stop painting, I think and I think that I paid membership dues to the Norway Artists Association every year, and they give out stipends, but I've never applied for one, because I never needed to, but maybe I can apply for one too and even get one, since I've never applied for one before, that's why I never got one, aside from the artist's stipend I got when I went to The Art School, I think, because there are various stipends you can apply for, and I believe there's a stipend for deserving older artists too, and I guess that's what I am now, I'm older anyway, however deserving I might be, yes, well, opinions vary on that, but now do the members, or some of the members, of the Norway Artists Association think I deserve their support, well, no, I don't think so, they probably think I don't, they probably think I've been a hack my whole life who's just smeared up paintings for money, yes, I'm afraid that's how they see me as a painter, but anyway I can apply for a stipend from the Norway Artists Association, it's worth a try, and then I'm also a member of something called West Norway Artists, and I think they also have a little money in stipends to give out, and in that case I can apply for a stipend from them too, I think and it won't be that many years before I can collect a pension, and I'm really looking forward to that, getting money every month whether I do anything or not, anyway I'll probably be one of the people who gets the lowest amount but that'll be more than enough for me, I think, because if I stop painting and I don't need to buy painting supplies anymore then I won't have big expenses at all, and it'll be good to get a little money regularly every month, because to tell the truth I've never had that happen to me in my whole life, I've painted pictures to sell them and that's how I made the money I needed, I think, and I have everything I need, the house is mine, and I have a good car, a car I bought only around five years ago, so I'll have it as long as I live, or as long as I'm still allowed to drive, I think and it feels good to think that I'm not going to paint anymore, that it's over, that I've done my part, what I wanted to do was paint and I painted, year after year, and all those years I was actually painting away at the same picture, and the closer I got to my own picture deep inside me the better I painted, and these unfinished pictures are really most likely finished too, in their way, yes, in fact precisely because they're not finished, because it doesn't feel right to stop when something's finished since my inner pictures in their own picture are always pointing towards something beyond themselves, there is a kind of longing for afar in all the pictures, and at the same time what the pictures are yearning for is always in them already, I think and I stay there looking at the picture of Ales, I haven't painted many portraits, just this one of Ales plus one more, I think, because back when I lived in Herdis Åsen's apartment I painted a portrait of her and was paid well for it, we agreed that I could not pay rent for six months as payment for the picture, and since I moved out after just a couple of weeks I was paid in cash instead, and the picture of Herdis Åsen wasn't so terrible either, it was a bit forced, a bit fake in a way, but the portrait I painted of Ales is just how she was, how she was with her light, I think and it's also the only picture I'm going to keep, not because it's a picture I painted but because it's a picture of Ales, I think, because I only painted that one portrait of Ales and I did that after I'd painted the portrait of Herdis Åsen and Ales didn't like that I'd painted a portrait of Herdis Åsen and not of her, I think and

I stand there and look at the portrait of Ales and I go and sit down in the chair I have up there a few steps away from the chair where I have the picture leaning against the back, and I look at the portrait of Ales and I see Asle running down the stairs from the room he's renting now at 7 University Street and he thinks that it was kind of too bad that Herdis Åsen had baked a cake and sort of prepared a moving-in party and then he just left, but Ales is on the street outside waiting for him, isn't she, and the only thing Asle wants is to see Ales again, to be with her, he thinks and he goes out the front door and he doesn't see Ales anywhere, no matter where he looks, and a feeling of despair starts to come over him and he thinks no, she can't have just left, no, not again, no, not this time too, no, not that, Asle thinks and then he hears Ales shout Asle and then he sees her sitting on a bench a little way up University Street, there's something like a little park there, and Asle runs over to Ales and he sits down next to her and she puts her arm around his shoulders and she says no, he can't live there, in that room there, the landlady there is totally impossible, and it was pretty obvious that she couldn't stand her, Ales says, it was like she'd done something terrible to her even though they'd never seen each other before, not that she can remember anyway, Ales says, no, she's never seen her before, she says, and then she looked rather slovenly, like a drunk, yes, like an old tart, to be honest, Ales says and that comes as a surprise to Asle, he'd never thought anything like that about Herdis Åsen, he saw her more like an educated older lady, maybe she did drink rather a lot, she certainly smoked too much, that's for sure, he practically never saw her without a cigarette in one hand and an ashtray in the other, and she always took very deep drags of her cigarette, he thinks and Ales says the smell, yes, it stank of old alcohol, and perfume, and smoke pouring out into the main stairwell of the building, she says, no, he can't live there, but she, yes, she might be able to find him another place to live, Ales says and she puts her other hand on Asle's belly and then he puts his arm around her shoulders and then they sit there with their

arms around each other and then Ales brings her mouth over to his
ear and then she whispers to him

Asle and Ales, she whispers

and he whispers into her ear

Ales and Asle, he whispers

and she says that it's strange that they have such similar names,
the letters are the same, you just have to move them around a little

And neither name's all that common either, she says

Ales isn't anyway, Asle says

and she says that Asle may be more common than Ales, but
she doesn't know anyone else named either Asle or Ales, so both
names are pretty unusual, she says and Asle says that he doesn't
think he knows anyone else named either Ales or Asle either and I
sit and look at the portrait I painted of Ales and I think that I can
drive all the pictures I have here that are done to The Beyer Gallery
as soon as today, because even the ones I thought of as unfinished
are actually finished, but I won't sell the portrait of Ales, I think
and I look at the portrait of Ales and I see Ales and Asle cross a
street and Ales says that the street is called Canon Street and she
points and says there's St Paul's Church, and she's been there a lot,
because her mother Judit was and is a believing baptized Christian,
yes, Catholic, and she's Catholic too, Ales says, yes, so now he
knows, she says and later they'll need to go into the church, maybe
even today, she says and then she gives Asle a sudden kiss on the
cheek and then she says look, The Bus Station's over there, and
there's the sign for The Bus Café, she says and she points to it and
she says that surely he remembers and she laughs and Asle says that
if there's one thing in the world he remembers it's that, he says, yes,
that's for sure, he says and Ales says that they should go back there
together sometime, but now she wants them to go to Ridge Street,
because that's where she lives, with her mother Judit, at 29 Ridge
Street, she's lived there her whole life, Ales says and it's not far from
here, she says and Asle feels afraid, feels a kind of terror and Ales
asks doesn't he want them to go to Ridge Street

Don't you want to see where I live? Ales says

Yeah, Asle says

But, he says

But what? she says

I'm kind of afraid to meet your mother Judit, he says

and Asle says that he doesn't know why but he doesn't feel like meeting her mother Judit, not today, there has already been so much today, he says and Ales says that they don't need to go into the house if he doesn't want to, they can do that later, some other day, and he can meet her mother Judit then, and then Ales can show him her pictures, she says and she is so looking forward to seeing his pictures, she says

They're in the old suitcase, Asle says

And if it weren't for that Herdis Åsen woman I could see your pictures today, Ales says

Yes, Asle says

and he and Ales keep walking and Ales says he can't stay in that room in Herdis Åsen's apartment and Asle thinks that he could have taken the suitcase with him and shown Ales his paintings outside, but he didn't think of it, he thinks

I can bring my suitcase of paintings outside, he says

That would be too ridiculous, Ales says

and then she says that there, over there, where Ridge Street starts, and she points and then they start to cross Ridge Street and Asle lets go of Ales's hand and she says he doesn't need to worry about her mother seeing them, she's at work, so he can feel free to hold her hand, she says and Asle takes her hand and then she holds his hand tight and they cross Ridge Street hand in hand and Ales points to a nice white old wooden house, the kind there are so many of in Bjørgvin, yes, Bjørgvin houses they call them, and she says that that's where she lives, and he remembers the address right? she says

29 Ridge Street, Asle says

Not bad, Ales says

and Asle says no not bad at all and Ales says that he doesn't
need to come home with her today, even if her mother Judit isn't
home, but before long he'll have to come look at her pictures and
meet her mother, her mother Judit, she says

But not today, Asle says

We can wait a little, he says

Yes, Ales says

and they keep walking and Ales says that now they can go to
The Bjørgvin Museum of Art, because there are lots of good pictures to see there, she says, but actually they could maybe do that
another day, because now they're pretty near The Beyer Gallery,
they just need to go up the next street, with the fitting name, Steep
Street, and then they'll be up on High Street and that's where The
Beyer Gallery is, which is without question the most important
gallery in Bjørgvin, and there's a show there now of paintings by
Eiliv Pedersen, yes, he was reading the review by Anne Sofie Grieg
of that show in *The Bjørgvin Times* at The Bus Café, yes, the first
time they met, and the only time they met before today, Ales says
and she says that it was a tremendous review and Asle says that
he really wants to see Eiliv Pedersen's pictures so nothing would
be better than going to The Beyer Gallery, he says and Ales says
that most of the reviews have been positive, almost too much in
her opinion, there was something hollow about them, but he, Eiliv Pedersen, is the one that Asle is going to have as his painting
teacher at The Art School, she says, and he's a very good painter
in her opinion, Asle mustn't misunderstand what she's saying, he is
without question the best painter living and working in Bjørgvin,
a leading light, and The Beyer Gallery is without a doubt the best
gallery in Bjørgvin, she says, it's one of the most important galleries in all of Norway even, yes, aside from being made Arts Festival
Artist at the Arts Festival in Bjørgvin and having an Arts Festival
Exhibition, having a show at The Beyer Gallery might be the most
prestigious place you can have a show in the whole country, Ales
says and she doesn't believe that she herself will ever have an exhi-

bition there but maybe Asle will have an exhibition there someday, she believes that, actually she's sure of it, she just knows it, Ales says, and Beyer himself is often there in his gallery, so if they're lucky he'll have a chance to meet Beyer today, she says, and she and her parents have gone to The Beyer Gallery ever since she was a girl because her parents were friends with Beyer, he's a widower and lives alone so it sometimes happened that he came over to their house for Christmas Eve, and when Ales and her mother Judit went to celebrate Midnight Mass in St Paul's Church Beyer and Father stayed home with their drinks, yes, that's how it was, Ales says, and only when she and her mother Judit came back home did Beyer go back to his own place and to his art, as he would say, because he had no other faith, no other religion besides art, Beyer liked to say, Ales says and she says that she must have seen every exhibition they've had at The Beyer Gallery since she was seven years old or somewhere around there, she says, and at home they have several paintings by Eiliv Pedersen, Ales says as she and Asle walk hand in hand and then she says that now it's not far to walk before they get to The Beyer Gallery, they can even see the building now, and she points to a big white wooden building up ahead, with a big parking lot in front of it, and big windows facing the street

Beyer lives upstairs, Ales says

And the gallery's downstairs, she says

He lives alone, he has ever since his wife died, she says

and then Ales and Asle walk hand in hand towards The Beyer Gallery and Ales opens the door and they go inside and then they stand there holding each other's hands and Asle sees that a man is sitting at a heavy old brownish desk at the back of the room and Ales whispers that that's Beyer and Asle thinks no, it can't be him! he can't believe the man sitting there is the one who bought so many of his pictures when he was a boy with a show at the Barmen Youth Centre, Asle thinks and he's barely changed at all in the years since, he thinks and Beyer looks at them and he stands up and he goes over to Ales and he says it's nice that she wants to see the Eiliv Pedersen exhibition again, and it's nice that you've got a boyfriend, he says and Ales says yes and then Beyer looks at Asle and he says he has a feeling that, yes, yes, he's seen him before, yes, now he remembers, Beyer says, you're the boy who had an exhibition at The Barmen Youth Centre several years ago and I bought five of your paintings, yes, now he remembers! no, is it really you! Beyer says and he holds out his hand to Asle and he shakes Asle's hand and Beyer asks if Asle has started at The Art School now and Asle says well he's about to and Beyer says that he's sure he'll do well because there was a lot of talent in the five pictures he bought that time and to tell the truth he has them hanging in his own apartment, every one of them, Beyer says and he says that they'll be talking again many times in the future, you can be sure of that, he says and then he holds out his hand to Asle again and they shake hands and Beyer holds Asle's hand for a long time and then he says that now they should look at all the paintings and neither Ales nor Asle says anything and Beyer goes and sits back down behind his desk and Ales and Asle go from picture to picture and Asle thinks that Eiliv Pedersen is really getting at something in his pictures, something he's never seen in the work of other painters, and he can't quite understand what it is he's getting at, and he does it almost without using colours, just a little blue or green maybe, or pink, otherwise it's all grey and white and black, yes, there's a muffled black colour in most of the paintings, Asle thinks and Ales asks him if he likes the pictures and he says yes, yes, they're really good, he says and Ales says yeah, yes, she likes them too, but there's something like a distance in the pictures, and she can't quite get on board with that, she says and they walk towards the door and then Beyer calls out we'll talk soon, we'll talk soon, no, wait a second, he calls out and he comes walking over to them and he tells Ales that it was nice of her to come in for another look at the Eiliv Pedersen show, yes, Pedersen rarely exhibits but one of the first exhibitions he ever held in his gallery, Beyer says, was of paintings by Eiliv Pedersen, he says and he looks at Asle and he says that he remembers it well, he says, it was hard to sell even a single picture, the people who bought art in Bjørgvin back then were extremely tied to traditional ways of judging what was a good picture or a bad picture, but eventually their eyes were opened to Eiliv Pedersen so after a few years all the pictures from the first exhibition had sold, and this time the paintings all sold the first day, but like always he'd given some buyers the right of first refusal, because the best customers and art collectors get their pictures in advance, you need to take good care of your good customers, Beyer says, and they, these select good customers, and friends, he might add, had seen the exhibition the night before the opening and by the end of that night more than half the pictures had been sold already and the rest sold before the first day they officially went on sale, damn if they didn't, he's never seen anything like it, Beyer says and Ales says that since Asle's going to start at The Art School, in Painting, she thought she'd show him the exhibition by the painter who's going to be his teacher, she says

You'll have the best teacher you can have in Eiliv Pedersen, Beyer says

No, it was so nice to see you again, he says

and then Beyer says that he'd really like to see Asle's paintings when the time comes and Asle says thank you, and that he has some finished paintings in an old suitcase he brought with him to Bjørgvin and Beyer starts to laugh and Ales says that Asle got into The Art School without an examen artium, she says, he got in because of those pictures, she says and Asle nods and Beyer remembers it well, he says, he hated high school too, so he can certainly understand why Asle would have dropped out of high school, and in that case the pictures Asle has already painted must really be good, otherwise he wouldn't have been admitted into The Art School with just them, Beyer says and he says that it must have been Eiliv Pedersen who thought that Asle should start at The Art School, but Asle probably doesn't remember the name of the person he showed his pictures to, Beyer says and Asle says yes he doesn't remember

No, it was really great seeing you again, Beyer says

But now I shouldn't keep you any longer, he says

and then Beyer says that he'll always be more than happy to look at Asle's pictures and Asle says he really appreciates that, thank you, and he says that he can bring the suitcase to the gallery sometime and Beyer laughs and says he should definitely do that and Ales says yes, really, she and Asle will come by one of these days with the suitcase and Beyer says that he means it they should

It was really unbelievable seeing you again, Beyer says

Time just flies by, he says

The last time I saw you you were just a boy, and now here you are as a grown man, he says

and then Beyer says goodbye and that they need to come show him Asle's paintings as soon as they can and then Beyer goes and sits back down behind his desk and Asle stays standing there looking at a picture '

Should we go, Ales says

I just want to look at the pictures a little more, Asle says

and then Ales and Asle go over to one painting again and then the door opens and a woman with medium-length blonde hair comes in and it's like something comes over Ales and she tugs a little on Asle's hand and then they go to the front door and then they leave and Ales says that there's something she doesn't like about that woman, with the medium-length blonde hair, she runs into her so often, and the way she looked at Asle, looked at him like she'd fallen in love with him, to be honest, she saw that too, Ales says and Asle says he didn't notice and Ales says that was probably because he was so busy looking at the pictures and he says that he really liked Eiliv Pedersen's paintings, he's never seen anything like them, the pictures were really well painted, he says, and it's hard to believe there are so many greys, he says, because all the pictures were done in all grey, and then a little black in some places, and a little pink, and then the brushstrokes, they looked accidental in their absolutely precise movements, they were incredibly good paintings and almost all of them were of a woman sitting by a window, and all were entirely their own thing in a way, they were their own world, they all had this invisible thing that became visible in them, but in a different way in each different picture

I wonder who that woman is, Ales says

Unbelievably good pictures, Asle says

I run into her all the time, Ales says

I don't understand, she says

And I've never liked her, and then the way she looked at you, she says

I'm lucky I'm going to have Eiliv Pedersen as my teacher, Asle says

and Ales and Asle cross High Street and Asle says that the paintings were awfully expensive and still they all sold, he says and Ales says he'd already met Beyer before and Asle says it's a stupid story, but when he was a boy he put on an exhibition in The Barmen Youth Centre, yes, he grew up in Barmen before he moved to Aga to go to The Academic High School, and Beyer was passingthrough and he stopped and came in and looked at the paintings and then he bought five of them, and then it was Beyer's relatives or friends who bought the rest, he says, but he had no idea that the man buying the pictures, whose name he didn't even remember, ran a gallery in Bjørgvin, or maybe he hadn't even said his name at the time, the thought hadn't ever crossed his mind and he almost couldn't believe his eyes when he saw the man he'd sold five paintings to sitting there behind the desk, he says and Ales says that Beyer would never have done that, bought his paintings, yes, if he hadn't thought very highly of them, she says, and didn't he also say that he had the pictures hanging in his apartment, she says, and that's saying something, she says and she says that every single one of Eiliv Pedersen's paintings has already sold, and that's how it almost always is at The Beyer Gallery, Beyer almost always manages to sell all the pictures in an exhibition, yes, he could probably sell anything, she says, but they say, and it's true, she knows it's true, she says, that a picture with a slip of paper underneath it saying Sold may not actually be sold, it's so that the people in the gallery will believe that there's a lot of interest in the pictures, because the next day there won't be a slip of paper there and there'll often be a slip of paper saying Sold under a different picture, yes, she's seen that herself, many times, because she often went to see the same exhibition several times, Ales says, but now why is she telling him about that, Ales says and then she says that she doesn't understand why she always feels uncomfortable when she runs into that woman with the medium-length blonde hair, the one who came into the gallery, she says and they turn left and Asle sees a sign that says The Lane and Ales says that he probably remembers that they went down this little alley the last time he was in Bjørgvin, when they met for the first time, she says and she says that Asle will definitely like going to The Coffeehouse, lots of artists go there during the day, but never in the evening, because they don't sell beer or wine at The Coffeehouse, and there are lots of people from the country-side there too, people waiting to take the express ferry either north or south and Asle says that he'd love to go to The Coffeehouse, and he says wow this is a narrow lane and Ales says yes it's not called The Lane for nothing, she says, and when they get to the bottom of The Lane Ales points to the intersection to the right and says that over there, a little way down the side street, is The Country Inn, and on the ground floor, with a view of The Wharf, is The Coffeehouse, so they're almost there, she says and Ales and Asle walk hand in hand over to The Coffeehouse and it's totally empty and Ales goes to a table all the way in the back, in a nook by a window, and with a view of The Wharf, and Asle puts his brown leather shoulderbag down on a chair at the table and then they go over to the counter and Ales says she'll have a cup of black coffee and Asle pours coffee for both of them and then puts a little milk in his cup and then he says that he's kind of hungry, so he'd be happy to get something to eat, maybe an open-faced ground-beef sandwich, he says and Ales says that she's not hungry and Asle tells

the woman sitting at the cash register that he'd like an open-faced
ground-beef sandwich

Then that's what you'll get, she says

I'll bring it over in a minute and the silverware's over there,
she says

and Asle pays and Ales is already on her way back to the table
they'd picked and Asle gets a knife and fork and a napkin and follows her and Ales sits down with her back to the room so that she's
looking straight out at the street or diagonally out at The Wharf
and she says that this is her favourite place to sit, at this table, and
with her back turned to the other customers, if there are any, and
even if there aren't, but there'll be plenty of customers here soon,
because it's getting close to the time when people come to The
Coffeehouse to get lunch, and there are some customers who eat
lunch at The Coffeehouse practically every day, Ales says and Asle
says that he'll probably start coming to The Coffeehouse a lot

Yes, Ales says

I thought so, she says

and she says that she thought she wanted to live outside of
Bjørgvin, and that, if they have children, she says and she stops and
she blushes and she says yes so if she ever becomes a mother and
she gives a little laugh and then they sit there and Ales puts her
arms on the table and reaches out towards Asle and he takes her
hands and then they sit there like that for a moment before taking
a little sip of their coffees and Ales says that she so likes sitting in
The Coffeehouse and looking out at The Wharf, at the fishing
boats being moored and unmoored, at the people walking past, at
the express ferries docked there, just sitting like this and looking,
and it often rains, but not today, and that's probably because Asle
moved to Bjørgvin today, Ales says and she says that today is one
of the great days, one of the days when something happens, yes,
an event, because it's so strange, day after day goes by and it's like
time is just passing, but then something happens, and when it happens the time passes slowly, and the time that passes slowly doesn't

disappear, it becomes, yes, a kind of event, so actually there are two kinds of time, the time that just passes and that really matters only so that daily life can move along its course and then the other time, the actual time, which is made up of events, and that time can last, can become lasting, Ales says and she says that that's how her mother Judit talks about it, how she divides up time, she says, because she and her mother Judit talk about all kinds of things together, Ales says and Asle thinks that his Grandmother died yesterday, but he doesn't want to tell Ales that, not now, he thinks and Ales says here she is babbling away and Asle says that he thinks he understands what she means and then Ales makes the sign of the cross sitting there and Asle has never seen anyone make the sign of the cross before and Ales says that now they're boyfriend and girlfriend

Yes, says Asle

Ales and Asle, he says

Asle and Ales, she says

and Asle looks up and he sees the woman who was sitting at the register come over to their table with an open-faced ground-beef sandwich and she hands it to him and he starts eating right away and he says that it tastes really good, and that he's very hungry, he says and Ales says that the ground-beef sandwiches and the meatballs are both good at The Coffeehouse, they sure know how to make them, she says and Asle asks if she wants some and she says no thanks and then he silently keeps eating and then he looks up and he sees the woman with the medium-length blonde hair, the one who came into The Beyer Gallery, walk in the door of The Coffeehouse and she takes off her scarf and drapes it over the back of a chair at a table by a window a few tables away from them and Ales asks what is it and she says he doesn't need to say it, she knows already, and then Ales turns around and she tells Asle she knew it, and now she's standing there staring at him, fuck, that woman, Ales says and Asle quickly eats up the rest of his open-faced sandwich and drinks up the rest of his coffee and he says he can tell Ales wants to leave and she says yes and they get up and Asle puts his leather shoulderbag back on and then they head straight for the door and Asle can tell that the woman with the medium-length blonde hair is looking at him but he doesn't look back and when they get outside Ales says of course, of course she had to show up and had to look at him with eyes full of admiration like she was in love, she says and Asle says that he didn't look at her and Ales says no why would he and then they stand there outside The Country Inn and Ales asks if he wants her to walk him back to his rented room and Asle says that if he's going to go back to his room she basically has to come with him because otherwise he'll never find it, he says and then Ales throws her arms around him and then Ales and Asle stand there in front of The Country Inn hugging each other and I sit there in the chair and I look at the portrait of Ales that's leaning against the back of the other chair and I think that I can't drive the pictures down to Beyer today, because it's Little Christmas Eve today and tomorrow on Christmas Eve Åsleik and I are taking The Boat to Øygna, up by Instefjord, so I probably need to pack soon and get ready, and the dog, yes, what about the dog? what should I do with Bragi? yes, I hadn't thought of him, but obviously he has to come with me, because he can't just stay home alone here, no, impossible, I think and I stand up and I go downstairs and I go into the main room and I see Bragi lying there on the bench and I call him and then he comes shuffling over to me and I think that he's showing his age, the dog too, he has lots of grey hairs around his snout, in the fur on his body too in some places, yes, he's so old now that he can barely manage to stand totally steady on his feet after he's been sleeping, I think and then I stroke his back and I think that now I need to light the stove soon, warm up the room, and even the electric heater is off, even though it's so cold, I think and so I have to take off my black coat and hang it where it goes in the hall, and just think, I slept on the bench last night, in my coat, no, that's just not right, and I can't remember ever having done that before, I think and so I need to pack, I think and there's probably not much I need to bring, but I do need to dress up a bit for Christmas Eve, put on a suit and tie, I think and I go into the bedroom and I take down my old suitcase, the same one I brought with me when I moved to the rented room, and that belonged to my grandparents, the one that carried my paintings that I brought with me when I was trying to get admitted to The Art School, and when I moved to Bjørgvin, and I carried them in this same suitcase when I went to show my paintings to Beyer, I think and I take the suitcase down from the top shelf and lay it on the bed and I open it and then I put a suit and white shirt and tie in the suitcase, then I put my nice shoes that are in a black bag into the suitcase, and there's probably not much more that I need to take, I think, yes well the book I'm in the middle of, I need to bring that, and once again I'm reading Meister Eckhart and the book I'm reading now is called *Unity with God*, I just started it, but it really is worth reading even though I hardly understand anything, neither of Meister Eckhart, whom I've read again and again over all these years, nor of life, or maybe I should read Meister Eckhart's *From Whom God Hid Nothing* again, I think, but I can just take both, and aside from those two books I'll only take a toothbrush and toothpaste, but I need to pack that in the morning, I haven't brushed my teeth yet today, I think and I shut the suitcase and then I carry the suitcase into the main room and I put it down between the hall door and the kitchen door, where the stack of unfinished paintings used to be, and under the peg where my brown leather shoulderbag is hanging, and I stand and look at my chair on the left by the round table and I look at Ales's chair and I see her sitting there, I think and I go sit down in my chair and I look at the fixed spot I always like to look at in the water, my landmark, the tops of the fir trees in front of my house go in the middle of the middle windowpane in the right-hand part, because the window is divided in half, and it can be opened from either side, and each half of the window is divided into three panes, and it's the middle third in the right-hand half that needs to line up with the tops of the fir trees, that's how I take my bearings, and I look and look at my spot in the Sygne Sea and I notice that Ales is sitting in her chair next to me and she's holding her hand out to me and I take her hand and I look at my spot out there in the water, I look at the waves and I see Ales and Asle walking, hand in hand, over to St Paul's Church, because Ales has said that they should go into the church, they have to do that, she said, because for her there is so much of life bound up with the church and nothing but the church, and it's not an especially big and grand church, it's definitely not a cathedral, it's just a small and rather dark church, but there are so few Catholics in Bjørgvin, actually in all of Norway, that they didn't need to build a big church and didn't have the money to either, Ales says and she says that she was baptized in this church and went to first communion here

That means when you go to the altar for the first time, she says

Yes, first communion, she says

I've never been to a first communion, Asle says

and Ales says that right over there, he can see it, yes, there's The Bus Café, she says, and the day they met was the first time she'd been in there, like she said, she'd walked past it lots of times and then she decided she wanted to see what it was like inside, because The Bus Café doesn't exactly have a great reputation, the rumours are that women sell their bodies in there and stuff like that, but that's at night, Ales says, and the fact that she would go into The Bus Café on just that day, at just the time Asle was there too, so that they could meet, no, it couldn't be an accident, there was providence in it, God's providence, it was predestined, Ales says and Asle hears what she's saying and he can sort of understand what she means, maybe, but he can't follow all of it, even if, strangely, ever since he met Ales he's noticed that he's been thinking about something like God's nearness, but that doesn't need any church, any first communion, it doesn't need any God who became man and was crucified and died and rose up from the dead and was taken up to Heaven by the God he in a way also was, because he was God, yes, part of God, he didn't really need any other God to take him up to Heaven, Asle thinks and he says that he'll have to go to mass with her sometime and Ales says yes, they should, but there's no mass happening now at St Paul's Church, but she'd still like to go inside the church with him, because the church is always open, she says and they go up the steps to St Paul's Church and Ales lets go of Asle's hand and she opens the door to the church and Asle walks in and it's totally dark in the church, and all the way in the back left corner, under a statue of the Virgin Mary with the child Jesus in her arms, there are a lot of little candles burning and at the front of The Church there is a little red light, behind the altar, above a cupboard there, and to the right of the door there's a basin of water and a similar one on the left and Ales says softly that it's holy water in the basins and Ales goes over to the basin on the right and she dips two fingers of her right hand into the water and then she slowly puts her fingers first on her forehead and then on her chest and then to her left shoulder and then to her right shoulder and then she looks at the red light and then Ales kneels and then she gets up and then she stands looking at the red light up ahead above the altar

There's something there, she says

and then she bows her head and then she takes Asle's hand and brings him with her into the half-darkness under a staircase that must go up to a gallery or something, Asle thinks and then she kneels and Asle just stands there and he feels filled with something, yes, something takes him and lifts him up in a way and then he rests in this lifting up, and everything is completely silent, and it's like the silence is filled with something, and it's like what fills the silence is filling him now, Asle thinks and then he kind of doesn't think anymore and he is just there in the silence until it's finally something he doesn't even feel, he's just there, in the silence, he is the silence, he thinks and then Ales gets up and she looks at him and then she goes and lights two candles under the statue of the Virgin Mary with the child Jesus and then she goes and dips two fingers into the basin of holy water on the right and crosses herself and Asle also dips two fingers of his right hand into the basin of holy water and then Ales takes his hand and she moves it to his forehead, to his chest, to his left shoulder, to his right shoulder and then she walks towards the door and again she makes the sign of the cross and Asle does too but he's a little unsure if he's doing it right and even so he feels the power of the sign of the cross fill him and then Ales takes his hand and then they go outside and Ales shuts the door behind them

Now we're married, Ales says

and Asle nods

In reality we're married, she says

and Asle nods and Ales says that now she can take him back to his rented room on University Street, it's not far to walk, just a little way on Canon Street, where St Paul's Church is, and then University Street is the first street on the right, Ales says and then Ales and Asle walk away from St Paul's Church hand in hand and Ales says that they'll see each other again tomorrow, but she has to go to school tomorrow, she can't cut school every day, she has to finish at the academic high school and take her examen artium if she's going to have any chance of getting into The Art School, but then, after she's done with school tomorrow, then they can meet outside where she lives, Ales says and Asle says that he'd rather they meet at The Coffeehouse and Ales says that he'll never find the way there alone, but he can always just ask people, and if he gets totally lost he can always take a taxi, but he's going to have to learn to find his way around on his own, at least to The Art School and to The Coffeehouse, Ales says and she laughs a little

I'll do my best, Asle says

So we'll meet at The Coffeehouse at three tomorrow? Asle says

and Ales and Asle stand in front of the door at 7 University Street and then they hug each other and Ales finds his mouth and his tongue and they kiss for a long time and then they let each other go and Ales says that she's not too happy that he's going up to that Herdis Åsen woman or whatever her name is, but that's what he has to do, he has his room and his things there, but they should find another room for him soon, or, yes, maybe they can move in together? she says, she isn't too Catholic for that, she says, and she laughs a little, and in reality they're married now, they're married before God now, she says and then she kind of tears herself away and Asle stays standing there and watches her go and when she's very far away from him she stops and turns around and she raises her hand and waves and he raises his hand and waves and then she blows him a kiss and he blows her a kiss and then he sees her disappear around the streetcorner they'd just come around and then he stands there in front of the door to 7 University Street and he unlocks the door and goes inside and he locks the door behind him, because he thinks Herdis Åsen told him he should do that, or maybe she didn't say it, he doesn't totally remember, Asle thinks and he goes up step after step until finally he gets to the sixth floor and he sees that the nameplate says Borch on the door facing the one that says Herdis Åsen and he unlocks the door where it says Herdis Åsen on the nameplate and he goes inside and he locks the door again and then there's the sound of footsteps and he sees Herdis Åsen come walking towards him, she is wearing a white house coat, and she has pink slippers on, and she has her cigarette in one hand and her ashtray in the other hand and she says that it was nice of him to come back, yes, he sure took his time with that female, she says

And remember, no girls in the room, Herdis Åsen says

No, Asle says

But I thought you'd come home later, she says

and Asle hasn't thought about the time at all and Herdis Åsen says so then, it's not too late to have a coffee and some cake maybe, after all she'd baked the cake for his arrival, because he was moving into her apartment, it was to mark that, yes, to put together a little moving-in party, that's why she had baked a cake, and so it was too bad that none of the cake had been eaten, and for no other reason besides that female, Herdis Åsen says and then she says that the cake could wait until tomorrow but it'd taste better today, it's best to have cake freshly baked of course, she says and Asle takes his shoes off and puts his brown leather shoulderbag down on the floor and Herdis Åsen says that it's fine that he's taking his shoes and bag off in the hall this time but in general she'd like him to keep both his shoes and his bag in his room, but now he should come with her, Herdis Åsen says and she goes and opens the door to the living room and Asle walks in after her and the round table in the living room is set for two people, plate and knife and coffee mug and wine-glass, and he sees that the wine bottle on the table is almost empty, and that there's just a little wine left in one of the glasses, and he sees Herdis Åsen stub out her cigarette and put the ashtray down on the table and then take her glass and drink a little of it

I prefer white wine, Herdis Åsen says

And this is a good white wine, she says

And it wasn't cheap, she says

and then Herdis Åsen says that she thought she should have a little since they were supposed to celebrate his moving into her apartment, but because of that female it didn't go how she'd imagined it, Herdis Åsen says and she asks if he'd like to have a little wine and Asle says yes thank you and then Herdis Åsen pours wine into the empty glass and he raises his glass and takes a little sip and the wine tastes good and has a long aftertaste

Isn't that a nice wine? Herdis Åsen says

Yeah, Asle says

and then she says they should toast, yes, toast to his moving into her apartment, she says and they bring their glasses together and clink them and say cheers and then Herdis Åsen says that it's nicer if he doesn't hold his hand around the glass itself but holds the stem like she's doing and then Asle puts the glass down on the table and picks it up again by the stem and then they toast again and then Herdis Åsen says that he should have a seat

Go ahead and sit on the sofa, she says

and Asle goes over to the sofa and sits down and then Herdis Åsen goes out to her kitchen and she comes back in with a cake on a dish and Asle has never liked cake, and damned if he knows what kind of cake it is, but it's big in any case

The coffee's almost done, and then we can eat, Herdis Åsen says

and she asks if he usually takes milk and sugar in his coffee and Asle says he likes a little milk in his coffee and Herdis Åsen says she does too and then she goes out to the kitchen and she comes back with a little pitcher and puts it on the table

So you can just have a seat at the table, she says

and Asle goes and sits down on the chair at the place setting he took the glass from and Herdis Åsen pours his coffee and pours herself coffee and she puts the pot she has the coffee in down on the table and then she hands him the little pitcher of milk and then he pours a little milk into his coffee and hands the pitcher to Herdis Åsen and she pours milk into her coffee and then she says that now he should help himself to some cake and Asle sits there a little confused and then she asks him to pass her his plate and then she cuts a big piece of cake and puts it on the plate and hands it to Asle

I hope you like it, she says

and Asle takes the plate and since there's a fork on the table he realizes he's supposed to eat the cake with a fork, something he's not used to, because he's always eaten cake with a spoon to the extent he's eaten cake at all, and he takes a bite and it tastes like cake, yes, nothing more and nothing less, so it doesn't taste good, and he chews and chews and then he has a sip of coffee and washes the cake down with it and with the coffee the cake tastes better

So you're going to get married too, Herdis Åsen says

and Asle knows that when you put a piece of cake on a plate then if it's standing on its side the person whose plate it is will get married, and he sees that his piece of cake is standing on its side, he thinks

Just as long as it's not to that girl I met today, Herdis Åsen says

That was no kind of girl for you, she says

I could see right away that the two of you don't belong together, she says and she picks up her plate and her piece of cake is lying on the plate

No, I'll never get married, she says

And that's probably for the best, she says

and then Herdis Åsen eats her cake and she asks Asle if he likes the cake and he says yes, yes the cake is really good and he chews and chews and washes it down with coffee

Now you need to eat up, as you can see there's lots of cake, Herdis Åsen says

and Asle doesn't say anything and Herdis Åsen has finished her piece of cake and she says cake's not the worst thing now is it, so he mustn't be shy, he should eat up, she says and then she raises her glass and she says in her opinion both white wine and coffee go well with cake, and especially both together, she says and Asle sees that he's barely managed to get half his piece of cake down and he takes another bite and chews and chews and then washes it down with wine, yes, he empties the glass and Herdis Åsen says she needs to open up another bottle of wine and then she takes the empty bottle and goes out to the kitchen and Asle hears a cork being pulled out and then Herdis Åsen comes back in with a bottle of wine and she says that this is a reasonably priced wine, but definitely drinkable, she says and she pours him a glass and she says he's eating so little and Asle says that he wasn't very hungry

Or maybe you don't like cake? Herdis Åsen says

Not usually, but this cake is very good, Asle says

Well you're polite at least, Herdis Åsen says

and then she pours wine into her own glass and then she raises her glass to Asle and he raises his and she says that she's glad to have a man in the house again, she likes it better when she doesn't have to live alone in this big apartment, she says, and so what if he doesn't like cake, real men usually don't, Herdis Åsen says and she says that tomorrow she has some substitute hours at the school, and cake will certainly go over well in the break room, she says, and besides it was mostly to celebrate him moving in that she'd baked a cake, of course, and plus she likes baking, especially cakes, there aren't many feminine chores she bothers with much, she can't even knit, and she's never even tried to crochet, but baking, and especially cake, yes, she's always liked doing that, Herdis Åsen says and now Asle can just take his glass and have a seat on the sofa again and then she'll just take the cake away, yes, the failed cake, she says with a laugh, and the plates and all the rest of it, Herdis Åsen says and Asle goes and sits down on the sofa and he drinks wine and he feels that he's already getting a little tipsy and he looks around the room, it's packed with pictures, big paintings, small paintings, and he sees at least two that must have been painted by Eiliv Pedersen, and there are also several Norwegian Romantic paintings, and a portrait of Herdis Åsen as a young woman, and then there's the big heavy built-in bookshelves, brown, and then there's another book cabinet in the same style as the bookshelves, and he hadn't noticed that that one was there before, and both the book cabinet and the bookshelves seem to be what they call Jugendstil, Asle thinks and he finishes his glass and damn that was good wine, the first wine was clearly the better of the two but the second wine was good too, yes, he hasn't drunk too much wine in his life, but now he's drunk wine, and he can choose, he's always picked red wine before, yes, red wine is better than white wine, no doubt about that, he thinks and Herdis Åsen comes in and she takes her glass and she drinks up the wine in it and then she refills her glass

Oh I didn't notice you'd finished yours, yes, what a hostess I am, she says

and then she refills Asle's glass and puts the bottle down on the coffee table and then she sits down on the sofa next to Asle

I see you have pictures by Eiliv Pedersen, Asle says

Ah, you know his work, Herdis Åsen says

Of course you would, she says

Yes, now that I think about it, she says

and then Herdis Åsen says that when she was young she knew Eiliv Pedersen well, very well indeed she might say, so she got those paintings from him personally, as a present, but even if the pictures were painted by the young Eiliv Pedersen they're still his, he's still him, she's recently been to see his latest exhibition, yes, the one at The Beyer Gallery now, and Asle should go too, Herdis Åsen says and then she points to the portrait of herself as a young woman

Yes, I was pretty back then, she says

and no one says anything and Herdis Åsen lights a cigarette and she asks if Asle could bring her the ashtray, it's on the living room table, she says and he does and then he stands and looks at the portrait of Herdis Åsen as a young woman, and it is of a beautiful woman, and the picture is painted well, he thinks and Herdis Åsen says that it was a young man who painted that, and no one says anything, and Herdis Åsen says that when she sat as a model it took forever, at least that's how it felt, she says and she gives a short laugh and Asle takes out his packet of tobacco and he rolls himself a cigarette

I didn't know you were a smoker too, Herdis Åsen says

and Asle says that he's smoked almost since elementary school, and he'd liked it from the first time he ever smoked, it was a friend who stole a pack of cigarettes from his grandfather and then they went out to a boathouse and that's where he smoked for the first time and he liked it from the first puff, but his friend got sick and threw up and kept on vomiting and said that he'd never be a smoker and so he gave Asle both the pack of cigarettes and the box of matches, yes, that nice tingling in his body, and how after he's smoked a kind of calm spreads all through him, Asle says and Herdis Åsen says it wasn't like that for her, she can remember her first smoke very well, she remembers it like her first kiss, she says and laughs, but they probably shouldn't talk about things like that, about kissing and things like that, she says and gives a short laugh and then she says that they were still kids in the street, and one of them had managed to get a packet of tobacco, he must have stolen it somehow or another, she doesn't know, but all the kids rolled themselves something resembling a cigarette, it wasn't easy, it took a lot of cigarette paper to do it, and if she remembers right they eventually ran out of cigarette paper, but they all got something to smoke anyway and to tell the truth she threw up, yes, embarrassing isn't it, she couldn't keep going, she threw up, and it was a long time until the next time she smoked, and then it was a cigarette, not rolling tobacco, and that went great, that was when she was a student in Berlin, she was studying German, because she's taught German and Norwegian all these years, as she'd said, yes, Herdis Åsen says and she has a sip of wine and then smokes more of her cigarette, and she says that she's smoked since her time in Berlin, but never rolling tobacco, just cigarettes, she says, and she smokes too much, she tries to keep herself to a pack a day but it often happens that she starts a second and that's too much, she says and then she stubs out her cigarette and then they both drink wine

And then it's not hard to have too much wine too, she says

and no one says anything

I live alone, she says

and again no one says anything

That's how it is, she says

and then she says no, she shouldn't complain, she has it good, as good as she can have it probably, she says and besides, yes, she just thought of something, yes, maybe Asle can paint a portrait of her? and Asle thinks that he doesn't want to but that he probably has to say yes now that she's asked

I could do that, he says

Of course I'd pay you, she says

and she says maybe they can start it tomorrow, if Asle wants to and if he has time, and he asks her how big she wants the portrait to be and she says it doesn't need to be that big, but maybe Asle could paint her while she's lying in the high rosemaling canopy bed, because that bed is really her favourite place to be, Herdis Åsen says and she gets up and she takes her wine-glass with her and goes into her bedroom and she says that Asle should come and he stubs out his cigarette and gets up and follows her and then Herdis Åsen lies down, in her white house dress, and with her pink slippers on, and with her glass in her hand, on the bed, a rosemaling canopy bed, and with lots of pillows, and she half sits half lies in bed and she asks Asle to sit down on the chair next to the bed, the one with the high back, and Herdis Åsen finishes her glass of wine and she asks if Asle can go get the bottle and pour her a little wine and Asle says yes and then he puts his glass down on the floor and he goes and gets the bottle and it's almost empty and then he pours what's left into Herdis Åsen's glass

So we finished that bottle too, she says

I'll have to go buy some wine tomorrow, she says

and Asle picks his glass up from the floor and he finishes it and then he says thank you very much for the cake

It was nothing, Herdis Åsen says

And for the coffee, he says

And the wine, he says

and Asle says that it's probably time for him to go lie down, it's been a long day, he says and then Herdis Åsen says it has, but he should remember what she said, that he doesn't have permission to have girls in the room, she says and Asle says that he understands, yes, and Herdis Åsen says it must sound like she's just nagging and griping and Asle doesn't says anything and she says maybe she's had a little too much to drink, she says and she hands the empty wine-glass to Asle and he takes it and then she says it would be nice if he'd put the bottle and glasses in the kitchen and Asle says he'll do that and then he stands there with the empty bottle in one hand and the two wine-glasses in the other and he says good night and Herdis Åsen says that it would be good for her if they could start on the portrait tomorrow, and maybe it would work better if she sat for it in his room, but she'd really rather he paint her lying in bed, because it's less tiring to lie down than sit, she says and Asle says that should be fine and then Herdis Åsen says that she wants to make herself look nice and put on make-up, she doesn't want to look slovenly in the portrait, she says

I'll do my best, Asle says

And I'll make myself look as good as I can, Herdis Åsen says

But it's not so easy to look good when you're as old as I am now, she says

And as wrinkled, she says

They say that women who smoke get more wrinkles than women who don't, she says

I got mine anyway, she says

and Asle says good night and Herdis Åsen says good night and then Asle goes and puts the empty bottle and the two glasses in the kitchen and then he goes out into the hallway and he picks up his shoes and shoulderbag and then he goes into his room and he puts his shoes and shoulderbag down on the floor and then he stands there and looks at the bed and then he makes the sign of the cross, but he doesn't remember exactly how he's supposed to do it, and he tries several times, and then he does it right, he thinks, and again he brings one hand slowly to his forehead, to his chest, to his left shoulder, and to his right shoulder and he feels something happen to him, he feels filled with a strength, or something, or whatever you'd call it, but he is filled with something, something that wasn't there before he made the sign of the cross, Asle thinks and he gets undressed and he puts the clothes on the chair by the desk and then he lies right down in bed and he can feel the good strong rush the wine gave him and he closes his eyes and he breathes slowly and regularly and he thinks that tomorrow he and Ales will meet at The Coffeehouse at three o'clock, he thinks and I sit here in my chair and I look at my fixed spot in the water, at my landmark, at the waves, and I'm still in my black coat, and I still haven't lit the stove, and Bragi is lying in my lap, and now I need to light the stove soon and take off this black coat of mine, I think and I look at the waves and I see Asle walk into The Coffeehouse and at first he doesn't see anyone there and then he sees the woman with the medium-length blonde hair sitting just inside the door and she's sitting and looking out at The Wharf and The

Bay and Asle thinks that she always has to be here and that Ales is not going to like that she's sitting there, Asle thinks and he pours himself a cup of coffee and puts a little milk in the cup and then he goes over to the register to pay and then he goes and puts the cup down on the table all the way in the back and he puts his shoulder-bag on a chair and then he sits down with his back to the woman with the medium-length blonde hair, and he can feel very clearly that she's looking at him, and there was a suitcase next to her, and some shopping bags, so maybe she's sitting there waiting for the express ferry, and so she lives either north or south of Bjørgvin, because one boat goes south and one goes north, Asle thinks and he takes out his tobacco pouch and he rolls himself a cigarette and he lights it and it tastes good and feels good, coffee and a cigarette, he hasn't eaten anything yet today but he's not hungry, he doesn't like food in the morning, it's only much later in the day that he likes to eat, often not until evening, he thinks, so he can't understand people who eat breakfast, he has never done that, all right maybe when he was a little kid but he can't ever remember having eaten breakfast later, the first thing he has in the morning is a cigarette, and then another cigarette, and then maybe a cup of coffee, Asle thinks and he looks at his watch and it's only two-thirty, so he's early, he is always early when there's somewhere he has to be, yes, usually, but when he was in elementary school he was never early, he was always a little late, always, Asle thinks and he drinks his coffee and smokes and then he hears footsteps and he turns around and he sees Ales coming over to him and he gets up and he walks towards her and they meet and they hug each other and they kiss each other and he can feel both the woman at the register and the woman with the medium-length blonde hair looking at them and Ales says that he's here early and Asle says he always is, and he's bought himself a coffee, and does she want anything, he asks and Ales says that she'd like a cup of coffee, she says and Asle goes to pour another coffee and then Ales hurries over to him and says quietly no, she doesn't want anything, because they need to leave, because, yes, she, the woman who's always looking at him, who's always there, yes, they'll never get away from her, Ales says, so they should just leave, and she can't follow them, probably, Ales says and Asle puts the cup back and then he goes and gets his tobacco pouch and Ales says he should just finish smoking the cigarette in the ashtray and drinking his coffee, of course, and Asle puts out his cigarette and puts it in his tobacco pouch and then he gulps down the rest of his coffee in one sip standing up and Ales says he should take his time, she didn't mean it like that, she says, they don't have to leave right this second, but still, that woman, with the medium-length blonde hair, she's here again, she says and Asle puts his brown leather shoulderbag on and then Ales takes his hand and then they walk to the front door and Asle doesn't look at the woman sitting there in the corner, the woman with the medium-length blonde hair, he opens the front door with his free hand and Ales leaves and then he leaves and the door shuts behind them and Ales says that it's a nice day so they can just go down The Wharf, because there are benches where they can sit, she says, and she has so much to tell him, she says and they go and find a bench to sit on and they sit down and sit there and look at The Bay, the water is dead calm and the houses on the other side of The Bay are mirrored in the water

It's not often the water's so still, Asle says

No, no, almost never, Ales says

And the houses on the other side are mirrored in the water, she says

and then she says that it's probably for them that the water's so still today and Asle doesn't say anything and then they hear a motor start growling and Asle sees that one of the express ferries is leaving the quay and then the wake from the boat makes the dead calm water move and the mirror image of the houses turns into fragments and disappears and Ales says now he needs to listen and Asle takes out his tobacco pouch and takes the half-smoked cigarette out, yes, now you need to listen, Ales says

You have to meet my mother Judit today, she says

Your mother Judit? Asle says

and he's both surprised and startled, because that was sudden, everything's happening so fast now, kind of, and he feels like he's not entirely ready to go along with her

We're going to go to my house in an hour and then you'll meet my mother Judit, Ales says

But do we really need to be in such a hurry? Asle says

Yes, Ales says

and no one says anything, and then Asle says that the express ferry that just left is going south so the one that's still there must be going north, he says and he hears how meaningless what he's saying is, it's as if he's just saying something to say something and Ales says yes and then she says that he has to meet her mother Judit since they're married now, because they are, yes, in a way, she says

Yes, Asle says

Yes, exactly, Ales says

and then she says that they were married yesterday in St Paul's Church, so they are married before God and Asle thinks that maybe they did that, yes, got married yesterday in the church and he thinks that it's not always so easy to understand what Ales means, and he can probably think that way too, but he does feel that this is all very strange, taken together, sitting like this on a bench and looking at the water, at The Bay, and hearing Ales say that they are married before God and that he has to meet her mother Judit today

And you remember we live on Ridge Street, Ales says

and she says that Asle has to meet her mother Judit before the two of them move in together, and Asle hears what Ales is saying but he doesn't understand it, they're going to move in together? cohabitate? and he's just moved into the room at Herdis Åsen's, he thinks

Because you can't keep living there with that Herdis Åsen, Ales says

It's fine, Asle says

No, Ales says

No it's not fine, she says

and that's why she's rented a little apartment for the two of
them, yes, actually it was her mother Judit who helped her, because
a friend of Judit's has a house in The Hills and there's a basement
apartment in the house and at first her mother Judit thought she
was too young to move out and live by herself, and then she'd
thought that she certainly couldn't move in with a man she'd just
met, no, impossible, you can't do something like that, her mother
Judit had said and then Ales said that she was completely certain
that this was the right thing to do, she just knew it deep inside, and
her mother Judit had looked at her and then she'd fallen into her
silence, because mother Judit could kind of just fall into herself and
become silent, it seemed very strange to other people, but she was
so used to her mother Judit going into her silence that she almost
didn't even notice it, and she herself had also started to go into a
wordless silence sometimes, or maybe a better way to put it is fall
into it, yes, she says

I understand, Asle says

and after her mother Judit had been in that silence, and maybe
she herself too, her mother Judit had said that it was probably right,
what Ales was saying, and then her mother Judit had said that she
knew a friend who had a house in The Hills with a basement
apartment that was empty now, her daughter had lived there while
she was studying in Bjørgvin, but now she was married and they'd
moved to Oslo, it was just a couple of years ago, but the friend
hadn't been able to bring herself to rent out the apartment, it was
just standing empty, but she'd often spoken about how she had
to hurry up and rent out that basement apartment already, but it
had never gone beyond just talk, she dreaded putting an ad in the
paper, having people who might consider renting the apartment
come by to look at it, having to talk to them, that was one thing,
and the other thing was that she hated having people she didn't
know living so close to her, but for whatever reason her friend had

never managed to rent out that basement apartment, and it's in a nice location, with a view over the whole centre of Bjørgvin, and you can see a lot of The City Fjord from there, it was a nice little two-room apartment, with a very big main room and a very small kitchen, her mother Judit had said and then she'd said that maybe Ales could rent it, it might be good for her to live alone, but she wasn't entirely sure if it was right for Ales to live there with a man, with a man she'd just met and she didn't really know, she had just fallen so much in love that she didn't know what was best for her, she'd said and Ales had said that she'd decided, and so her mother Judit said that she'd call up her friend and ask if Ales, yes, if they could rent the apartment in the basement

Do you know what the friend does, Asle says

She works with my mother, Ales says

She's a nurse too, she says

And a widow too, she says

And she has a daughter, like I said, who lives in Oslo now, but the daughter's a lot older than me, she says

and she says that her parents were old when she was born, but she's probably already said that, Ales says and she says that now Asle needs to listen and then she says that her mother Judit had called this friend, whose name is Hjørdis

That's almost like Herdis, Asle says

Yes, right, Ales says

Yes and so my mother Judit's friend said that it was great for her if I wanted to rent her apartment, that was a better arrangement for her too, because it wasn't so nice living alone in a big house, she'd said, she says

And then my mother Judit said that I, yes, that you and I would move there together and then the friend, Hjørdis, yes, gave a big laugh and said that that was wonderful, because they could use a man in the house, there was always something in an old house, she had often thought about selling the house for just that reason, she'd said, Ales says

But I, Asle says

You won't need to do anything, Ales says

It's just, I'm really clumsy, Asle says

That doesn't matter, Ales says

and she says that maybe they can shovel the snow for her mother Judit's friend in the winter, if there's any snow, because there's often no snow in Bjørgvin, so it probably wouldn't be that often, but she, the friend, yes, Hjørdis, had mentioned shovelling snow, it was because she said it, Ales says and she says so now she's found and rented an apartment for them, and they can move in whenever they want, she says and Asle hears footsteps and he turns around and he sees the woman with the medium-length blonde hair come walking along The Wharf and she has a suitcase in one hand and shopping bags in the other and Ales turns around too and she says she's always there, she doesn't understand it, why would she always be wherever we are? she says and they look at her and they see her go on board the express ferry that's docked at the quay

At least she doesn't live in Bjørgvin, Asle says

That's good, Ales says

But I don't understand why I see her so often, she says

Yeah, Asle says

Well so let's go and you can meet my mother Judit, Ales says

And after that we'll go look at the apartment, and if the friend isn't home we can see it from the outside at least, she says

Yeah, Asle says

So let's go, Ales says

and they stand up and walk hand in hand along The Wharf and I sit and look at my spot out there in the water, I look at the waves and as I see Ales and Asle walk along The Wharf I think that Ales and I weren't given that many years together but I'm grateful for the years we did have, I think and Ales is sitting next to me and we're holding hands and I feel her so close so close, I think, and I still haven't taken off my black coat, and I still haven't lit the stove, it's crazy, I think and I look at my landmark in the water, at the waves there, and I sit and hold Ales's hand and we stay sitting like that for a long time just holding hands and then Ales lets go of my hand and I look at the waves and I see Asle standing there, he is wearing a black suit, a white shirt, and a purple tie, and Ales is in a white dress, and her mother Judit is in a purple dress, and Ales and her mother Judit are sitting to one side of the altar, each in their own chair, and sitting on the other side of the altar is the woman Ales and Asle are renting the basement apartment from, Ales's mother Judit's friend, and Father Brochmann is standing in front of Asle dressed in a priest's white robe, and a friend of mother Judit's is standing behind Asle, Asle doesn't know him, but he's the same age as mother Judit and he's a doctor at The Hospital, and he's Catholic, he converted to The Catholic Church, and he has his hand on Asle's right shoulder, and Asle thinks that he didn't know who he could ask to be his witness when he decided to convert and be confirmed, he didn't know any Catholic he could ask, and so mother Judit said she could ask someone she knew and he'd said he'd be glad to be a witness and now he's standing behind Asle with his hand on Asle's right shoulder and Father Brochmann is standing in front of Asle and Asle thinks that it was mother Judit who suggested that Asle go to Father Brochmann once he'd decided that he wanted to convert to The Catholic Church if possible, and it was mother Judit who first got in touch with Father Brochmann, he is actually German but he's worked in Norway pretty much his whole life, Asle thinks and he and Father Brochmann met a few times, Asle thinks and he'd said that it was Ales who really wanted him to convert, but it wasn't like he didn't want it himself too, and he'd said that it was Ales who'd brought him to mass, and also they'd often gone into the church just to sit there and one time there was a woman there and she was kneeling, deep in prayer, and this picture, of the kneeling woman completely lost in prayer, and her collectedness and the power, or whatever you'd call it, coming from her lodged inside him, Asle had told Father Brochmann, and Asle thinks that this picture is sometimes sitting on the top of his collection of all the pictures he has in his head, he thinks, and there it sits speaking silently to him, Asle thinks standing there in front of Father Brochmann, and Asle thinks that he'd told Father Brochmann that this kneeling woman, alone in St Paul's Church, one Monday morning, around ten-thirty, had meant so much to him and actually it was then and there that it was decided for him that he might convert, he'd told Father Brochmann and then he told Father Brochmann, Asle thinks, that everything else about the mass, the sign of the cross when you go into the church, and when you leave the church, the sign of the cross when the priest starts the mass and when he ends it, and then, right at the end, when the priest says Go in peace, yes, all of that spoke to him, and filled him with peace in a way, Asle had said, he thinks standing there in front of Father Brochmann, and then the silence when the bread and wine were held up and then seeing Ales and the other people, and usually there weren't that many, falling silent one after the other and walking in silence up to the altar to take the body of Christ and the blood of Christ and then walking with head bent back down the centre aisle in the nave of the church after having received the host, with hands folded, and then sitting back down where they'd been sitting before with their hands together in prayer, some kneeling, some sitting with heads bent, but everyone deep in prayer, and then the grand silence that filled the church, yes, Asle wanted, if possible, to become a part of that history, that community, he'd said, he thinks standing there in front of Father Brochmann, so if it was possible he would really like to be accepted into The Catholic Church, yes, become part of the Catholic community, Asle had said, he thinks, and then he and Father Brochmann had met a few times and talked about faith, about what it meant to become Catholic, and then Father Brochmann wrote to The Bishop in Oslo and recommended that he accept Asle into The Catholic Church, Asle thinks and now here he is standing in front of Father Brochmann and now, right now, Father Brochmann is drawing a cross on Asle's forehead with the consecrated oil, and the cross sticks to him, it sticks to his forehead, it sticks inside him, in all of him, Asle thinks, and from now on he will feel that cross wherever he is, he thinks, a cross drawn with consecrated oil, Asle thinks and then he goes and sits down next to Ales and the man who had put his hand on Asle's right shoulder goes and sits down next to mother Judit and then Father Brochmann says This is my body and he raises up the host and he raises up the chalice and says This is my blood and then Father Brochmann walks over to them and then Asle holds out his hands placed like a cross, left hand over right, like a throne, the way both Ales and Father Brochmann had told him to do it, and Father Brochmann places the host in his hand and Asle says Amen and then he puts the host in his mouth and he folds his hands and bows his head and shuts his eyes and in a silent prayer without words he sits there and he feels peace spreading through his whole body, Asle thinks, and then, finally, after a long silence, Father Brochmann begins to speak and says a prayer and then at the end he says Go in peace and everyone answers Thanks be to God and then they get up and everyone's happy and then they take a taxi home to mother Judit's where she's left a lamb roast in the oven to keep it warm and she's also invited Beyer to the celebratory meal, and he comes, and then they eat and drink red wine and then Father Brochmann has to go since he has to hold mass that evening, he says and Beyer says to Asle that maybe it's time to start thinking about an exhibition now and Asle doesn't say anything and then Ales says that Asle has had a picture accepted for the West Norway Art Exhibition and one for the Autumn Exhibition and Beyer says he'd like to see Asle's new pictures as soon as possible, today even, yes, that's how impatient he is, Beyer says and I sit in my chair by the round table and I look at the waves out there in the Sygne Sea and I see Ales and Asle walking with Beyer up in The Hills

It's a small apartment, Ales says

And it's all messy right now, she says

That doesn't matter, Beyer says

and they go into the apartment and Ales apologizes again for all the mess, because there are canvases and easels and tubes of oil paint and a worn-out sofa and it's like nothing goes together and Ales asks Beyer if he'd like a cup of coffee and he says no, no, he's already been fed enough today but he'd really like to see the pictures, both hers and Asle's, he says and Ales says that she doesn't want to show him any of hers, because when you're busy working on something, yes, something just for yourself, it can kind of destroy it, or the painting can sort of get stuck, if you show it to anyone and Beyer says that he understands, but he does need to see Asle's paintings, after all that's why he, an old man, dragged himself up into The Hills, to see the pictures, he says and they go into the living room and then Asle shows him one painting after another, he has nine finished paintings in the room, and then he has quite a few more in a storeroom down in the cellar, he says and Beyer says that there is not the slightest doubt in his soul, yes, Asle simply must have his debut exhibition and it has to be in the spring, and then, Beyer says, he can use the fact that Asle has had pictures accepted in both the West Norway Art Exhibition and the Autumn Exhibition, but if he had room in his schedule, yes, he would show Asle's pictures right away, because talent shines from these pictures, he can see it, and he can always see right away if an artist has talent, and it all depends on talent, it's a gift, yes, a gift of grace the Catholics would probably say, and he has to admit that if there's anything that could make him believe, believe in something big, something bigger than life, yes, it's when he sees talent in a picture, and in Asle's pictures there is such obvious talent that he's never seen anything like it, he says, yes, Asle's talent is so self-evident that he will definitely encounter a lot of resistance, because it's like great talent awakens opposition, yes, it scares people, and irritates them, and it gets bad reviews, but for whatever reason it's different with the people who buy pictures, they buy what they like and what they think is worth the money, and what they buy, with few exceptions, are pictures that show talent, Beyer says, anyway

JON FOSSE

that's how it is in his gallery, he says, and Beyer asks if he can also see the paintings that are down in the cellar storeroom right now and so Asle and Beyer, both wearing a black suit and tie, go down the steep old steps to the cellar and in the light that there is down there Asle shows Beyer the paintings he's keeping there and Beyer says that Asle already has enough pictures for two shows, so there'll be two, but there has to be a year between them, and now that he's seen these paintings too he's changed his opinion somewhat, he wants Asle to exhibit them in the weeks before Christmas, he should be able to squeeze in an exhibition during Advent, Beyer says, because that's when pictures sell the best, he says and he says that he feels strongly that Asle's pictures will sell well and Asle doesn't know what to say and doesn't say anything

If that works for you, of course, Beyer says

Yes, Asle says

and he thinks that he'd realized he would have to exhibit his pictures sooner or later, have his debut exhibition, but he'd imagined his first show would be after he'd graduated from The Art School, because that was how it was usually done, but Asle's painting teacher, Eiliv Pedersen, had also told Asle that he already painted well enough to have his first show, he thinks and just then Beyer says that Eiliv Pedersen had mentioned a student of his who was good enough to have a show already and that must have been Asle, even though he didn't say the student's name, and Beyer hadn't thought anything more about it, he says, but now, yes, today, now it was decided, Asle would have a Christmas exhibition this year and another one next year, Beyer says and he looks at Asle who stands there and looks down at the floor and then Beyer says that there sure are a lot of empty bottles of spirits here in the cellar and Asle doesn't know what he should say and then Beyer says that Asle mustn't drink too much, he has seen alcohol destroy all too many great talents, and it was often the greatest that alcohol took, and if it didn't destroy the talent it still eventually destroyed the person, so he needs to be careful about alcohol, Beyer says and Asle doesn't

129

know what he should say, because he probably does drink too much, yes, Ales says so too, because it's now up to a half-bottle of spirits a day, but he doesn't start drinking before five o'clock, and he never paints after he's had something to drink, he thinks, but Beyer's probably right, and Ales too, because once it hits five o'clock, yes, well, it's time for a glass, kind of, it's turned into a habit, and there aren't many days he doesn't drink, and then he really craves a glass, Asle thinks and then Beyer starts to go up the stairs and Asle follows him and when they're upstairs Beyer says yes he has certainly seen enough pictures today for two exhibitions, and he will have two exhibitions, the first one before Christmas this year and the second before Christmas next year, he says and I sit here and I look at the water, at my spot out there in the Sygne Sea, at the waves out there and I think that today is Saturday and it's Little Christmas Eve and Åsleik came over yesterday to have lutefisk, and the food was good, yes, but I wasn't really feeling my best, I think, and it's ridiculous that even now, so late in the day, I haven't even lit the stove and that I'm still sitting in my black coat, yes, I even spent the night on the bench in my coat, what is wrong with me? I think, and tomorrow I'll go with Åsleik and celebrate Christmas at Sister's house, and I really don't feel like doing that, but now that I've said I'd go with him to Sister's house to celebrate Christmas I have to do it, I think, and then I need to quickly call The Hospital and ask if I can visit Asle, I think and I look at my landmark out there in the Sygne Sea, always, I'm always sitting and looking at my landmark and I look at the waves and I see Asle standing and looking at a picture that's on an easel, and he thinks that no sooner has he moved into Herdis Åsen's apartment than Ales found a basement apartment for them in The Hills, or else her mother Judit arranged for them to rent a basement apartment from a friend of hers, Asle thinks and he thinks that he really isn't looking forward to telling Herdis Åsen that he's going to move out, he thinks and I sit and look at my landmark, and now I almost can't stand looking at it anymore, because I'm just sitting here looking and looking, I think and I look at the waves and I see Asle standing in the hall in front of Herdis Åsen

That's too bad, you're moving out already, so soon, you only just moved in, she says

and Asle says that he's sorry about that, but he and his girl-friend, yes, the woman she'd met, were going to move in together into a basement apartment in The Hills, he says

It was quite a short stay, if you can put it like that, Herdis Åsen says

and then she says that she thought it was too bad that Asle was moving out, they got along well together, she says and so what'll happen with the portrait of her he was going to paint? she says

Yes, I need to paint it, Asle says

As soon as I saw that girl I knew that it'd end up like this, Herdis Åsen says

and she says it's that female who made him move out and Asle stands there in front of Herdis Åsen and looks down

I'm right, aren't I, Herdis Åsen says

and Asle doesn't answer

There's nothing wrong with you, it's just that girl, she says

and Herdis Åsen says that Asle probably wanted to be able to bring her to his room, naturally he wanted that, she thought so, and that was why she said that the only rule was that he couldn't have girls in his room, but she wasn't generally prudish and she'd made up that rule on the spot, because of course it had sometimes happened that previous renters had had girls in the room with them, it was a normal thing, but she just couldn't tolerate that from the girl who was standing there in the doorway before he even moved in and that was why she'd said that, Herdis Åsen says and Asle says that since he was moving out so soon, well, if she really wanted him to paint her portrait he would probably have to do it now, he says

Now? Herdis Åsen says

Yes, before I move out, he says

And when will that be? she says

Soon, Asle says

and Herdis Åsen says that in that case they should probably get started right away, he can go get his things ready, and she wants to be painted sitting in her bed, and with a glass of wine in her hand, she says and Asle goes into his room and takes the canvas he thought he'd use, that he'd already stretched on a stretcher, and he puts the painting supplies he'll need in one of the boxes he had with him when he moved in and that he'd kept, in the wardrobe where he kept his clothes, and he picks up the easel too and then he goes out into the hall and he thinks that he'll stand and wait there, because he obviously can't just walk into Herdis Åsen's living room, and certainly not into her bedroom, of course not, he thinks and so he stands there and waits with the stretched canvas in one hand, the easel in the other, and the box of painting things on the floor at his feet and he thinks that now she really needs to come soon, he thinks and then Herdis Åsen comes out into the hall, and her lips are bright red, and her eyebrows totally black, and somehow or another she has managed to cover up almost all the wrinkles on her face, and she's wearing a red dress, and it's as low-cut as a dress can possibly be, and it clings to her body, and it's very short and Asle thinks that she doesn't look right at all, he thinks

So now we can start, Herdis Åsen says

and she goes into the living room, and into her bedroom, and Asle follows her and she goes over to the nightstand and raises a glass with a long stem that she's filled with wine and then she lies down on the bed, outstretched, she lies on her side with one foot over the other and she's propped up on one arm and with her other hand she sort of holds the long narrow wine-glass out in front of her, like she's about to hand it to someone, and Asle asks if she wants him to paint her whole body or just her face and she says he should do it however he wants and Asle thinks that he wants to paint her head and upper body, her face and the long wine-glass create a balance in the picture and he starts painting and then Herdis Åsen starts telling him about all the men who've pursued her, and it still hasn't stopped, don't think it has, there are still some men who send her flowers or invite her out to dinner at the finest restaurants, she says and Asle doesn't say anything and she tells him about one after another of these men and he hears her say this and a picture of her face has lodged in his head, of her upper body with her small breasts held firmly in her bra, and that low-cut red dress showing just about everything, and then the bent arm sort of offering the long narrow wine-glass, and Asle thinks that there is something so helpless, so human, about what he's seeing, yes, something so beautifully ugly that it kind of lifts up the picture he's painting, yes, it'll be beautiful, because the picture of Herdis Åsen as he just saw her in the hall has entered him and lodged there, he thinks, so he is painting so to speak both the inner picture lodged inside him and the one he sees in front of him and Asle looks at Herdis Åsen every now and then but it's mostly to be nice to her, he thinks and then he paints her younger than she is, she almost looks like a woman who's younger than forty anyway, yes, younger, Asle thinks and it's quick and easy to paint the portrait, and Asle himself feels that it's turning out to be a good painting, and then he paints an A in the bottom right corner in black, and it blends together with the still-wet oil paint, the way he likes it to do, and then he says that she can come look at it now, if she wants

You're done already, Herdis Åsen says

I think so, Asle says

You can really do a good job that fast, I don't know, Herdis Åsen says and she gets up and comes over and stands and looks at the painting and Asle can tell that she is more than satisfied, she is really and truly happy, yes, delighted to see the picture, and that makes Asle glad too and Herdis Åsen says that since Asle has painted such a beautiful portrait of her he won't have to pay any rent, since he hardly lived in the room anyway, and of course she'll pay him too for the picture and she asks him what he wants for it and Asle says an amount and Herdis Åsen says that's way too little and then she goes and gets her purse and she pays him double what he'd asked for and she says that the picture probably needs a while to dry and Asle says it does and Herdis Åsen says that she wants to hang the picture up on the wall across from the bed, that's where it'll hang, and she asks if Asle can help her hang it up and then the picture can hang there and dry, because it smells so good, the oil paint, she says and Asle says he can do that, she must have a hammer and nail lying around somewhere, he says and Herdis Åsen says she does, yes, and then Asle says that he'll move out tomorrow

You're in that much of a hurry, Herdis Åsen says

We arranged it like that, me and Ales, that's her name, yes, who I'm moving in with, he says

and then he turns the picture over and then he paints *Herdis Åsen* in thick black oil paint on the top of the stretcher and then he puts the painting down leaning against the wall where Herdis Åsen said she wanted the picture hung and then he puts his painting things in the box and folds up the easel and Herdis Åsen stands and looks at the portrait and she says that he was so nice, really, because she's not as beautiful as she is in the picture, and then there's such a remarkable feeling of elevation in the picture, of being lifted up, she says and Asle says that if she gets the hammer and a nail they can figure out where she wants the picture and Herdis Åsen leaves the room and Asle stands and looks at the portrait, and he's happy with what he sees, it turned out to be not just a good portrait but a good picture too, he thinks and then Herdis Åsen comes back with a hammer and a nail and Asle holds the picture up and asks if it's good like that, and Herdis Åsen says yes the picture should hang just like that, she says and then Asle picks up the hammer and nail and he hammers in the nail and then Asle lifts up the picture and hangs it there on the nail and Herdis Åsen says that she's very happy with the picture and thanks him very much, she says and I sit here and look and look at the water, at the waves, at my spot out there in the Sygne Sea and I close my eyes and I open them and I think that my not having lit the stove, and not even turning on the electric heater, and not taking off my coat, yes, sleeping in it even, there on the bench, this is falling apart, nothing less, I think and I think that I should have called The Hospital and asked if I could go visit Asle, asked how he's doing, but I've already done that, and not that long ago, or maybe I haven't just called? I think and I'm not sure if I did or not, and that must be because I've already done it so many times, and every time I get the same answer, that Asle needs rest, and that it would be best if I didn't come see him, I think and I think that in that case Asle will have to be in The Hospital over Christmas and maybe it's better that way, because otherwise he'd probably have been alone in his apartment, the way he usually spends Christmas, and he didn't think that was so bad, he'd said, he spent it like a normal day, he thought almost nothing about it be-ing Christmas, but it was hard to completely not think about it, he'd said, because it was like everything around him was saying it was Christmas, he'd said, and a person shouldn't be alone at Christ-mas, that's somehow been decided once and for all, he'd said and I pet Bragi's back and then I fold my hands so that the thumbs make a cross, yes, a St Andrew's Cross as Åsleik says, *St Andrew's Cross, St Andrew's Cross,* but now I want to just be silent, I think and I breathe calmly in and out and then I say Our Father who art in Heaven Pater noster qui es in cælis and I think what do I mean? why am I saying these words? who am I turning towards? I think and it's just words, yes, images, metaphorical language, they call it, that means something other than it says, because God is obviously not a father, I think, but when I say these words I feel clearly, yes, even more clearly, this nearness, yes, the nearness of God, and of Ales, I think and I think that it's this wordless nearness I'm talking to now, that of God, who is near me and who is in me, I think and I think about Meister Eckhart who said that without human beings God would not exist, and without God human beings would not exist, because I, and everyone, and everything come from God, and if God withdraws back into himself then I and everything else will disappear, Meister Eckhart wrote, I think, and God is nowhere, because he is outside of everything that is, and at the same time he is in everything that is, and people say that the place where he is is up in the sky, because human beings look up and if humanity can find any word for where God, who isn't anywhere, must be, yes, then it's up in the sky, in the heavens, Our Father who art in Heaven Pater noster qui es in cælis and yes, there, outside time and space, outside creation, and in all of creation, and inside me, right in the middle, and in other people, yes, in everyone, is the uncreated, that which has never been born and so it can never die or else it is born again and again all the time, I think, yes, Meister Eckhart wrote that it's Jesus Christ who is born again and again inside the soul, down at the bottom, in the soil, the foundation, the abyss, and we rise up from the dead all the time in the same way, I think and I try to stay perfectly still and silent, and I listen to the silence, and I say Hallowed be thy name Sanctificetur nomen tuum and a blessing settles over everything all at once, everything is hallowed, everything becomes whole, everything becomes sacred and I say Thy kingdom come Adveniat regnum tuum and may it be so, and it's going to happen, and it's happening right now, because the kingdom of God is already between us, and inside us, and just as there once was the kingdom of God so too there will be the kingdom of God again, and then creation will no longer be separate from the creator, but united with him in uncreated love, but then won't God disappear? won't everything disappear? turn to nothing? I think and I think that it's not like that, but it can be thought of like that, and interpreting, yes, saying something about God, and about the kingdom of God, yes, is always very close to misusing God's name, so God forgive me, because only silence can say anything about God, about the kingdom of God, because God hides in silence, I think, and also in love, I think and I feel that Ales is near me and then she puts her arm around my shoulders Thy will be done Fiat voluntas tua and God's will is love, peace and love, and I try to get rid of words, get rid of pictures, and I feel how right it is to pray that God's will be done, yes, on earth as it is in Heaven,

Sicut in cælo et in terra and I feel that that's enough, what it means becomes clear and I understand what it means, and still I can't manage to say it, I think, yes Fiat voluntas tua sicut in cælo et in terra and I think that that's how Jesus Christ taught his apostles to pray, and in so doing also taught me how I should pray, and The Son of Man was someone you can talk to, he was God who became man and who died, to share our suffering, our death, and who rose up from the dead, and vanished into the kingdom of God, and with him all people, all, yes, all, everyone who ever lived, everyone who's alive now, everyone who's going to live, yes, everyone is of God and comes from God and will go back to God, to the kingdom of God, and it doesn't make sense, it's total foolishness, but it is foolishness we preach, as Paul wrote, I think, and maybe God is closest of all to those who are poor in spirit, those who never think about God, yes, because they shall inherit the kingdom of God, as is written, I think and it's always these words, yes, these words that only have meaning when they contradict each other, and Meister Eckhart has thought almost everything I think before I did, I think, but isn't every human being a unity of opposites, yes, a paradox, they call it, coincidentia oppositorum, they call it, with a body and a soul, like how Christ was both human and God, yes, Jesus Christ is himself the paradox that contains the paradox that all people are, I think, so that the cross is the symbol of the paradox, I think and I think that since faith is paradoxical, self-contradictory, they call it, it can never be understood with reason, because reason has to follow the usual logic where A and not-A, as they put it, can never be true at the same time, while in faith they are both true, three is the same as one, the way it is in the Three-in-One God, in the trinity, they call it, I think, and always these thoughts, these thoughts that never go anywhere, I think and I say Give us this day our daily bread Panem nostrum cotidianum da nobis hodie And forgive us our trespasses as we forgive those who trespass against us Et dimitte nobis debita nostra sicut et nos dimittimus debitoribus nostris And lead us not into temptation Et

ne nos inducas in tentationem but deliver us from evil Sed libera
nos a malo I think and I say Amen and then Ales lets go of my
shoulder and she takes my hand and I think that today is Saturday
and that it's Little Christmas Eve and tomorrow Åsleik and I are
going to take The Boat to Øygna and Åsleik's going to call me
tomorrow when he thinks it's the right time to set out, I think and
I think that now it's Christmas again, now it's Christmas again, and
the years go by faster and faster, I think, Christmas again, Christmas again, I think and I think that for the first time I'm going to
be with Åsleik celebrating Christmas at Sister's house, at the house
of the woman named Guro, I don't even know how many times
Åsleik has asked me if I wanted to come with him and celebrate
Christmas at Sister's, and this year I said yes, and I don't totally
understand why, I think, but anyway tomorrow Åsleik and I are
going to go on his Boat to see Sister who lives in Øygna, way up
in Sygnefjord, on a bay, not far from Instefjord, I think and I need
to bring a Christmas present for Sister, I think, but what should it
be? I think, I'm so old that I could forget something as obvious as
the fact that I need to bring a Christmas present for Sister, the
woman named Guro, since I'm going to spend Christmas with her
and Åsleik, I think but I didn't buy anything I can give her for
Christmas so I'll just have to give her a painting too, and I have a
painting, they're all packed up in the storage room, but I need
those for the exhibition, and so what else can I give her? I think
and I think at the same time how little I want to give her anything
else so I guess I'll just paint a picture now and give it to her, paint
it quickly, because a picture can be painted fast, or I can keep
working on it forever until either I finally feel happy with it or
paint over it in white, that's how it is, but now I need to quickly
paint a picture I can give Sister as a Christmas present, I think, and
it should be small, and I have to paint it not too thickly so that the
paint will be dry by tomorrow morning when we get on board
Åsleik's Boat to go up Sygnefjord to Øygna, no, the paint won't be
dry by then but it has to be dry by Christmas Eve itself, and I have

no desire at all to paint another picture, I feel such distaste at the thought of it that I almost can't stand up, I think and I let go of Ales's hand and I stand up and Bragi tumbles onto the floor and again I forgot he was lying asleep in my lap, I am never going to learn to remember that, I think and then I go up to the attic and I find the smallest canvas I've already stretched and I go downstairs and put it on the easel, but what should I paint? it should probably be a kind of portrait of a woman's face, I'll paint the face of the woman named Guro who watched the dog that night, I think and then I call Bragi and he comes over to me and I pet his back, I grip and tug at his fur, and I have several pictures of the face of the woman named Guro lodged in my mind, one of them that's lodged there was when she raised her wine-glass to her mouth back at Food and Drink and I'll paint that picture, I think and I pick up the palette and I think that I'll paint the picture in different grey colours and then with a little pink and maybe just the slightest bit of blue, I think and I paint as fast as I can and I see that it's turning out to be a good painting, of a twisted face, a face with pain and suffering in it, but with a clear longing in it, I think, and I see that I've painted it thicker than I thought, that's not good, because it's Little Christmas Eve today and the paint won't be dry by tomorrow morning, but anyway it'll be dry enough to bring on The Boat, I think, and then it'll dry more in the boat and then I'll wrap it before we get back on land, I think, and it feels good to paint a picture, but now I don't want to paint anymore, not for a long time in any case, maybe never again, I think and I think that I might as well carry all the tubes of oil paint, yes, all the painting supplies into The Parlor, where Ales used to be with her painting things, and where the books are, but no, no I don't want to do that, because that room should stay the way it was when Ales left it, I think, but today's the day to carry things out, get rid of things, now's the time to make decisions and changes, I think and I go out to the kitchen and get some shopping bags that are in the cupboard under the sink and I put the tubes of oil paint and brushes and all of the painting

things I have in the main room into the shopping bags and I go up
to the attic and I put the bags into the storage room where I have
painting things stored, boards, tubes of oil paint, brushes, palette
knives, turpentine, rags, scrapers, I have all of that stored up there
and I go back down to the living room and then I take the picture
I just painted off the easel and put it down over there next to the
kitchen door and then I fold up the easel and I carry it up to the
attic and put it down in the storage room and I think so that's over
and done with, I think and I think that I've already packed my
suitcase and so I'm ready for my trip, and the suitcase is standing
where the unfinished paintings used to be, between the door to the
bedroom and the door to the main room, under the peg where my
brown leather shoulderbag is hanging, and the painting I'm going
to give Sister, the woman called Guro, for Christmas is standing
there to dry next to the kitchen door, and it'll probably have to lie
out drying in The Boat too, because I used a lot of oil paint and
painted in thick strokes, so I'll bring a little paper and string in the
suitcase and then I'll wrap the painting on The Boat just before
Åsleik and I tie up The Boat to walk up to Sister's, I think and I go
out to the hall cupboard, the one under the stairs, because I have a
roll of brown packing paper there, and I unroll it and tear off a
length of it and then I get a length of string and a black marker and
I go into the main room and open the suitcase and lay it flat on the
floor and then I put the brown packing paper, the string, and the
marker into the suitcase, on top of the suit, and then I shut the
suitcase again and put it back against the wall, in the middle, under
the peg where my leather shoulderbag is hanging, and it's the good
old suitcase that has come with me through all these years, I think
and I go and sit down in my chair over by the round table and after
a while I look at the empty chair there next to me and I see Ales
sitting there and I take her hand and I look at my landmark and I
look at the waves and I see Asle standing by the window in an old
brown house and he's looking out and he sees that it's just starting
to get dark and I sit there and look at the waves and I see Ales and

Asle stand and look at the brown house, it's tall and narrow and it's on a beautifully built foundation wall

It really needs a paint job, Asle says

Yes, Ales says

and then she says that it's pretty now too, but it's true, the house should have been repainted a long time ago, she says

It's almost falling apart, she says

But it might be nice inside, Asle says

and he says that he doesn't understand how anyone could let such a nice old house just fall apart and not rent it out, not do anything to maintain it, he says and I sit and look at my landmark out there in the middle of the Sygne Sea and I think that I'm always just sitting and looking at the water, and that it's so good to feel Ales's hand, I think and I still haven't lit the stove, I think and I look at the waves and I see Asle standing and looking out the window in the brown house, and he sees that it's slowly started to get dark and he thinks that again it was Beyer who came to his aid, he'd told Beyer that both he and Ales were thinking they needed a bigger place to live, it was a bit cramped in the little two-room basement apartment since they both wanted to both live and work there, and then Beyer helped them find this house to rent, Asle thinks standing there looking out the window at the trees on the other side of the road, and now the leaves have turned such beautiful colours, and he doesn't want to think about colours, he wants to just look at the colours and see them get darker the more the day darkens, Asle thinks and he thinks that it's hard to believe but all the pictures in his debut exhibition had sold, unbelievable, Beyer had said and then he'd said that since Asle had told him that they'd like to live outside of Bjørgvin he'd spoken to a friend who had a house that Ales and Asle could rent, it was this friend's childhood home, ten or fifteen miles, drive north of Bjørgvin, the friend's mother had lived there until a few years ago but ever since she died the house has stood empty, and the friend who's lived all these years in Bjørgvin, he was a doctor at the hospital, yes, Sande was his name, was also one of his best clients, Beyer had said and then Ales and Asle had rented the house, and then they'd moved to the old house, ten or fifteen miles north of Bjørgvin, Asle thinks standing there looking out the window and he sees a car drive past on the road, a small van, and he's seen this car or van several times, Asle thinks and he thinks that Sande, the doctor who'd rented them this house, had said that they should arrange things however they wanted, Asle thinks, and he thinks that he and Ales got the keys to the brown house and they drove to the house and let themselves in and it smelled stuffy in the hall and they opened the door to the right and there was a little kitchen, with an oven and refrigerator, and old cupboards, and an old table with old chairs, he thinks and then there was a door to the living room and the living room was empty, only a sofa, a coffee table, and an armchair were still there, and then a dining table with six chairs, and through the living room there was a big bedroom and there was a double bed in there with a duvet and a pillow with no sheets or pillowcase and there was a door from the bedroom out to the hall and there were stairs from the hall up to the attic and there was a little hallway with a door to the left and a door to the right and there was a bed in each of the two rooms and then Ales and Asle went back downstairs and then they sat right down on the sofa and sat there and looked at all their stuff on the floor in the middle of the room, they'd left some in the hall but brought most of it into the living room, and now there was a whole heap of it standing there, and both he and Ales were tired, Asle thinks, and so they lay down on the sofa and they lay there with their arms around each other, he thinks and then Ales said that she wanted to stop going to The Art School and Asle asked why and she said that she didn't think she was ever going to paint well enough and Asle said that he thought she was a good painter and Ales said that's just it, she was good, just good, no matter what she painted it turned out just good, somehow, dutiful and good and totally without anything that made it stand out, she said, because what was necessary, what it needed, wasn't there, yes, what made art art was missing, what went beyond the picture and made it something other than just a picture, Ales said and Asle asked if she was completely sure that she wanted to stop and he said that if she stopped going to The Art School then he would too, he said, because he didn't feel that he was learning anything new anymore, and then it was so distracting to have to stand there in The Painting Hall with the other students and paint there, he said and then Ales said that in that case they would both stop, because she was also sure that Asle already had what he needed to be able to paint the way he wanted and should, because actually there was just one thing he needed, and whatever it was, yes, he had it, she said, but she didn't have that one thing, Ales said and Asle didn't say anything, and Ales said that he could just keep painting but she on the other hand thought she should start as a student at The University, she wanted to study art history, and especially icons, and then she wanted to start painting icons, because as long as she could understand what an icon was and how it was painted she was sure that painting icons was the right thing for her to do, she felt something almost like a calling to do it, if she could use such a big word, she said and Asle said that she should think it over and Ales said that she didn't know if he'd noticed, he often spent so much time in his own world, but she'd recently been reading lots of books about icons, both histories and books about how icons are made, and there was no one in Norway as far as she knew who painted icons, no one from Norway anyway, and you had to order from abroad what you need to paint them, she said and Asle said that he'd always liked icons and Ales said that she knew that icons were what she should paint, not paintings, she'd be an icon painter, not an art painter, she was just as sure of that as she was of the fact that he and she belonged together, she said and Asle said that he'd support her as well as he could whatever she wanted to do, he said and Ales said that she'd been a little worried about telling him, but now she'd said it at last, and she wasn't worried about telling The Principal at The Art School that she was going to stop

going there, and Art History was an open major at The University
so she could start going to lectures there right away, and one of the
professors there was also an expert on icons, she said, he wrote his
dissertation about something to do with icons, and he often came
to mass, so Asle must have seen him, he has long grey hair and a
long grey beard, she said, and Asle said that he'd certainly noticed
the man with the long grey hair and the long grey beard, he said
and he said that in that case it was decided, then, yes, they'd both
stop going to The Art School and then she'd start as a student at
The University and learn how to make icons, that was probably
best, and he would keep painting his pictures, Asle said and then he
said that they could go see The Principal at The Art School as soon
as Monday and tell him they were quitting, he said, Asle thinks as
he stands there in front of the window watching it slowly get darker and darker outside and he thinks that then Ales and he were
standing outside the door to The Principal's office at The Art
School and they knocked and he came and opened the door and
Ales said first that she'd decided to stop going to The Art School,
she didn't want to paint pictures, but icons, she said and as a first
step she wanted to study art history at The University, she'd said
and The Principal had nodded and said that she knew best, and of
course he would accept her decision, he said and Ales thanked him
and then Asle had said that he was going to stop going too, he
wanted to be a full-time painter and The Principal said he could
understand why Asle would want that, and he just had to accept it,
he said and then Ales and Asle shook hands with The Principal and
they thanked him and The Principal wished them the best and
they left The Principal's office and Asle said that he wanted to go
see Eiliv Pedersen and thank him for all his teaching and Ales said
that she would go straight up the hill to The University and register as an Art History student and then they each went their way,
Ales left The Art School and walked up the hill to The University
and Asle walked into The Painting Hall where everyone taking
Painting was standing and painting, and actually that was what

bothered him the most, that he had to stand there with all the others and paint together, it distracted him so much, it was downright destructive for his pictures, Asle thought and he saw Eiliv Pedersen standing there saying something to one of the other students in Painting and Asle waited until he was finished and then went over to Eiliv Pedersen and said that he'd decided to stop coming to The Art School and Eiliv Pedersen said that he could understand that, because Asle was such a good painter that he at least didn't have much he could teach him, he said, yes, probably the other way around would be more accurate, he said and Asle didn't know what to say and he thought that it was all wrong but he couldn't say anything to contradict him and then Asle said that he just wanted to thank him for all the lessons, he had learned a lot from Eiliv Pedersen, and not least from his paintings, seeing them had been very important for him, Asle said and Eiliv Pedersen said again that he's known for a long time that Asle has reached where he's going, yes, or in any case gone as far as The Art School can take him, and now there's just the enormous, lifelong work of painting picture after picture, now he needs to just keep doing it and doing it and not care about what art critics or other people who supposedly understand art have to say, but Asle probably learned all that after the exhibition he'd had at The Beyer Gallery, because he must never care about reviews, or else he should just listen to criticism from people who can paint, yes, who have painted excellent pictures themselves, because actually it was only the people who've done something who can judge whether something is good or bad, and then there weren't more than a few so-called normal people who had a kind of access to the understanding of art that let them say something about the quality of a picture, and quality, that's what it's all about, Eiliv Pedersen said and then he said that Asle had chosen a hard life by choosing art, but in his case it was the right choice, Eiliv Pedersen said and then he held out his hand to Asle and Asle held out his hand to Eiliv Pedersen and then they shook hands and then Eiliv Pedersen said that he wished Asle the

best, Asle thinks standing at the window in the brown house looking out and he thinks that it's getting darker, but slowly, and it's
beautiful watching the leaves, in all their colours, yes, autumn is his
time of year, Asle thinks and then he sees the old big car or small
van drive past on the road again and I sit here in my chair by the
round table and I look at my landmark out there in the middle of
the Sygne Sea, at the waves out there, I hold Ales's hand and I look
at the empty chair where Ales liked to sit, because we sat like this
a lot, just sat without saying anything, I think, and it's good holding Ales's hand, I think and I look at the waves and I see Asle standing there in front of the window

You've been standing there long enough now, Ales says

and she goes over to the window and she takes Asle's hand and
then they stand there hand in hand and they look out the window
and then Ales asks why don't they go for a walk, before it gets
totally dark, she says and Asle says yes they must do that, he says
and then they go out into the hall and Asle puts on his long black
coat and Ales takes a scarf out of a box and she hands it to him and
she says he needs a scarf and then Asle puts on his brown leather
shoulderbag and Ales says you can't go anywhere without that bag,
she says and they go out and then, hand in hand, they start walking
down the country road

Look over there, there's a playground, Ales says

There sure is, Asle says

That's strange, you can't see a single other house, she says

But there are swings and seesaws and a sandbox, she says

and Ales asks why don't they go down to the playground and
Asle says they should, and there's a path down to the playground
and it runs over a hill and ends at a hilltop

There must be houses with children on the other side of the
hill, Asle says

Yes, there must be, Ales says

and she and Asle walk down the path and they go into the
playground

Now it's almost dark, even if it's only afternoon, but soon it'll be evening, Asle says

Yes, Ales says

and then she goes over to the swing and she sits on it and then she asks Asle to give her a push and he goes and grabs the ropes holding the greying wooden seat that Ales is sitting on and he pulls her slowly back, and then he lets go and he pulls her back again and he lets her go

More, harder, Ales says

and Asle pulls and gives a stronger push

Even harder, Ales says

and Asle pushes even harder

More, harder, Ales says

and it's like she's screaming and Asle pulls as hard as he can and Ales flies as high as the swing can go and then Ales shrieks and he lets go of the swing and then Asle steps back and then he sees a man come walking down the path, and he's in a long black coat, and he has long grey hair tied back in a hair tie and Ales says that was really great, she says, it was like being a child again, she says

And there's a seesaw, she says

And there's the sandbox, she says

and the path of the swing gets shorter and shorter and then Ales stops the swing entirely with her feet and Asle goes over to her and he puts his hands on her shoulders

I'm just like a child again, Ales says

and Asle says nothing and I sit there in my chair by the round table and I look at my landmark out in the water, I look at the waves, at the eternal waves, I think and I think that I want to go to mass, and I should have driven into Bjørgvin so I could go to mass on Christmas Day, the way I usually do, but there'll be none of that this year, since for some strange reason I said yes to celebrating Christmas with Åsleik and Sister, whose name is Guro, and what's said is said, a promise is a promise, I think and then I think that yes, now that I've decided that I'm going to stop painting I can drive to Bjørgvin today and drop off these nine pictures too, the ones I kept, to be sold at the next exhibition at The Beyer Gallery, I think, and then I can go to mass in the evening and then, yes, I don't know how many times I've called to try to get permission to see Asle, but they always say the same thing, that he can't have visitors, but maybe if I just show up in person at The Hospital and say that I want to see him they'll let me, I think, so then I have three things to do in Bjørgvin, deliver my paintings, go to mass, and go to The Hospital and ask if I can see Asle, I think, and then I can spend the night at The Country Inn and then drive back home early tomorrow, yes, at the crack of dawn, so that tomorrow morning, yes, when it gets light, Åsleik and I can go in his Boat to Sister's to celebrate Christmas, and I think that Beyer will probably be surprised if I show up with new paintings already, so maybe it's best if I call him, but if he isn't in his gallery I can probably just bring the pictures into The Beyer Gallery myself, and if the side room, yes, The Bank, is locked I'll just put the pictures in some other place, maybe behind the desk, but I have to talk to Beyer in any case, I think and Ales lets go of my hand and I get up and I go out into the hall and I look up Beyer's phone number in the phone book, and the truth is I haven't called him that many times, I think, and I pick up the receiver and I dial the number and I hear Beyer's voice say Beyer here and I say

It's me, I say

Well, it's you, Beyer says

Yes now this is unexpected, he says

The guy doesn't call all that often, he says

and he says that if I'm wondering how it went with the sale he is happy to report that it couldn't have gone better, because all the pictures are now sold, so as far as that goes he could have shut The Beyer Gallery and taken Christmas off, but he'd said that he'd be open both today, on Little Christmas Eve, and tomorrow, Christmas Eve, because there are always people who are late buying Christmas presents, and it's often people who are flush with

money and bad with time, Beyer says and he laughs and he is getting on a roll with his chatting away like Bjørgvin people do and I
say he needs to listen to something

Yes, Beyer says

I'd like to bring by nine paintings for you today, I say

and there's silence on the telephone

I have nine paintings here, four of them are pictures I didn't
want to sell, for various reasons, maybe they're strange, but I've
probably told you about them, I say

and Beyer says that he doesn't recall that I have, but it sounds
very interesting, he says, and I then say that there are four pictures
I set aside to work on more but now I think they're done

But is it really so urgent, Beyer says

Yes, I say

and I think that I'm not planning to say that I'm not going to
paint any more pictures, because then Beyer will only say that it's
just an idea, I'll definitely paint more, of course I will, I'm just tired
and feeling a bit rundown, he'll say and Beyer says that even if this is
unexpected he is obviously, when it comes to me, always happy to
see me and my pictures, and then, he says, yes, then maybe he can
take down some of the ones that have already sold and hang up some
of the ones I'm bringing, because the ones he has stored in The
Bank he's already promised that Kleinheinrich could show in Oslo,
or Huysmann in Nidaros, but damn if he wasn't tempted to get two
or three of the pictures and hang them, he must admit, Beyer says,
but now we'll just see if we can get a few more pictures sold before
Christmas, he says and Beyer's all eager now and he says the best
thing would be if I could come as quick as I can, and I said that I'd
thought these pictures could be for next year's show, and Beyer says
that there'll be more pictures for next year's show, so everything'll be
great, and I say that in that case I'll just wrap my paintings in blankets
and carry them out to the car and then drive down to Bjørgvin right
now, I say and Beyer says that in that case he'll be waiting for me in
the gallery even if I get there after closing time, because he needs

to keep the gallery open tomorrow, even though it's Christmas Eve tomorrow, even if it's a Sunday this year, because that's the day of the year when he usually sells the most pictures, he says and I say thank you so much and then we say we'll see each other soon and I hang up the phone and I think that the best thing to do would be to call The Country Inn and see if they have a room free tonight and I find the phone number in the phone book and I dial it and I ask if they have a room free and I say that 407 is my usual room at The Country Inn and The Bjørgvin Man says that they do have room for me, as always, and Room 407 is free, he says, so then I can have my usual room, he says and I say that in that case I'll reserve the room and The Bjørgvin Man says certainly and I hang up the phone and I go up to the attic and get blankets from the attic room I use as a kind of storeroom and I go into the other attic room where I keep paintings in crates and I wrap each and every one of them in its own blanket and then I carry them downstairs and I step into my shoes and I go outside and put them in the back of the car and I feel how good it is to be getting all the paintings out of the house, so now the only picture I still have is the portrait of Ales, which is still leaning against the back of the chair up in the attic room, and then the picture of Guro that's drying next to the kitchen door, but that'll be out of the house first thing tomorrow, I think and I go inside and I call Bragi and he wakes up and looks at me with his dog's eyes and then I say come and he comes and he stops next to me and then I put my brown leather shoulderbag on and I think now what's wrong with me, sleeping all night on the bench in my coat, and I haven't taken it off yet today, and now I'm going to drive back to Bjørgvin again, I think, and under my coat I'm wearing my black velvet jacket, so I slept in that too, I think and I go out to the kitchen and Bragi follows me and then he drinks up all the water that's in the bowl and I give him fresh water from the tap and he drinks a little of that too

You were thirsty, weren't you Bragi, I say

and I think that he needs a little something to eat too, and I cut a slice of bread and crumble it into pieces and put the pieces in the bowl and Bragi goes and sniffs a little at the bread, but he doesn't eat any and I think that he probably isn't hungry then, and I go to the hall door and I say come on Bragi and he reluctantly follows me and I turn off the kitchen light and the hall light and I go outside and Bragi goes a little ways out onto the hill and first he raises his right back leg and he takes a good long piss and then he squats and then stays like that to shit and he clearly doesn't really need to because he squats and pushes several times but then it works and then I open the back door of the car and Bragi hops in and lies right down on the back seat and I shut the door and I get into the car and I start it and it hasn't snowed for several days and the roads are well cleared, with firm dry snow, so they're good to drive on and I think that it'll be good to get rid of the paintings, finally, finally get rid of them, and then it'll be good to go to mass tonight, I think, and not least to go check on Asle, I think and I drive and I don't think about anything, that's maybe what I like best about driving, that the thoughts sort of go away and I get absorbed in just driving, that I fall into a kind of stupor and get a kind of break or rest or whatever it is, I think and then I see snowflakes start to land on the windshield one by one and I'm getting close to the playground and I see two people walking hand in hand towards me along the road and I think that those are the people I saw down in the playground when I was driving back from Bjørgvin not so long ago, and he has medium-length brown hair, and she has long dark hair and Asle thinks here comes that car again, a small van, yes, he's seen it several times, there aren't that many cars he notices but he remembers seeing this particular one before

I've seen that car a bunch of times, Asle says

I don't remember seeing it before, Ales says

and I think that it's not so far to the playground, and to the turnoff, but I don't feel tired, and the young couple step off onto the side of the road and stop and stand there, and I see that he's wrapped his arms around her back and snowflakes are slowly coming down over them and now it's not far to drive to the old house

Ales and I rented, first there's the playground and then the turnoff and then I drive by the old brown house, I think, and no one has lived there since we moved out and moved to the old white house in Dylgja, I think, and the house has become more and more run-down and I don't like looking at that good old house just falling apart and that's probably why I don't want to look at it, I think and I look at the two people standing on the side of the road and snowflakes are landing in his medium-length brown hair and in her long dark hair and I drive past them and I get closer to the playground and I don't want to look down at it or at the turnoff and I get to the brown house and I do look at the house after all and it is a lot more rundown than it was when we lived there, now the little house is about to collapse, yes, some shingles have already fallen off the roof, and I don't like looking at the house, and yet I almost always do it, I think and I see a young man with medium-length brown hair standing in the window looking out and I look straight ahead and I try not to think about anything, or to just think that now I'm going to drive to The Beyer Gallery, drop off the paintings with Beyer, and then take a taxi to The Hospital to see Asle, and if they don't let me in now then yes well I don't know, I think, and after I've seen Asle I'll take a taxi to St Paul's Church and it'll be fine if I get there early, then I can sit in the church and listen to the silence, because it's in the silence that God is nearest, I think and then I'll be there for mass, and it's been a long time now since I've taken communion, I think and then I'll walk to The Country Inn, and I know how to get from St Paul's Church to The Country Inn very well, I've done it so many times, I think, it's very easy, I should be able manage that, anyway it'll be fine, I think and I drive and I fall into a stupor and I'm absorbed in just driving and before I know it I've reached The Beyer Gallery and as soon as I stop the car Beyer is standing in the door and he waves to me and he comes walking over to me and he holds out his hand and we shake hands and he says no, this is a surprise, but actually it'll work out splendidly, as they say, because, like he said, yes, he's sold all of the pictures in the Christmas exhibition, he says, and he can most likely get a few of the ones I'm bringing him now sold tomorrow, on Christmas Eve day itself, he says and I open the door to the back of the van and Bragi starts barking and I say hush, quiet now, I say and Beyer asks if I have a dog now and I say it's just a dog I'm taking care of and Beyer says that I've said so many times that I thought I should get a dog, especially after I became a widower, he says, but I never did, Beyer says and he asks if I like looking after dogs and I say it's fine, and he asks if I've thought about getting a dog of my own now and I say I may do that and then Beyer says that the door to The Bank is already open

And Doctor Sande, yes, you remember him, Beyer says

Yes, you rented a house from him, he says

Yes, he bought three pictures this year, he says

Three pictures, he says

and I don't say anything

But what made you decide all of a sudden that you wanted to drive down and deliver some pictures to me, Beyer says

and I don't answer

No, well, if you don't want to tell me then don't tell me, he says

You've never been a big talker, he says

and I don't say anything and then Beyer and I start to carry the pictures inside and he says we'll put them right in The Bank and that he'll look at them tonight, after the gallery has closed for the day, he says and it doesn't take long to carry all the pictures inside and I stand there with blankets in my hands and Beyer asks what I'm going to do now and I say that first I'll go to The Coffeehouse and get a little food and Beyer says I should do that, yes, like usual, and I can tell he wants to ask me more questions about why I came so soon with new pictures, and why I drove down to Bjørgvin today at all, and he tries to let it go, but he can't contain himself

Is it something about a woman? he says

and Beyer is sort of whispering to me

Since you've lived alone all these years it's about time, he says

and I shake my head and then I think that maybe Beyer's kind of right about it, because that woman Guro, who lives in The Lane, no, it's not exactly a thing about a woman like Beyer says but it is kind of like that a little, I think, but I promised to be eternally faithful to Ales so I can at least keep that promise for the length of a human life

But it's none of my business, Beyer says

and then I say Merry Christmas and Beyer says Merry Christmas and then he says he can't remember my pictures ever having sold so quickly any other year, he says, and he says that when pictures sell so well it's fun to be a gallerist, he says, and he was already going to be open tomorrow too, on Christmas Eve itself, even though it's Sunday, maybe it's not exactly legal, for all he knows, but never mind about that, he says, since Christmas Eve, he says, is the day when he sells the most pictures all year, because there are always some of the wealthier Bjørgvin men who wait till the last minute to buy something for the lady of the house, he says and I don't say anything

No, I won't hold you up, Beyer says

and then he opens the door for me and I go outside and I think that now all I have to do, as I've done so many times before, is cross High Street and then take a left down The Lane and then I'll pass by the house where Guro has an apartment on the ground floor and I think that it'd be really bad if it's like Beyer says and I'm involved in something to do with a woman, but if I am then it'd have to be with Guro, I think and in my long black coat, and with my brown leather shoulderbag, I cross High Street, and then I take a left and start to walk down The Lane and right away I realize that there's a smell of something burnt and I see that the windows are broken and the woodwork is burnt in an apartment there, on the ground floor, and I think that can't be Guro's apartment where there was a fire, can it? yes, it looks like it, and I stop and I stand there looking at the broken windows and the burnt-up wood panelling and I see how the grey and black burn marks are almost screaming at the white, it's almost like most of the places are grey, and there's a strong burnt smell and I think that that really is Guro's apartment that caught fire, and then this strong smell of smoke, it smells burnt, nothing else, and it must be Guro's apartment where there was the fire, I think, and Guro smoked so much, she would roll a cigarette, smoke it, stub it out, roll a new cigarette, smoke it, stub it out, roll a new cigarette, she smoked constantly, I think, so she was probably smoking in bed and that's probably how the fire started, I think, and now that too is just too horrible, I think and I see an older Bjørgvin man come walking up The Lane and I say excuse me but I see there's been a fire

It's just too horrible, he says

and he shakes his head

Yes, I say

And someone died in the fire too, he says

Someone died? I say

A woman, middle-aged, he says

She'd lived in that apartment for years, he says

And then, yes, it must have been the smoke that killed her, he says

Was her name Guro? I say

Yes, he says

and we stay standing there looking at the burnt-out apartment

These things happen, he says

Yes, I say

and then he wishes me Merry Christmas and I thank him and wish him the same and then he keeps walking and I stay standing there looking at the burnt-out apartment and then I think now Guro's dead, yes, it's sad, it's always sad when someone is taken away forever, but now Guro is with God, now she's resting in God, in God's peace, in God's light, I think, I'm sure of it, so when I look at it more clearly it's not so sad, not that Guro went to church or was a Christian or anything, no, far from it, she probably wasn't a believer at all, but she had a lot of God in her, and now that part of her is back with God again, like she is, like what was deepest inside her is, it's impossible to understand it but that's how it is, I think, now Guro is part of God and at the same time herself, I think and then I make the sign of the cross right there in front of the burnt-out apartment and then I walk farther down The Lane and I think that not many of the people who believe they're inside really are, but many of the people who are outside, those are the ones who are inside, the first shall be last, as is written, I think and then I walk over to The Country Inn and I think that now I'll go check in and then I'll have The Bjørgvin Man, it'll of course be him sitting there at the reception desk now, call me a taxi, and I walk into the lobby and of course it's The Bjørgvin Man sitting there at reception

So, here you are again, he says

It hasn't been so long, he says

And you want Room 407, he says

That's what you said on the phone anyway, he says

and I nod and The Bjørgvin Man stands up and takes a key off the hook on the wall behind him and he hands me the key and I thank him and then I ask if The Bjørgvin Man can call me a taxi and he says of course and he calls and then he says the taxi will be here right away and I hand the key back to The Bjørgvin Man and he hangs it on the hook behind him and then I go outside and I stand there and I'm not thinking anything, I just feel empty, and the smell of something burnt reaches all the way to The Country Inn, and then I see the taxi coming and I get in the back and I say I'd like to go to The Hospital and The Taxi Driver asks if I'm visiting someone there and I just answer yes and he says that that must be rough to be in The Hospital over Christmas and I say yes and then he keeps quiet and he stops in front of The Hospital and I pay and I go into The Hospital and straight to the reception desk and I ask if there's any way I can get to see Asle, he's a good friend, and the woman sitting there says she is so sorry, he died last night, he passed away quietly and peacefully, she says and I turn around and I go outside and the taxi is still standing there and I ask The Taxi Driver to take me to St Paul's Church and he says that'll be fine and I realize that I can't think clearly, I'm not sad, I'm nothing, just empty, just an empty blackness, I think and The Taxi Driver stops by St Paul's Church and I pay and I go into the church, dip my fingertips into the basin with the holy water, make the sign of the cross, and go to the third pew from the back on the left, I kneel and then sit down at the end of the pew and I think that I always sit there, because that was where Ales always sat, and where we always sat together, I think and then I bow my head and I fold my hands and then one by one people come into St Paul's Church, all of them silently, and they all kneel or bow their head before they sit down and I try to be as silent as I can and I sit there on the outer edge of the third pew from the back on the left in St Paul's Church and I realize that Ales, even though she's been dead for so long, is sitting next to me, the way she used to, and I take her hand and I hold her hand and I shut my eyes and now I just want to be silent and I breathe calmly in and out and then I fall into myself and I think that Asle is dead, and Guro is dead, and I sink into the usual course of the mass, and tonight it's a Latin mass and it's Father Brochmann who is celebrating mass and the familiar words feel comforting, drained as they are of meaning in the usual sense, instead they have a kind of silence inside them and they fill the silence with meaning, with God's closeness, and the close human community is a shining unity when the people there in the church, about ten people, stand up and pronounce the beautiful words Kyrie eleison Christe eleison, first Father Brochmann, then the congregation, it's said three times, and then the congregation says the Pater noster together and when I and the others kneel for the consecration, when Father Brochmann in persona Christi says Accipite et manducate ex hoc omnes Hoc est enim corpus meum quod pro vobis tradetur and then lifts up the host that has now become Christ's body, become all of him, gathered into his transfigured spiritual body, become Christ's mystical body, and the moment of transformation happens I see a halo appear around the host, and Father Brochmann says Accipite et bibite ex eo omnes Hic est enim calix sanguinis mei novi et æterni testamenti qui pro vobis et pro multis effundetur in remissionem peccatorum Hoc facite in meam commemorationem and lifts up the chalice and the wine is transformed into Christ's blood, into everything Christ is, gathered into his spiritual transfigured body, it is one with God, I see a flash of light come from the chalice in the moment of the consecration, and then the deep feeling of truth when the Mysterium fidei is recited, and faith, hope, and charity fill the congregation sitting there and Father Brochmann says the Peace Prayer with Christ's words Pacem relinquo vobis Pacem meam do vobis and Father Brochmann says Pax Domini sit semper vobiscum and I feel how good it is to hear Father Brochmann pray to let me, me, Asle, receive God's peace and I know that before long I will go up to the altar and then Father Brochmann will put the host in my left hand that's crossed over my right hand as he says Corpus Christi and I will say Amen and put the host in my mouth and then with my hands together in front of me I will go back down to my place, there on the outside of the third pew from the back on the left, and then I will fold my hands and bow my head and close my eyes and as the host, Christ's body, dissolves in my mouth I will gather everything I have into a prayer for God to take both Guro and Asle into himself and for them to find peace in God, find rest in God's light, that they might become part of the kingdom of God, again and again I think that and then I give thanks for my life and for letting me meet Asle and I give thanks for having met Guro and then I just say thank you and then I pray that the pictures I've painted might be a help to others, and I fall silent inside myself and then Father Brochmann starts to pray a prayer and everyone stands up and then finally he says in Norwegian Go in peace and I sit down and I close my eyes and one by one people leave the church and again I pray for Guro and Asle to find peace in God, that they might become part of God's kingdom, God's light, and then I stand up, bend my knee, and then I go and dip my fingertips into the basin of holy water and I make the sign of the cross and then I leave St Paul's Church and I start to walk straight to The Country Inn and I think that as soon as I get there I will lie down and go to sleep, and I feel so tired that it won't be hard to get to sleep at all, I think and then tomorrow at the crack of dawn I will drive to Dylgja, because tomorrow Åsleik and I are going to take The Boat to Øygna, way up in Sygnefjord, not far from Insteljord, almost all the way up Sygnefjord, to celebrate Christmas at Sister's, as Åsleik always says, but her name is Guro, I think and then I remember that Bragi is alone in the car, and he needs to be walked, needs something to drink, but he'll probably manage all right alone for a few more hours, a short night, because right now I so don't want to go up The Lane and see the broken windows and the burnt-up walls of the apartment that used to be Guro's, and then that burnt smell, I think and I go straight to The Country Inn and once I get to The Country Inn I just nod to the woman who's sitting at reception now, because now The Bjørgvin Man is off for the night, and the woman sitting there now is someone I've never seen before as far as I can remember and I say 407 thanks and she stands up and takes the key off the hook and hands it to me and I say thanks and I go take the lift up to the fourth floor and I walk to Room 407 and I turn on the light and it's nice and warm in the room, and it feels good to walk into a warm room after having sat in the cold church, and having walked from St Paul's Church to The Country Inn through the cold night, I think and I take off my shoulderbag and put it on the floor and then I take off my black coat, and now I've definitely been wearing it for more than a full day, because last night I slept in my coat on the bench in the main room back home in Dylgja, and then I take off my black velvet jacket, and I've been wearing that even longer, I think and I drape it over the back of the chair next to the desk and then I pick up the brown leather shoulderbag and put it down on the chair and then I take off my scarf

and pullover and trousers and put them on the chair and I lie down
on the bed and oh it is so good to lie down in a bed with fresh
clean sheets, I think, no, how can something so normal feel so
good, I think and then I turn off the light and then I hold the cross
at the bottom of the rosary I have hanging around my neck, that I
got from Ales once, with brown wooden beads and a brown wood-
en cross, and while I hold the cross in my hand I say out loud Ave
Maria and I say to myself Ave Maria Gratia plena Dominus tecum
Benedicta tu in mulieribus et benedictus fructus ventris tui Jesus
Sancta Maria Mater Dei Ora pro nobis peccatoribus nunc et in
hora mortis nostræ and then I breathe slowly in and out and then
I slip into sleep and I sleep, I wake up, and I think that I was so tired
last night that I fell asleep right away, and I slept heavily and peacefully, I think, and today it's Sunday and it's Christmas Eve day itself,
I think and I think that now it'll be good to take a shower, because
I really feel dirty all over, and I get up and I take a shower and then
I dry my long grey hair with a hair dryer and I tie my hair back in
a ponytail and then I get dressed and I think I should have brought
fresh clean clothes with me, but later today I'll dress up in my best
suit, because today is Christmas Eve, I think and then I put on the
black velvet jacket and I drape the shoulderbag over my shoulder
and I drape the coat over one arm and then I take the lift downstairs and I walk into the place that's The Coffeehouse during the
day but in the morning it's the breakfast room for guests at The
Country Inn and I get myself a little coffee with milk, but I don't
feel like eating and then I go and drop the key off with the woman
who's sitting at reception and I pay for my room and then the
woman sitting at reception and I wish each other Merry Christmas
and then I put on my black coat and I go outside and I don't look
at Guro's burnt-out apartment, I just walk straight ahead and then
I cross High Street and there in front of The Beyer Gallery is my
car and I unlock it and right away Bragi wakes up and jumps up
and down and wags his tail and then I open the back door and pull
him out and Bragi runs like crazy around the parking lot and I call

Bragi and he comes right away and hops in the back door that I'm holding open and he lies down on the back seat and I get in and sit down in the driver's seat and I start the car and I drive out of the centre of Bjørgvin, the difficult way that Beyer taught me a long time ago, and I drive north and I approach Sailor's Cove and I don't want to look at the building where Asle used to have his apartment and I drive past the building and I drive north and I look at the white roads and it's a cold, clear morning with shining stars and a practically full moon and I think that I don't want to look at the house Ales and I rented and lived in, I think and I drive north to Dylgja and I think that now, now I want to just drive and be empty, and not think about anything, not about Asle, not about Guro, I think and I don't want to look at the turnoff, not at the playground either, I think and I think that it wouldn't surprise me if Åsleik had already called to say I should get ready and we should set out soon, because it's light so few hours a day in this time of year and we have to use those hours, I think and then I just drive and I don't think anything and I look up at the brown house and I see a young man with medium-length brown hair standing and looking out the window and then a young woman with long dark hair comes and stands right next to him and then they stand there and look out and Asle thinks there's that car again, that small van, he thinks and I think that now I mustn't look at the two of them in the window, I think and I look at the white roads in front of me and I keep driving and then I get to Instefjord and then to Øygna, and now it's almost totally light out, I think and I think that I don't want to look up at Sister's house, where the woman named Guro lives, and I look at the white roads and I drive slowly onwards and then I'm at Dylgja and I drive past Åsleik's house and then up the driveway to my own house and I park the car in front and I open the back door and pull Bragi out and as usual he can't wait to jump out into the snow and lift his leg and there's an ugly yellow spot in the snow behind him and then he bends his back and shits, and I stand there looking at him and then I open the door and I call

Bragi and he comes leaping over and I go into the kitchen and then I hear the phone ring and I go out into the hall and pick up the receiver and it's Åsleik and he says where was I? or was I sleeping that heavily? did I forget that today is Christmas Eve and that we're supposed to take The Boat to Øygna to celebrate Christmas at Sister's? he says and I say no I didn't forget and Åsleik says that he's called several times, because we should set out soon, we agreed that we'd set out as soon as it was light, he says, and it's a long trip to Sygnefjord, and it'll get dark early, we need to go while it's still light, yes, like we agreed, so now I need to come right over to his place at once, because sailing in the dark is no fun at all, not to mention tying up to the dock, Åsleik says and I say I'll come right over

Yes, right away, Åsleik says

Yes, I say

But why didn't you answer the phone? he says

and I don't say anything, but anyway it's good I finally answered, Åsleik says, because didn't he say that we had to leave early, we had to set sail as soon as it was light out, he'd said and I say yes, yes, I know, I remember he said that, I say and of course we need to, it is much better to take The Boat when it's light out than when it's dark, of course, I say

Yes, Åsleik says

So you need to come over now, he says

and I hear in his voice that he's a little annoyed, and I say again that I'll come right over and Åsleik says that he's ready and that it would be best to set out as soon as we can, he says and I say I'm going to hang up the phone and then drive right over and then Åsleik says that in that case he'll go down to The Boat and wait there for me to come and then we'll set out, he says, because there aren't that many hours of daylight at this time of year, yes, as he's said, and as I know perfectly well, he says and I say I'm coming right over and then I say I'll see him soon and I hang up the phone and then I go into the main room and I touch the picture I painted for Sister and it's almost dry and I pick it up and then I pick up the suitcase that's standing there between the bedroom door and the hall door and then I call Bragi and he comes running and I go outside and Bragi follows me and I shut the front door behind me and I think that no one in Dylgja locks their door, it's the custom in Dylgja to leave your door unlocked, I think and I go over to my car and then I put the suitcase in the back and then I lay the painting that's still not totally dry on top of the suitcase and then I open the back door and Bragi hops in and I get into the car and then I drive off to Åsleik's farm, and there's a short narrow path running down to the boathouse and his dock, and I drive down it and then I park next to the boathouse and I see Åsleik standing on the deck of his Boat, of course it had to be a boat like that, with a wheelhouse in front and a deck in back, and I pick up my shoulderbag and go out and I hear thumping from the engine of The Boat and I drape the leather shoulderbag over my shoulder and I open the back of the car and I take out the painting and the suitcase

Don't you ever take off that black coat, Åsleik says

Or that shoulderbag, he says

and I shut the hatch of the car and Åsleik again shouts that he knew it, he knew I was going to show up with that brown leather shoulderbag and wearing that black coat and with a scarf around my neck and I'm probably wearing that black velvet jacket under my coat too, he says, and now here I am, he was right, but a suitcase in the boat, no, a suitcase on a boat is bad luck no matter how old and nice a suitcase it is, don't I even know that, Åsleik says, suitcases and women are bad luck on boats, he thought I knew that much, only sailor bags belong on a boat, and in the old days sailor trunks on big boats, Åsleik says, and his sailor bag is already stowed in its place on the part of the deck closest to the bow in the cabin, he says and I walk towards The Boat and Åsleik, and the motor says thump thump and I see a black cloud of exhaust rise up from the stern and then I hand the suitcase to Åsleik and he says that since I didn't know any better, or couldn't help it, we'll just have to hope for the best, better a little luck than a lot of brains, he says, and then I hand him the painting and I say that he needs to be careful because the picture isn't totally dry yet so he has to lay it paint side up and he takes the painting and he says that this is a nice portrait I painted of Sister and that Guro will be very happy to get it, and it's unbelievable that it can look so much like her when I've only seen her once, in The Coffeehouse recently, Åsleik says and I say I was thinking I needed to bring a Christmas present for Sister and I couldn't find anything to buy her so I thought I might as well paint a picture for her, I say and I say that I don't know if it's good or bad, and I say that I think the face I painted both does and doesn't look like Sister, I say, because I've never met her, strangely enough, or not before I saw her in The Coffeehouse recently, I say, because that probably was Sister I saw then, I say and Åsleik says that anyway it's a picture of Sister I painted, so it definitely must have been her that I saw sitting at The Coffeehouse, with her suitcase and shopping bags, he says and I say that I don't know if she'll like the picture but the important thing is that I've brought her a Christmas present, I say and Åsleik says that Sister will be very happy to get the picture, he says and I say that I have wrapping paper for the picture in my suitcase and then Åsleik says that the picture I've painted looks exactly like Sister down to the last detail, it's absolutely unbelievable that I was able to paint her so accurately having only seen her once in The Coffeehouse, he says and then he puts the painting up on the square box covering the engine and I see that the picture is shaking a little up and down with the thumping of the engine and then Åsleik says again that the picture looks just like Sister down to the last detail, so if I really saw her just that one time then yes he doesn't understand how I could have painted it, that I was able to do that, because he's never showed me a photograph of Sister anyway, he doesn't even have one, he says then I hear Bragi bark

Mustn't forget the dog, Åsleik says

Yes, Bragi, he says

That would have been bad, I say

and I go open the back door of the car and Bragi hops out
and I slam the door shut and then I go over to The Boat and Bragi
follows me and he looks scared of The Boat and then I pick him
up and hand him to Åsleik and Bragi whines and whimpers and
whines and Åsleik takes him and puts him down on the deck and
Bragi lies right down and then he's lying there shivering and looking up at me with his scared dog's eyes

Doesn't look like much of a ship dog, Åsleik says

He's lying there shivering and whimpering so low you almost
can't hear him, he says

and I untie the front mooring and I throw the rope to Åsleik
and he coils it up nicely and then he lifts up the front fender and
right away the bow starts to drift away from the dock and Åsleik
says we're lucky, we have the current with us, the trip up Sygnefjord goes much quicker with the current than against it, it can
take almost twice as long if it's running against you, Åsleik says
and I untie the rear mooring and I coil the rope as I walk towards
The Boat and I hold tight to the rope so that the stern of The
Boat is right up next to the dock and Åsleik holds The Boat close
to the dock too with a boathook and then I step down onto the
gunwale and then down onto the deck and Åsleik shoves off with
the boathook and right away The Boat moves out into the water
and already we're a few feet from land and Åsleik brings the stern
fender on board and then he goes into the wheelhouse and turns
the wheel so that the bow is pointing straight up Sygnefjord and
I take the suitcase and painting and go into the wheelhouse and
Åsleik says again a suitcase on a boat, like I'm on a cruise, yes, like
this was some kind of luxury yacht I was vacationing on, one of
those ships that's constantly sailing up into Sygnefjord and back
down out of Sygnefjord on summer days, he says and he says that
he's often thought about what it would be like on board a ship like
that, and what it would be like on the bridge steering a ship like
that, pulling into shore must be really hard, you'd have to steer it

very precisely, because there are lots of skerries in the water, so it'd be a real tricky business, Åsleik says, yes, he who has spent his whole life sailing in these waters knows them well, but there were not a few skerries he's passed over that weren't on any charts and that he hadn't known about before, he says, but the skippers used well-known routes that had been taken many times, because cruise ships have been sailing up into and back down out of Sygnefjord all these years, so they had their fixed routes, and that's why it always went well, he's never heard about a single cruise ship running aground on any skerry, Åsleik says and I go into the cabin and Bragi comes slinking after me and he is moving as little as he can and once he's in the cabin he lies right down in the corner on the port side next to the door to the wheelhouse and I put my suitcase up in the bow, behind Åsleik's sailor bag, and then I lay the painting on top of the suitcase and then I put my shoulderbag down on the deck and then I go out of the cabin and I stand next to Åsleik there in the wheelhouse and he says that the weather is good, couldn't be better, almost, there are always some little billows but once we get some water astern it'll give The Boat a little extra speed, and with the current the trip'll be fine, Åsleik says and he says that yes, yes, it'll be all right, he says

Are you scared, Åsleik says

Are you scared of the water? he says

No, I say

You seem a little scared, he says

No I wouldn't say I'm scared, I say

Just a little nervous, Åsleik says

Yes, I say

and then it's silent and Åsleik sits down at the wheel and he holds the wheel in one hand and he says that it's not often I'm on board a boat, is it, and I say that I practically grew up in a boat and Åsleik says that he knows that perfectly well, he was just thinking, because I grew up in Hardanger, by Hardanger Fjord, he says and I say I was in a boat the whole time I was growing up, in a pointed boat, a so-called Barmen boat, I say and Åsleik says that he must be getting old because I've told him that many times, he says and I've often said that I wanted to get a boat of my own, but I never did get a boat, he says and I think that now that I've stopped painting I need to get a boat, because I need something to do and something to keep me busy, so I need to get a boat, a Barmen boat with a pointed bow and a flat stern and with a little outboard motor

I think I should get a boat, I say

You've said that before, Åsleik says

and he says that as long as he's known me I've talked about how I should get a boat and a dog, I've even said that a person needs them for a good life, yes, a boat and a dog, he says and it's silent again and then I sit down, because in the wheelhouse there's a chair at the wheel on the starboard side and another chair on the port side, and in between there's the door that leads into the cabin and that can be shut with a hook on the starboard side, and behind Åsleik there's a little hot plate and I look at it and Åsleik says that it's good to have a primus stove, you can boil yourself some coffee, and fry up bacon and eggs, get something warm in you, and that can be good, because it can get cold on the water, but he has a little stove and when it gets too badly cold he turns the stove on, and he says that the stove is firmly attached to the deck behind me and I turn around and I see the stove and Åsleik says maybe he'll warm it up a little? he says and he asks me if I can take the boat and I go over and take the wheel and it's a small wheel, with pegs around the rim, and Åsleik points at a little holm near the middle of the fjord way up ahead and he says I should steer towards that, he says and I sit down at the wheel and I let go of the wheel and right away The Boat starts to head towards land and I straighten the wheel up again and steer towards the holm in the middle of the fjord way up ahead

Now it should get a little warmer soon, Åsleik says

and I see him go into the cabin and then he comes out and he has a bottle of beer with him and he goes and opens a drawer

under the primus and he takes out a bottle opener and he opens
the bottle and then he sits down in the chair on the port side and
he sits there for a long time and then he raises the bottle to his
mouth and drinks

It's not often that I'm not at the wheel myself, I can't even
remember the last time, it must have been when my father was still
alive, Åsleik says

and I say that's not true, because he and I have been on the
water together lots of times, we've gone to Vik to go shopping
lots of times, I say and Åsleik says yes that's true, he's so forgetful
nowadays, he says

But it's been a long time in any case, he says

Yes, I say

Maybe ten years, at least, he says

Something like that, I say

and Åsleik says that since he's always been at the wheel himself,
for at least ten years in any case, it's really nice now to be able to
just sit and be a passenger, because he could probably say that that's
what he was now even if it was he who owned The Boat, Åsleik
says and I say that it's been a long time since I've been at the wheel,
but everything's fine, it's good, I say and Åsleik takes a sip

It's nice with beer, he says

I almost never drink beer at home, but I do a lot in The Boat,
he says

and it's silent

I think it has to do with my always having been a little scared
of being in a boat, I've always been a little scared of the water,
Åsleik says

and I don't say anything

Yes, it's true, Åsleik says

It's not because I like being in a boat that I've spent so much
time in one, it's because I had to, he says

To make a living, he says

and it's silent for a moment

And that's probably about my father having been lost at sea, he says

Yes, I say

and it's silent for a moment

They never found him, Åsleik says

No, I say

and it's silent again

No you've got it better, just painting pictures, but you need talent for that, it's like you need a gift of grace, Åsleik says

But gifts of grace come from God and I never believed in that, he says

and I don't say anything

No, never, Åsleik says

Believed in God, I mean, he says

and it's silent and Åsleik says that no one can say anything for certain about the big things, the biggest things, sea and sky, life and death, he says and he drinks his beer and he says that all of that is like an unknown darkness, we come from an unknown darkness and we return to an unknown darkness, that's how it is, there's nothing more to say about that, and as for whether a person was something in the darkness before being born, and whether they turn into something there after they die, no one can say anything or know anything about that, so for him all that's possible is wonder, he doesn't have any answers, Åsleik says and he finishes his bottle of beer and then he gets up and goes out on deck and I turn around and I see out the porthole at the back of the wheelhouse Åsleik throwing the empty bottle into the water and then he stands on his sea legs in a wide stance and he opens his fly and takes out his penis and pisses into the water in a nice arc and then I suddenly think about the boy who drowned when I was little, his name was Bård, and he was from the neighbouring farm, and then he fell out of their Barmen boat, a two-oar boat, and into The Fjord and he couldn't swim and he clearly couldn't get back on board the boat, so he never got to be very old, I think and I start to think about my sister Alida, she also died so long ago, both Ales and Sister are dead, and my sister Alida died so suddenly, I think, and the night before last Asle died and I can't think about that, I really just can't, and then the woman Guro, who lived in The Lane and who died in a fire, I think and it's horrible to think about, I think and I see Åsleik come back in and he goes into the cabin and gets a new bottle of beer and he opens it and he says you need to drink on Christmas, it's an old custom, back in the old days people said you should drink on Christmas, when the sun turns you should celebrate it, celebrate that the light was going to come back, that the grass would be green again, yes, that spring would come, would have to come, that winter would have to be over soon, people thought, and that's why they drank and went on a bender and travelled to be together, often from far away, to be together, to drink on Christmas, that's how it was, and the same thing in summer, when the sun turns, you should drink your way through Midsummer's Eve and a long way into the next morning, Midsummer's Day, that was the custom in these parts, it was still like that in his youth, and there was a bonfire on Midsummer's Eve and you could see a bonfire burning from every corner of Sygnefjord, he says, yes, it was like people were greeting each other with the bonfires they lit on Midsummer's Eve, and then there was dancing and drinking, and then you needed a fiddler, and even if there wasn't a fiddler in every village you didn't have to go too far to find one, they used to say that every real village needed a shoemaker, a blacksmith, and a fiddler, Åsleik says, that's how it was, he says and I sit there and keep a straight course for the holm in the middle of the fjord and Åsleik says it's nice to have company, man is man's delight, as the saying goes, Åsleik says and I sit there and look at the holm out there in the middle of the fjord and then Åsleik says that the holm I'm steering towards used to be where they had executions, and that's why it's called Gallows Holm, the same as another small island near Aga, a lot of Satan's witches were burnt there, and a lot of Satan's henchmen, he says, it was a long time ago, but he can remember Grandfather telling him about it, Åsleik says and it's silent and I think and I look at the waves and I see Ales standing there in her white dress, because she wanted a white wedding dress, Asle thinks and he bought himself a black suit and black dress shoes at The Second-Hand Shop in Sailor's Cove, where Ales and he bought most of what they needed during all their years together, dishes, clothes, almost everything they needed they bought there

You look good in a suit, Ales says

Yes how could we have managed without The Second-Hand Shop, Asle says

and he gives a little laugh

You can say that again, Ales says

and I look at the holm, at Gallows Holm, there in the middle of the fjord, that apparently used to be a place of execution, and I think damn it's good that The Second-Hand Shop is there in Sailor's Cove, because often when I'm in Bjørgvin I look in there, there in Sailor's Cove, a little north of the centre of the city of Bjørgvin itself, I think and I think that I bought my black suit and white shirt and tie and dress shoes there when we were going to get married, and it's exactly the same suit, the same shirt, the same tie, and the same shoes that are now in the old suitcase up in the bow, I think, and Ales bought her beautiful white wedding dress there, and it's still in her clothes closet in the house up in Dylgja, I think and I look at the waves and I see Ales standing there in her white wedding dress and she is carrying a white wedding bouquet, because she so wanted one, so even though it was expensive we had to buy one, Ales had said, Asle thinks, and now Ales is standing there in her white wedding dress and with her white wedding bouquet and they took a taxi to St Paul's Church, where the wedding was to take place, and it was Father Brochmann, who would later confirm Asle, and who had earlier confirmed Ales, who would marry them, and the maid of honour and best man would be mother Judit, as Ales's maid of honour, and then Beyer, as Asle's best man, Asle thinks and he thought that they didn't need to get

married, that cohabitating, as it was called, wasn't a deadly sin because they were married before each other, and they were married
before God, and he said that really they had been married for a
long time, ever since that day in St Paul's Church, there in the half-
darkness under the steps and Ales said that it was her mother Judit
who so wanted them to get married, yes, visibly married, they
should at least get married, mother Judit had said so many times,
Ales said, but Ales herself didn't think it was important that they
get married, yes, visibly, as it were, she said, since they had been in-
visibly married for a long time, before each other and before God,
she said and Asle had said that they could just get married visibly
then, since it was so important to her mother Judit, he thinks and
now Ales and Asle are standing there in St Paul's Church, he, Asle,
in his black suit and she, Ales, in her white wedding dress and Asle
has cut his hair and it's medium-length and brushed behind his ears
now, and Ales has put her hair up and I hear Åsleik say that it's been
a long time since I stopped drinking
    Yes, it was too much drinking, way too much, I say
    It was when you moved to Dylgja, Åsleik says
    No before then, I say
    But you probably don't want to talk about that, he says
    and I think, well, I can talk about anything, I think
    I was drinking way too much, I say
    And it could have turned out badly if I hadn't stopped, I say
    By the end all I was doing was drinking, I wasn't painting, I
didn't do anything but drink, I say
    and I say that Ales, my love, had a father who drank himself
to death, and Ales got me to stop drinking, and we rented a house
north of Bjørgvin so that I would stop drinking, yes, that was another reason for it, yes, before we took over the house from Ales's
aunt, old Alise, I say and Åsleik says that he remembers old Alise
very well, it was always nice to have a little chat with her, he says
and he drinks his beer and he says that beer, yes, beer and stronger
stuff too, are among the good things in life, and even if he's never

had any kind of drinking problem, yes, well, he had to admit that he did drink too much now and then, but then he never drank the next day, even the thought of beer or stronger drinks the next day just made him sick, he says

For a while before I stopped I was drinking round the clock, in the morning, during the day, in the evening, yes, even in the middle of the night, I say

No that's no good, Åsleik says

No it wasn't, I say

and I say that I even had what they call delirium tremens, the shakes, yes, he's probably heard about those, I say

Yes, Åsleik says

And I shook and shook and saw the most powerful visions, and the sharpest colours, and the strangest shapes, and I wasn't sure where I was, I say

You can die from something like that, Åsleik says

And I shook and shook, I say

and it falls silent and Åsleik says that he can understand very well why I totally stopped drinking, he says

But why did you drink so much? Åsleik says

It's like it wasn't me who drank, in the end it was the alcohol that was doing the drinking, not me, I say

and I say that I have nothing against other people drinking, it's not like when they drink I feel like I want a beer or glass of wine or something stronger, not at all, on the contrary, I'm happy that other people are drinking and I can see that it's good for them in a way, I'm never going to be for temperance or anything, I say

You were drinking yourself to death, Åsleik says

Yes I believe I was, I say

and it falls silent and I say that after lying with the shakes for a few days and seeing all the colours in the world I saw something white inside me and I held tight to it and then and there, in the middle of the shakes, in my delirium, my delirium tremens, I decided, while holding tight to that white colour, I made an agreement with myself that I wasn't going to drink anymore, and I didn't either, I say and Åsleik says that he still has a little spirits left in a bottle and he wants to have it, he says and then Åsleik goes into the cabin and he comes out again with a bottle that has just a little in it, down at the bottom, and he says that every Christmas he gets a bottle of spirits as a Christmas present from Sister, from Guro, yes, whom I'm finally about to meet soon, and it's about time, and some of it gets drunk on Christmas Eve afternoon, because they usually hand out their presents before the meal, to tell the truth there are only two presents, the picture Sister gets from him and then the bottle of spirits he gets from Sister, and whatever doesn't get drunk on Christmas Eve he takes home with him, but you couldn't call him a heavy drinker, no, because there's still, after a year, a little left in the bottle, and that's how it usually is every year, he usually brings the rest of last year's bottle with him when he comes to eat dinner at my house and when he sails to Sister's to celebrate Christmas, and he usually drinks up the last of it on the trip there, Åsleik says and he twists out the cork and he takes a swig

That tasted good, he says

And it feels good, he says

and then Åsleik drinks a little beer and then he says that now that we're near Gallows Holm I should take my bearings from the headland over there, he says and he points, and I turn the wheel and we glide slowly on towards the headland

This isn't exactly an express ferry here, Åsleik says

But it'll get there, he says

and Åsleik says that the trip to Sister's isn't all that long but we've hit a bit of cross-current now, he says, I can feel The Boat starting to rock back and forth a little, he says

Yes, I say

So we'll get there a little later, I say

Yes, Åsleik says

and then it's silent

You used to smoke too? Åsleik says

Yes, I say

But you quit that too, Åsleik says

Yes when we moved to Dylgja, I say

Why'd you quit? Åsleik says

and I say that Ales didn't smoke, and even though she never said she didn't like my smoking I had a feeling she didn't, I say, and then I also smoked way too much, it turned into a problem for myself as well as Ales, sometimes I'd even get up in the middle of the night to smoke, I say

Yes you were a real smoker then, Åsleik says

Yes, I say

Wasn't it hard to quit smoking? Åsleik says

Actually it wasn't, I say

When I quit smoking I started taking snuff, I say

and then it's silent

I never smoked, Åsleik says

I've never even tasted a cigarette, he says and I say that really it was Ales who got me to both quit drinking and quit smoking and Åsleik says yes and then it's silent and I look at the waves and I see Ales and Asle standing there outside St Paul's Church, and now they are married, so now what God has joined together no man can put asunder, Father Brochmann said, Asle thinks and now Beyer has gone to find two taxis, now they'll go home to 29 Ridge Street, and there's food there, a festive meal, it's almost ready, because there's mother Judit's lamb roast keeping warm in the oven and they've bought the best red wine, and it wasn't cheap, mother Judit said, Asle thinks and mother Judit says well it's not every day that your only daughter gets married is it, she says

This is a great day, Father Brochmann says

and Ales and Asle stand there holding each other's hands, and they're both shivering a little

It'll be nice to get back inside, Asle says

Yes, really nice, Ales says

and Asle holds Ales tighter and he rubs her back and she says

175

that feels good, really good and I see Åsleik raise the bottle of spirits and he takes a big swig and then he goes out on deck and he throws the empty bottle into the water and I hear him say farewell and then he comes back in with beer bottles in one hand and says that he can take The Boat now for a bit, so I can take a little rest in the cabin if I want, he says

And so you can wrap the picture you want to give Sister, if it's dry enough, he says

and I get up and Åsleik sits down at the wheel with one hand on the wheel and the beer bottles in the other and I stay standing next to him and I tell him that when I was young there was a neighbour boy, his name was Bård, and he drowned, he pulled the family boat in towards land, got on board and then pulled the boat out into The Fjord with him in it and then somehow he fell into the water and he couldn't swim and he couldn't get back on board the boat again, I say, and he hadn't even started school, I say

Lots of lives have been lost at sea, Åsleik says

I just suddenly thought about that, I say

It's the kind of thing you never forget, Åsleik says

No, I say

and there's silence and then I go into the cabin and I see Bragi lying there in the corner where he went and lay down when we set out, and now he gets up and goes and lies down on the deck up at the very front of the ship, at the bow, and he curls up and damn, it looks like he's shaking a little too, I think and I touch the picture and it's almost totally dry, anyway dry enough to wrap if I don't press the paper against the paint and if I use a good amount of paper and wrap it loosely, I think and I pick up the picture and put it on the berth and I open the suitcase and I take out the brown packing paper, the length of string, and the black marker and I carefully wrap the picture in the paper and then I write To Guro and under that Merry Christmas and under both From Asle and then I tie the string around the package and I put the rest of the packing paper and string and the black marker back in the

suitcase and shut it and then I put the wrapped picture on top of
the suitcase, behind Åsleik's sailor bag and I think that I'd imagined putting the picture in the suitcase but the best thing to do
would be to carry it under one arm, since the paint isn't entirely
dry and, worst case, the paper might stick to the picture, I think,
but if I walk in with a picture under my arm then Sister, Guro,
will know what she's going to get for Christmas from me as soon
as she sees me, so maybe I will put the picture in the suitcase, I
think, but in spite of everything it's probably better if she knows
what she's getting than if she gets a ruined picture, I think and I
leave the picture lying on the suitcase and I lie down on the berth
in the cabin and I shut my eyes and I see Ales standing in front of
Asle and she's saying she wants to move to the old white house in
Dylgja, where her father's sister lives, old Alise, and that it's already
been decided that she'll inherit the house, because there aren't any
other heirs, she says and she says that they might as well move
there now, because old Alise would be happy to have someone
else living in the house, she's old now, and frail, she's many many
years older than Father, and she can use help with so many things,
and they can live in two rooms up in the attic, that both have storage spaces, and then old Alise can live downstairs the same as she
does now and then they'll share the kitchen, and the toilet and the
shower that Father had put into the house, because when he was
growing up they had an outhouse, and when they needed to wash
up Mother heated up water and they bathed in a zinc tub, Father
had always said, Ales says and then Asle says that he doesn't want
to live with anybody else, it's not nice, and it's so distracting, he
says and I hear Åsleik shouting and asking if everything's all right
and I answer with my eyes closed that everything's fine, I just lay
down for a bit, I say and I lie there with my eyes closed and I see
Ales and Asle sitting in mother Judit's car, Ales sitting in front next
to her mother Judit and Asle sitting in the back and he's thinking
that now they're going to drive out to Dylgja to go to old Alise's
funeral and then they're going to go look at the house where old

Alise had lived and Ales wants them to move into and I hear Åsleik
say as long as I don't fall asleep now and I say I'm just resting a little
and I see Asle looking at the house where old Alise had lived, it's a
nice old house, painted white, up on a rocky hill and with a view
of the Sygne Sea and I see Ales come and take Asle's hand and then
they walk into the house together with mother Judit and Ales says
that everything in the house is the way it was when old Alise lived
there, because she lived at home until the end, but then she had a
stroke and she couldn't manage at home alone anymore and then
she was moved to The Hospice in Vik, and after that it wasn't long
before she died, Ales says, and how many bodices for the national
folk costume had old Alise sewed, and how many tablecloths and
table runners in Hardanger embroidery, no, nobody knew, because
that's how she made a living as best she could, Ales says and Asle
says that it's a beautiful old house, and no damage like there is to
the house they're living in now, he says

So you can imagine living in this house, Ales says

Yes, Asle says

I can hardly think of any place better to work and to live, he says

and then mother Judit says that in that case it's decided, yes,
they would move into the old white house and Ales says that it
won't be long before she finally takes her art history exams, about
the place of icons in the Norwegian Christian tradition or rather
their lack of place there, and after that they can move to Dylgja,
she says and I hear Åsleik shout to ask if I can steer for a minute
and I get up and go out the door from the cabin and go into the
wheelhouse and Åsleik is already standing in the middle of the
wheelhouse with one hand on the wheel

I really need to piss, he says

And besides the bottle's empty, he says

and Åsleik holds up the empty beer bottle and then he lets go
of the wheel and I take it and I see that it's still a good long way
to the headland we're steering towards and Åsleik says that when
he takes The Boat alone he usually lets it drift when he goes out

on deck to piss and I sit on the chair at the wheel and I notice that Ales is standing next to me and I say to her that we had it good then, in that time, in those years, when we lived together in the house there in Dylgja, it's just it was so few years, too few, I say and Ales doesn't say anything and I look at the headland and I steer towards it and Ales stands close to me and she says it won't be long before we're together again and I say that I've lived alone in the house long enough now, yes, for many years, I say and she says I moved in right after old Alise's funeral was over while she was preparing to take her art history exams, about icons in Norway, and in addition to the usual required reading she had also read everything she could find about icon painting, and right after she quit The Art School she'd sent away to Sweden for the things that she needed to paint icons and then she started painting icons too, yes, as she's sure I remember, Ales says, and it didn't take long before she'd painted her first icon, she says and I hear Åsleik say damn if I'm not sitting here talking to myself and he can take the wheel again now, he says

I was talking to myself? I say

Yes, Åsleik says

and he says we're getting close

It took its time, this trip, I say

The more times you take it, the shorter it feels, Åsleik says

It's like that with everything, probably, I say

The first time you walk some path, it feels the longest, Åsleik says

And it's like that in a boat too, he says

and I go back into the cabin and I lie back down on the berth and I close my eyes and I see Ales sitting there in The Parlour in the white house in Dylgja and she's working on an icon and Asle thinks that now it'll soon be a year that they've been living in Dylgja and he thinks that no one taught Ales anything about painting icons, she learned it all herself from books, he thinks and Ales looks up at him

How's it going, Asle says

Not bad, she says

The icon I'm working on is of John in the cave on Patmos, and I think it'll turn out beautiful, yes, as it should be, Ales says

Yes, Asle says

But you don't feel like painting again, he says

No, Ales says

Now I paint icons, just icons, she says

and then she says that it's good he paints pictures that they can sell, because how will she ever sell these icons of hers, no, she has no idea, Ales says and Asle says that she can sell them eventually, no need to worry about that, he says

You think so, Ales says

I am absolutely sure of it, he says

For example, we could put up a sign on the bulletin board outside St Paul's Church saying that you have icons for sale, he says

and Ales says that she never thought these icons of hers were good enough that she could sell them, she says and I hear Åsleik shout and say he needs to piss again, his bladder's not that big, so it'd be nice if I could take over the boat now, he says and I go back into the wheelhouse and I take the wheel and Åsleik goes out and I hear him almost shout that yes, you know how when you start pissing you piss in one go, almost, he shouts and then he comes back in and sits down on the chair on the port side

I've drunk enough now, he says

Now I won't drink any more, no, not till the lamb ribs, he says

and he says that he feels hunger gnawing at him at the very thought, because Sister's lamb ribs taste unbelievably good, I should really be looking forward to them, he says, yes, so there's something good about Christmas too, he says and then he falls silent sitting there

Did you hear any more about that friend of yours, your Namesake, the one in The Hospital, Åsleik says

and I think that I can't remember having told Åsleik anything about Asle being in The Hospital, but I must have, because my memory's not so good, I think

He died, I say

and it's silent

So, he's dead, Åsleik says

Yes, I say

He died the night before Little Christmas Eve, I say

and then I say that I drove back into Bjørgvin

Yes, Åsleik says

To see your friend, your Namesake there, in The Hospital, he says

Yes, I say

And when you got to The Hospital they told you he was dead, Åsleik says

and I nod and Åsleik says that must have been very hard for me, because the two of us, me and him, my Namesake, had been good friends all these years, he knows that, he says

Yes, I say

So it's really good that you're not home alone on Christmas, Åsleik says

and I don't answer, and it's silent for a long time

So you drove to and from Bjørgvin today too, Åsleik says

No, I spent the night at The Country Inn, I say

You drove to Bjørgvin yesterday and then drove back home early today, Åsleik says

Yes, I say

So that's why you didn't pick up the phone, he says

I heard it ringing as soon as I walked in the door and that's when I picked up, I say

and it's silent and then Åsleik sighs and says that he'd already called lots of times by then and he has to admit he was a little worried about me, he thought maybe something had happened to me, because I usually always answer the phone when he calls, he says and he says he thought for a minute about maybe taking the tractor and coming over to my house and it's silent and then Åsleik says yes, it must be very hard for me that my Namesake is dead, because my Namesake and I knew each other for so long, he knows that much, he says, but I'm not really someone who lets many things slip, and he doesn't even know if my parents are alive or dead, he says

They're dead, I say

and Åsleik doesn't say anything and it's silent and then he says that when we're past the headland he'll take over The Boat, since from there it's just a short way into a bay, and all the way up in the bay there's a dock, because even if Sister's house isn't on the water, it's up on a steep hill, as I've seen myself lots of times of course, her property still includes both a boathouse and a dock, but hardly anyone's been to the boathouse in a generation, yes, he's taken a look inside, and there were two old Barmen boats in there, and the boats looked nice and undamaged, so if someone just waxed them and took a little care of them, and let the wood swell for a few days, they'd be truly shipshape, but no one ever took them out onto the water anymore, because The Fiddler, the one who skipped out, the one from East Norway, he had no interest in the sea or in boats, but then again he was an East Norway man from inland, from far to the east in Telemark somewhere, Åsleik says and then it's silent and I think that maybe I can buy one of those Barmen boats from Sister, and then one day I can go over there and wax it and fix it up

I should get a boat, I say

I'm sure you can have one of Sister's Barmen boats, Åsleik says

But I want an outboard motor on the boat, I say

and Åsleik says that even if it has a pointed bow and stern there's always some way to find a solution so that I can have a little outboard motor on the boat, he says

Yes, I say

and Åsleik says that he can come with me and wax and fix up the boat, and then he can tow it to Dylgja with The Boat, he says and I say we'll see and Åsleik says I've been talking about getting a boat all these years but it never actually happened, I never got a boat, yes, I talked about wanting a boat and a dog and now that

my Namesake is dead his dog is probably mine now, Åsleik says
and I say yes and Åsleik says that in that case at least I have a dog
of my own now, now all that's missing is a boat, he says and then
there's silence

That's sad, about your Namesake, Åsleik says

And now there'll probably be a funeral in the week after
Christmas, he says

and again there's silence

Was he Catholic too? Åsleik says

No, I say

and again there's silence and I say he wasn't part of any religious
community, and he'll probably be buried without a ceremony, I say

Did he have family, Åsleik says

One daughter and one son, The Daughter and The Son, as he
used to say, and then The Boy, as he used to say, even though he's
grown up now, I say

He was married, Åsleik says

Twice, I say

And he lived alone, Åsleik says

Yes, I say

And then he drank himself to death, I guess, Åsleik says

I guess he did, I say

and I think that I never met any of Asle's children, and I don't have
an address or a phone number for any of them, I think and I look at
the headland and how am I supposed to know when he's going to be
buried? and where? I think, because I definitely want to be there, but
then I have to find out The Boy's phone number, I think and then
we've rounded the headland and Åsleik says he can take The Boat
now, and when we get to where we're going to tie up at the dock I'll
need to help him a little, it's much easier to tie up with two people, he
says and I see a boathouse and a dock there in front of us and Åsleik
takes the wheel and I sit down in the chair on the port side and I look
at the little waves there by the shore and I see Asle sitting outside a
door in a corridor in The Hospital and he's waiting for Ales

We're almost there now, Åsleik says

and I see Asle sitting and holding Ales's hand and she's lying there in a bed in The Hospital, and she's unbelievably thin now, he thinks, and she's sleeping, and Asle feels that he's about to start crying and then he places her hands carefully on the covers and then he goes over to the window and stands there and looks out, it's a cold autumn day, with a clear blue sky, and then he feels like a warm light is coming at him from behind and the light goes through him and he sees the light spread out like a beam, like a kind of column of shining golden dust the light spreads out across the blue sky and he doesn't understand what he's seeing and he sees that the light is dissolving and vanishing into the blue sky as infinitely many twinkles and Asle turns around and he goes over to Ales and he takes her hand and it's lifeless and he puts it back down and then he puts his hand in front of her mouth and he can't feel any breath and he kisses her cheek and then he pulls the cord you're supposed to pull if you need help and then he takes Ales's lifeless hand again and a nurse comes and takes Ales's pulse and she can't feel any pulse and then she says now she's finally at peace, now the pain has stopped, she says and she says that she needs to get a doctor and a doctor comes and he confirms that Ales is dead, I think and I dry my wet eyes with the back of my hand and Åsleik notices that something's wrong and he says we'll be docking soon now and I feel that Ales is so close so close, she is sitting right here in my lap with her arms around my back and then we give each other a kiss and then she leans into me and rests there and I know that she is resting in God now, yes, the way I am resting in God too, and that we are resting there together, and I never could imagine being with any other woman after Ales was gone, I think and Ales says that there was the two of us, that's just how it was, yes, as she knew, as she said the first time we met in The Bus Café, she says and then Åsleik says that a boat's what I need, he says, and now it's time for me to go out on deck and I have to just do what he says, yes, first put the fender out on the starboard side, and if there's a

current it can be hard to get right up next to The Dock so it'd be
nice if I took the boathook and stood ready to pull The Boat in
towards The Dock if needed and then I need to take the stern rope
with me and climb up onto The Dock and tie it to the bollard
farthest out on The Dock, Åsleik says and then he'll go up into
the bow and throw me the other rope and then I'll tie that to the
bollard farthest in on The Dock, Åsleik says, when there are two
people it's easy, it's worse when you have to do everything alone,
he says and I put my shoulderbag on and I go out on deck and pick
up the boathook and I pick up the rope sitting there nicely coiled
on the deck and Åsleik shouts that first I have to put the fender
out and I put the rope down and first I put out the fender that's on
the rear deck and then I climb out on the gunwale while I hold
on tight to the railing on the wheelhouse's roof and then I put out
the fender that's on the forward deck and I go back and pick the
boathook and rope back up and Åsleik shouts that he should be
able to manoeuvre The Boat pretty close to The Dock, but the
current is pushing us away from The Dock, so I'll need to be quick
and pull The Boat all the way in to The Dock with the boathook
when I can and then get up onto The Dock, and it won't be that
slippery, because there's still just dry snow on The Dock, Åsleik
says and he backs up The Boat, steers it in toward The Dock, backs
up again, then steers it in towards The Dock and when we're a
few yards from The Dock Åsleik backs up hard and then The Boat
gives a little jolt forwards and he puts the motor into neutral and I
grab the edge of the dock with the boathook and I pull The Boat
in towards The Dock and I take the rope and climb up onto The
Dock and I see the bollard sticking up from the snow and I tie the
line to it with two half hitches, they're called, and then I hurry in
on The Dock and Åsleik is already standing on the deck by the
bow and he throws me the rope and I pull The Boat in towards
The Dock and tie the line to the bollard with another two half
hitches and then I see Åsleik stand on the deck in the bow and he
says that that couldn't have gone better, he says and now he just

has to idle the motor and let it cool down for a bit, he says and he walks carefully aft on the gunwale while holding the railing on the wheelhouse roof

No, couldn't've gone better, he says again

Because it can be hard to bring her in, he says

If you're alone anyway, he says

But the worst is gusts and rain, he says

and then Åsleik disappears into the wheelhouse and then he comes back out with his sailor bag and he hands it to me and I take it and then he goes back into the wheelhouse and he comes back out with the picture I painted that he's going to give Sister and it's wrapped in Christmas paper with angels and fairies and whatever, and there's a red ribbon around the package holding a slip of paper that says To my dear sister Guro Merry Christmas From your brother Åsleik and he hands me the picture and I take it and put it down next to the sailor bag and then Åsleik goes into the wheelhouse and turns off the motor and it makes a few last thump thumps and Åsleik comes out of the wheelhouse and it's like he wants to climb up onto The Dock

My suitcase, I say

And the picture, my present, I say

And Bragi, I say

The suitcase, right, Åsleik says

and it sounds like scorn in his voice and he goes and gets the picture I'm going to give Sister as a Christmas present and he holds it up towards me

Didn't exactly go all out with the wrapping did you, he says

and I take the picture and I don't say anything and I put it down in front of Åsleik's picture and he holds up my old suitcase and puts it on the fender and I take the suitcase and put it down on The Dock and then Bragi comes running out on deck and Åsleik says yes you too, we mustn't forget you, no, he says and then he holds up the dog and hands him to me and I take Bragi, and oh how he's shaking, I think and I put him down on The Dock and he

stands there with his tail between his legs and then I take my suitcase and my painting and I walk in on The Dock with Bragi at my
heels and I hear Åsleik say that I'm quite a sight there in my long
black coat, and with that brown leather shoulderbag, and with my
grey hair tied in a little hair tie, and the hair just partly covers my
bald patch, and then with that dog padding behind me, he says and
I've reached land and I stop and I turn around and then I see Åsleik
putting one foot over the gunwale and onto The Dock and then
he holds onto the gunwale and he puts his other foot on shore too

My body's so stiff nowadays, he says

and Åsleik picks up his sailor bag and his picture and walks
slowly in on The Dock a bit stiffly and with his feet splayed and
then he stops and looks up at Sister's house, it's a little grey house,
and there's light in all the windows

Yes well it's Christmas again, Åsleik says

So it is, I say

You don't like Christmas, he says

No, I haven't liked Christmas since I was a little boy, I say

Me neither, Åsleik says

and then we start to walk on a snow-covered path up to the
country road and on the other side of the road a path has been
beaten to the grey house where Sister lives, and the house looks so
rundown, it should have been painted years and years ago, I think
and then Sister comes into view around the corner and she's wearing a Christmas pullover and she waves at us and Åsleik lifts up the
picture he's carrying and I lift up mine

Welcome to my home, Sister calls

Yes now it's Christmas again Guro, Åsleik calls

and she doesn't answer and I see her medium-length blonde
hair and I see that she's holding a lit cigarette and then she takes
a deep drag at the cigarette and to me she looks so much like the
Guro who lived in The Lane that I couldn't have told them apart if
I didn't know they weren't the same person, this Guro and the one
who just died in a fire, I think, and Asle is dead, I think, and I can't

think about that anymore, I think and then we get to the house and Guro shakes my hand and I say well we've never met and she says maybe not but she has seen me before, she's seen photographs of me in *The Bjørgvin Times* lots of times and then she saw me at The Coffeehouse in Bjørgvin

I always like to go there when I'm in Bjørgvin, I say

Me too, she says

I never go to Bjørgvin without stopping in at The Coffee-house, she says

And it hasn't been long since the last time I saw you there, she says

No, I say

and she says that she tries to make a living by sewing table-cloths, big and small, and table runners, short and long, in Hardan-ger embroidery, and then bodices for folk costumes, the decora-tive bodices, she says, and it's all right, she makes just enough for what she needs, just enough to keep poverty at bay, she says, and when she's finished sewing a bunch of tablecloths, table runners, and bodices, she takes the bus to Bjørgvin and brings them to The Craft Centre, and then she always buys there what she can't find at The Country Store in Instefjord, where she usually buys whatever she needs, and that's easy enough, because it's just a half a mile away or so, she says, and she doesn't eat much, so it's mostly tobacco and cigarette paper she needs to buy, and that doesn't add up to all that much, she says and she laughs

Yes, Merry Christmas, Åsleik says

Merry Christmas, yes, Guro says

Merry Christmas, I say

and then she says we should come in, and it's a roomy house, she says, she usually sleeps in the bedroom off the living room but there are two bedrooms up in the attic, and she's made up one for Åsleik, she says

You'll sleep in the attic room you always sleep in, she says

and Åsleik nods

And then I made up the bed in the other room for you, she says

and she looks at me and then she says with a laugh that her house is filled with pictures I've painted, no, she doesn't even know how many years it's been that Åsleik's given her a picture I painted for Christmas, and she understands that my paintings sell for good prices, so she's probably strictly speaking quite rich thanks to my paintings, and if she's not mistaken her collection of my paintings is going to increase by two this year, one of them bigger than any she has so far, and she likes my paintings so much, they give her a kind of peace, she says, so she'll never sell a single one if she doesn't have to, she says and I say I thought about how she has so many smaller paintings of mine, she must have more of them than anyone, and to tell the truth they are the very best small or smaller pictures I've painted, because she should know that her brother Åsleik has an eye for art, he chose the pictures himself and he always chose the one that I myself thought was the best, I say and I'm looking forward to seeing the pictures again, I say and then she says that she can show me every single picture, if I want, but now we need to come inside, she says and she goes and opens the front door and I go into the hall with my suitcase and the painting wrapped in brown packing paper and Bragi comes padding along at my heels

You have a dog too, she says

That's how it worked out, I say

and I see that several paintings of mine are hanging in the hall, and I feel them all again, there is a mix of newer and older pictures, and thought went into where they're hung and then I see a steep set of stairs going up to the attic and on the wall alongside the stairs there are more pictures I painted

Yes, you can see for yourself, Guro says

I have paintings of yours everywhere, she says

and she has a Christmas tree so she can put the present I brought under the tree, she says and I nod and I hand her the package and then she opens the door to the kitchen and goes away and there's a wonderful smell of smoked lamb ribs and I turn around and I see Åsleik coming into the hall with his sailor bag and with his painting wrapped in Christmas paper with angels and fairies and whatever and he says my goodness, he can't think of any food that smells better, Åsleik says and Guro comes back out and Åsleik hands her the wrapped picture

And here's a little present, or maybe a little bigger, he says

Because she probably wants to put the presents under the Christmas tree like usual, he says

and Guro takes it and disappears back into the kitchen

No food in the world smells better, Åsleik says

and Guro comes out into the hall and she says maybe before anything else she should show me the room where I'll be sleeping, she says

Hey, Guro, Åsleik says

Yes, she says

You have two boats sitting in your boathouse, well, in case you didn't know, two Barmen boats, and Asle has been saying for as long as I've known him that he wants a boat, so I was wondering if he could have one of yours, he says

and Guro says that if I want one of the boats then yes, I'd be welcome to take it, yes, take both for all she cares, but they'll sink as soon as they touch the water, she says

I, I don't know, I say

If you want a boat? Åsleik asks

Yes, I say

No, no, he says

You've been talking about it all these years anyway, he says

Yes, I say

and then there's silence

But if you want one of the boats, or both, you can have them, Guro says

and I say I don't know really and Åsleik says no well if I don't want a boat I don't want a boat, that's how it is, he says and I ask if Guro has pictures hanging in the living room, and she says yes, she has pictures hanging in both the living room and the bedroom where she sleeps, just through the living room, and I ask if I can see the paintings right now and she says of course and then Åsleik says that he'll take his sailor bag up to the attic room he'll be sleeping in and then he starts going up the stairs and I put the suitcase down and I follow Guro into her kitchen, and it's small, and there's smoke from a huge pan, and two more big pans are standing ready, in one there are peeled potatoes and in the other rutabaga cut into pieces, I think and then Guro picks up a glass of red wine that's standing on the kitchen table and then we go into the main room and there's a stove in one corner and it's warm and the room feels good and Bragi goes over and lies down in front of the stove and Guro says she didn't know I had a dog, Åsleik had never told her, but she likes dogs so it's great, she says and I see that there is brown panelling on the walls in the room and pictures I've painted are hanging on all the walls and in the middle of the room there's a scraggly little pine tree and the four gifts are under it and I go from wall to wall and I take a look at every picture as quickly as I can while Guro sips her wine and then Guro opens the door to the bedroom

Please come in, she says

and she laughs and I go into her bedroom and there's barely room for a bed and a nightstand and a wardrobe in there, and there too paintings of mine fill the walls, and I feel almost like it's too much and I go back out

It's gotten to be a lot of pictures over the years, Guro says

Yes, I say

and she asks if she can take me upstairs to the room where I'll be sleeping and I say yes thank you and then she starts up the stairs with her wine-glass and I pick up the suitcase and follow her and along the stairs too there are paintings, with maybe a foot and a half between them, and they're all good paintings, I think and up in the attic I see that there's not a single picture hanging in the upstairs hall and Guro points at a door and she says I'll sleep there and she opens the door and I go into a little white-painted room and I don't see a single picture in there either

I hung all the pictures either downstairs or along the stairs, Guro says

and then she says that she didn't put a single picture upstairs, not in this room and not in the room Åsleik is going to sleep in or in the hall either, yes, as I saw, she says and she says that she doesn't know why, but well that's how it's always been, she says and she drinks a little wine and I see that there's a bed with a nightstand in a corner, and next to the nightstand is a chair, and I put the suitcase down on the floor and I take my shoulderbag off and put it on the chair and I take my coat off and drape it on the chair and Guro says I could have hung up my coat down in the hall and I say it's fine to keep it on the chair and then I stand there in my black velvet jacket and Guro says that the food's cooking, so there'll be lamb ribs to eat soon, she says and she says that she's already had a couple of glasses of wine, she indulges in more than one glass every now and then, she says, anyway when it's Christmas, but I probably don't want any wine, because according to Åsleik I don't drink, she says and I say that I haven't had a taste of beer, wine, or anything stronger in many years

You used to drink too much, she says

Yes, I say

and she says I should make myself at home and arrange things however I want and then she leaves and she shuts the door behind her and I realize that I'm tired, and that the floor is kind of rocking a little, yes, like The Boat was, and I lie down on the bed, with my shoes and my black velvet jacket on, and I stretch out my legs and I put my folded hands behind my neck and rest my hands and head on the pillow and I feel how close Ales is, and Asle, and also how close the Guro who lived in The Lane is and I hear a knock on the door and I say come in and I see Guro come in and she is carrying a full wine-glass

When I have such fine folk in the house I have to talk to them a little, don't I, she says and she laughs and she sits down on the edge of the bed and then she says that she lived with a man for many years, he was from East Norway, and it didn't exactly cost nothing to have him in the house, but he always brought in a little something, he was a fiddler, and he was handy, he did a good job taking care of the house, he painted the house, managed things, mowed the lawn, yes, as long as he was living at her place everything was in order, as they say, but ever since he skipped out things have begun to fall apart more and more, Guro says and she drinks a little wine and she puts her free hand on my belly

And you're a widower, she says

and I nod

And you've been one for a long time, she says

and I nod again and then it's silent and she slowly moves her hand farther down towards my fly

Yes, I say

But my wife and I are still married, I say

You can't be married to someone who's dead, Guro says

and she rubs my fly up and down and she opens it and I take her hand away and I see her blush and then she says she really should go downstairs and check on the food and she wants a cigarette too, she smokes almost constantly, she smokes way too much, she says and I see the woman named Guro leave the room and she shuts the door behind her and I think that she talks and walks and is in every way like the Guro who just died in the fire in The Lane, and I should go to her funeral, but I won't do it, because I don't know when and where it will be, and I don't know who I can ask about it, I think and I lie on my side and I take out my rosary, the one I got from Ales once, with the brown wooden beads and a cross, and I think that now I need to sleep a little, rest a little, I think and I shut my eyes and I see Asle sitting in an attic in an outbuilding and he's paging through a book, and he's sitting in a boat with Father, and he's sitting on a bus and he's thinking about how a friend of his is dead, he just found out about it and I see Asle lying in a bed and reading around in a book, he draws, he paints, he drinks beer, he smokes, and then I see The Boy toddling around on the floor and Asle walks up and down the street, he drinks beer, she is naked and she is lying there in bed and he doesn't know what he should do he touches her and he feels he wants to lie on her and he does and he doesn't dare push into her something holds him back he doesn't dare because as soon as he gets close a fear comes over him and he pulls back and she just lies there and her name is Liv and he lies on her and then he's sitting at a desk and he stands there and smokes rolls a cigarette books a teacher is talking he asks the classroom tubes of oil paint and Åsleik who says *St Andrew's Cross* and who comes with dried fish her face all lit up so that you could see her angel roman-fleuve the other schoolchildren students and The Painting Hall girls boys coincidentia oppositorum cigarettes beer drinking beer talking and then just going there and waiting and then, finally, finally he's born, finally he comes out into the world, out into the light, and then Asle is a father, he is young, very young, but he has become a father and long brown hair and everyone else who is so much better than him he's worth nothing and she just wants to be with the others with all of them with all the others and it's over and he wants to lie down and go to sleep in the snow because it's so far to walk rubs and rubs Bragi's fur and he is so tired so drunk he sees the stars and then he and Father are in a boat they're fishing and books The Boat drawings paintings books and I want to get a dog and a boat, a Barmen boat, I think and painting just painting just that and beer alcohol that good rush Ales's face her eyes and her hand in mine Painting and the best first nothing special then Liv better and better and sister Alida who died Ales and him Drawing the neighbour boy who drowned Liv and Bård Painting and he hadn't even started school and I drink and she says I mustn't drink every single night a little rush every night and he trembles and shakes and it's like he's held tight by fear visions that there can be colours that happen inside him and he doesn't drink more painting money no money sells

pictures makes money doesn't have money exhibition exhibitions
shopping for painting things tubes of oil paint canvas always oil
paint and canvas always canvas stretchers boards stretchers tacks
canvas her and the woman who comes and sits down at the table
and they start talking and she's seen his exhibitions home with her
lying next to each other kissing her only son kissing her they take
off their clothes he pushes inside her they lie next to each other
they talk go home she's lying there the son is sleeping go home
she's lying there she's lying on the floor she's barely breathing ambulance boy crying The Boy cries howls ambulance he and the son
she writes him letters and he thinks he should get a dog and then
a boat a Barmen boat cries and cries they meet kiss eat together he
sits and drinks boat and dog that's what a person needs and she
comes and sits down exhibitions oil painting canvas stretchers need
to find a place to live and Åsleik says he can have one of the Barmen boats that's sitting in the boathouse and the boats boards nowhere to go pictures the others alcohol feeling warm beer and Ales
her warmth the mark of the cross on my forehead consecrated oil
there for all time always and another glass of beer her hand on my
fly talk about something alcohol laugh she comes in and it's Christmas lamb ribs summer her parents the house the white house silence and drinking smoking and then neither drinking nor smoking and Father who never spoke painting never gave up kept at it
people can say whatever they want he just kept at it dark eyes child
several children painting look there the house he sits and drinks
children painting their house should have been painted pictures
dog eyes tubes of oil paint days nights not getting to sleep and he
lies there and he shakes up and down jerking trembling shaking
and the man sitting there gets up and I sit there and then I lie on
the floor I lie there in the snow and my body jerks up and down
and I look at the picture no children had no children those two
lines that cross each other one brown and one purple Åsleik your
angel Ales your hand and there's nothing more to do on the picture
so I'll just put it away a good picture maybe disappear into the

picture if he can change into something way back there and I get
up and I go over to the picture the halo around the host clouds
grey clouds the sparkling of the chalice and then I lift the picture
off the easel and I put it back on the easel these pictures I'm working on and that I'm still not done with transformations brown
leather shoulderbag draped over if not always then often and he
presses his fingers against the shoulder of the man lying in the bed
and he just lies there and he holds his hand in front of the man's
mouth and he doesn't feel any breath and he feels for his pulse and
he goes out and now I need to get a little sleep soon and I don't
want to know what time it is, I think, but I'm so restless, I don't
know what's wrong and I see Ales's face, and it's the whole sky and
in the sky is Grandmother's face and she is so close so close and I
can't get to sleep I hold the brown cross on my rosary between
thumb and index finger and I think that I, what's I in me, can
never die because it was never born, because ich bin ungeboren,
Meister Eckhart wrote and I see the words before me nach der
Weise meiner Ungeborenheit kann ich niemals sterben, nach der
Weise meiner Ungeborenheit bin ich ewig gewesen und bin ich
jetzt und werde ich ewig bleiben, I think, because in jenem Sein
Gottes nämlich wo Gott über allem Sein und über aller Unter-
schiedenheit ist, dort war ich selber and I breathe evenly in and
evenly out and I say inside myself kyrie and I breathe out and eleison and I breathe in and christe and I breathe out and eleison and
I breathe in and I move my thumb up to the first bead and I say
inside myself Our Father Who art in heaven Hallowed be thy
name Thy kingdom come Thy will be done on earth as it is in
heaven Give us this day our daily bread and forgive us our trespasses as we forgive those who trespass against us And lead us not
into temptation but deliver us from evil and I think that I never
should have come with Åsleik to celebrate Christmas at Sister's
house, the woman named Guro, the other Guro, I think and then
I feel Ales lying next to me and she lies there holding me and I
move my thumb and finger back to the cross and I say inside myself

Pater noster qui es in cælis Sanctificetur nomen tuum Adveniat regnum tuum Fiat voluntas tua sicut in cælo et in terra Panem nostrum cotidianum da nobis hodie Et dimitte nobis debita nostra sicut et nos dimittimus debitoribus nostris Et ne nos inducas in tentationem sed libera nos a malo and I hold the cross and I grip the first bead between the cross and the three beads in a row and I say inside myself Our Father Who art in heaven Hallowed be thy name Thy kingdom come Thy will be done on earth as it is in heaven Give us this day our daily bread and forgive us our trespasses as we forgive those who trespass against us And lead us not into temptation but deliver us from evil and I move my thumb and finger up to the first of the three beads in a row and I say inside myself Ave Maria Gratia plena Dominus tecum Benedicta tu in mulieribus et benedictus fructus ventris tui Jesus Sancta Maria Mater Dei Ora pro nobis peccatoribus nunc et in hora mortis nostræ and I breathe slowly in and out and in and I move my thumb and finger up to the second bead and I say inside myself Hail Mary Full of grace The Lord is with thee Blessed art thou among women and blessed is the fruit of thy womb Jesus Holy Mary Mother of God Pray for us sinners now and in the hour of our death and I breathe evenly and I think yes like this nothing else nothing more because I didn't care about the others and I breathe slowly in and out and I move my thumb and finger up to the third bead and I say to myself Ave Maria Gratia plena Dominus tecum Benedicta tu in mulieribus et benedictus fructus ventris tui Iesus Sancta Maria Mater Dei and I a ball of blue light shoots into my forehead and bursts and I say reeling inside myself Ora pro nobis peccatoribus nunc et in hora

JON FOSSE was born in 1959 on the west coast of Norway and is the recipient of countless prestigious prizes, both in his native Norway and abroad. Since his 1983 fiction debut, *Raudt, svart* [*Red, Black*], Fosse has written prose, poetry, essays, short stories, children's books, and over forty plays, with more than a thousand productions performed and translations into fifty languages. *A New Name* is the final volume in *Septology*, his latest prose work, published in three volumes by Transit Books.

DAMION SEARLS is a translator from German, Norwegian, French, and Dutch and a writer in English. He has translated many classic modern writers, including Proust, Rilke, Nietzsche, Walser, and Ingeborg Bachmann.

Transit Books is a nonprofit publisher of international and American literature, based in Oakland, California. Founded in 2015, Transit Books is committed to the discovery and promotion of enduring works that carry readers across borders and communities. Visit us online to learn more about our forthcoming titles, events, and opportunities to support our mission.

TRANSITBOOKS.ORG

Printed in the USA
CPSIA information can be obtained
at www.ICGtesting.com
JSHW082150091023
49920JS00006B/6